HOW CAN SPOCK'S BODY SURVIVE WITHOUT HIS BRAIN?

HOW CAN KIRK AND HIS COMRADES SUCCESSFULLY TAMPER WITH TIME IN *STAR TREK IV: THE VOYAGE HOME*?

WHO ARE THE MOST DANGEROUS MONSTERS IN THE *STAR TREK* UNIVERSE?

Join your fellow *Star Trek* enthusiasts and experts in investigating these and other questions about everybody's favorite multimedia future universe. Learn more about allies and enemies, about the many unsung heroes and heroines, about medical marvels and technological wonders, about bloopers and errors big enough to fly the *Enterprise* through—in short, about everything that makes *Star Trek* so endlessly appealing to so many fans the world around.

THE BEST OF TREK® #13

THE BEST OF TREK® #13

A BRAND NEW COLLECTION FOR STAR TREK FANS

EDITED BY WALTER IRWIN & G.B. LOVE

A SIGNET BOOK

NEW AMERICAN LIBRARY

NAL BOOKS ARE AVAILABLE AT QUANTITY DISCOUNTS WHEN
USED TO PROMOTE PRODUCTS OR SERVICES. FOR INFORMA-
TION PLEASE WRITE TO PREMIUM MARKETING DIVISION, NEW
AMERICAN LIBRARY, 1633 BROADWAY, NEW YORK, NEW YORK
10019.

SIGNET TRADEMARK REG. U.S. PAT. OFF. AND FOREIGN COUNTRIES
REGISTERED TRADEMARK—MARCA REGISTRADA
HECHO EN CHICAGO, U.S.A.

SIGNET, SIGNET CLASSIC, MENTOR, ONYX, PLUME, MERIDIAN
and NAL BOOKS are published by NAL PENGUIN INC.,
1633 Broadway, New York, New York 10019

First Printing, May, 1988

1 2 3 4 5 6 7 8 9

PRINTED IN THE UNITED STATES OF AMERICA

ACKNOWLEDGMENTS

As always, thanks are due to the many, many readers, contributors, and fans who have helped make our magazines and books successful. Special thanks go to our patient editor at NAL, John Silbersack, and his associate editor, Christopher Schelling. Our warmest thanks go to the contributors in this volume; we couldn't have done it without you.

We'd also like to thank the following conventions for having us as guests during the past year. We enjoyed coming, and appreciate the opportunity to meet and talk with fans. Thanks to: Babel Banquet, Joyce Tullock, and Susan Weeks, Chairwomen; Vul-Con; Jim Mule; Chairman; SwampCon, Marine Fourrier and Carol DeWitt, Chairwomen; Enterprise II, Ray Tanyer, Chairman; and Trek Fest II, Rick Adams, Chairman. Special appreciation to the many fans who worked on and at these conventions—they're the ones who deserve the applause.

To all of the above, and especially you, our faithful readers, the following volume is dedicated. Thanks!

CONTENTS

INTRODUCTION

Thank you for purchasing this thirteenth collection of articles and features from our magazine, *Trek*. We have endeavored to make this collection just as exciting and entertaining as the previous twelve, and we hope that you will enjoy it.

These are exciting times for a Star Trek fan. *Star Trek: The Next Generation* premiered only days ago to critical acclaim, high ratings, and overwhelming fan approval. We here at *Trek* wholeheartedly approve of this new project of Gene Roddenberry's, and commend it to all Star Trek fans as a sterling example of IDIC (Infinite Diversity in Infinite Combinations) at its finest. *The Next Generation* is true Star Trek, presented just as Gene Roddenberry and his associates want it, without network interference or censorship.

If you want proof that *The Next Generation* is not intended to replace the old Star Trek we love, you can't do better than to know that Paramount has announced plans to film *Star Trek V*, with a scheduled release date of Christmas, 1988! All of the *original* cast will be included (indeed many have already been signed to contracts), and the film will be directed by none other than William Shatner!

The original series will still be shown in syndication throughout the nation and the world (albeit with a short hiatus while the new show gains a following), as well as continue to be released on videotape. Also continuing are the novelizations, original novels, and other Star Trek books.

As someone said at a convention recently, "This is a

great time to be a Star Trek fan! You have the old, the new, and the movies, too!" We heartily concur.

Speaking of the old and the new, we are happy to announce that we will once again be publishing *Trek* regularly, in a revamped format, beginning anew with Volume II, Number One. Naturally, we will be accepting subscriptions immediately! We invite you to turn to the ad elsewhere in this book for information on how to subscribe and order individual issues. (And, please, if you have borrowed this volume from a library, copy the information in the ad and leave it for others to see. Thanks!)

If you have enjoyed the articles in this volume and feel stirred to write one yourself, please do so and send it to us. We are *always* looking for new writers, with fresh viewpoints on Star Trek and related subjects. (Please, *do not* send us Star Trek stories or parodies! We cannot and will not publish fiction!) If you feel a little timid about submitting your work, remember that the vast majority of our contributors began by sending in articles after reading a previous *Best of Trek*. They made it; you can, too!

We want to hear from you in any event. We welcome your letters of comment, and we listen to what you have to say. It is only by these letters you send that we know what kind of job we're doing. Let us hear from you. Our address is:

Trek
2405 Dewberry
Pasadena, TX 77502

Thanks again, and we hope you'll enjoy *The Best of Trek #13!*

Walter Irwin
G. B. Love

MEDICAL PRACTICE IN
STAR TREK: CURES AND CATCALLS

By Sharron Crowson

We had the pleasure of finally meeting Sharron Crowson at a convention last year and found her to be a lively, lovely woman, with interests and opinions as diverse as her articles in these collections would indicate. This time around, she turns her attention to medicine in Star Trek. *In her cover letter with this article, Sharron, a registered nurse, said, "Some of the medical aspects of Star Trek were handled so well, I couldn't help wondering about the obvious blunders and outright errors that occurred."*

Medicine plays a big part in nearly every episode of *Star Trek*. It is integral to some stories, plays only a minor role in others, but Dr. McCoy and his staff are essential to developing the themes and magic of *Star Trek*. Like all magic, however, some illusions are spectacular, deserving our hearty appreciation and applause, while others miss, more or less spectacularly, earning jeers and catcalls.

Let's take a look at some illusions that are so believable modern medicine might actually be catching up to them. Computer-aided diagnosis and complex scanners may be a reality well before the twenty-third century. Today computers sort and store more and more data, thereby aiding physicians in their diagnoses. We have scanners, like the CAT (computerized axial tomography) scan, or the NMR (nuclear magnetic resonance), that are very sophisticated and efficient. It seems likely, then, that in the twenty-third century a device like the tricorder, on its own or linked to the *Enterprise*'s on-board computer, would be able to use a remote scanner the size of a salt-shaker to make an accurate diagnosis of internal injuries or disease processes. However, the whole-body scanner capable of analyzing down to the molecular level that appeared in *Star Trek: The Motion Picture* may take a little longer to realize, but is still not outside the realm of possibility.

Many of the "miracle cures" McCoy and his staff pull off seem entirely plausible, given the technology of today projected three hundred years into the future.

In "Miri," one of the best medical episodes, a planet's scientists tried to prolong life by using a series of diseases caused by an altered virus. Calling the changes caused by the virus "diseases" seemed odd, but perhaps understandable, since there were probably violent side effects (fever, rash, etc.) before the virus mutated to its final deadly form. The rationale that the virus would attack at the onset of puberty could be supported, assuming a certain level of reproductive hormones was required to trigger the final changes. Given all the information the landing party found in the ruins of the laboratory, McCoy, working with the biocomp and the *Enterprise*'s labs and computers, isolated the virus and formulated a treatment that would ultimately prove effective. While not standard medical practice, McCoy's decision to test the serum on himself was in perfect keeping with his own personality.

The only jarring note was the rapid disappearance of the blemishes caused by the virus. If they had looked like hives (an allergic reaction), it would have made sense, but those lesions appeared to involve breakdown of both skin and tissue, and so would logically take as long to heal (without some additional topical treatment) as they did to occur.

Another episode with a solid medical basis is "Plato's Stepchildren." McCoy is called upon to treat an infected injury sustained by a remote colony's philosopher-king, Parmen. McCoy matches the bacteria causing the infection to a known strain and comes up with an effective treatment. During the course of treatment, the landing party discovers the inhabitants of this little "utopia" have psychokinesis (all save Alexander, a dwarf). Realizing their need for a physician, Parmen demands that McCoy stay. When the doctor refuses, at Kirk's order, Parmen tries to convince him by using his psi powers against Kirk and Spock.

The solution to this problem is once again McCoy's trusty tricorder and efficient interview techniques by all the members of the landing party. A skilled researcher must learn to ask questions that will illuminate the problem, and listen carefully to each answer. Questioning Alexander, they determine when the powers were first exhibited by the colonists and relate Alexander's lack of power to his deficiency of pituitary hormones, which also caused him to be dwarfed. McCoy distills the psychoactive element, kironide, from available fresh fruit and vegetables, and gives everyone twice Parmen's power level. The effects of the kironide are not instantaneous, which adds a little realism and increases the episode's suspense.

"Miracle cures" occur in several other episodes, and some are more miraculous than others. In "The Tholian Web," McCoy must find something that will help the crew withstand the effects of a "distortion" of the space around them, making them hostile and subject to seizures of uncontrolled fury and paranoia. As McCoy gives his concoction to Spock and Scotty, he says it works by deadening certain nerve inputs. To which Scotty replies, "Any good brand of scotch will do that for you." When McCoy remarks that the drug does indeed work better when mixed with alcohol, Scotty takes the beaker off to see how it mixes with scotch. Mixing drugs with alcohol is a bad idea at any time, since alcohol may increase a drug's effect or cause unpredictable reaction. A drug powerful enough to overcome the serious physical and psychological symptoms exhibited by the crew would probably render them incapable of performing their duties safely.

In "Journey to Babel," the medical section gets a good workout, and some care was taken to make the medical aspects as logical and believable as possible. McCoy diagnoses a life-threatening heart defect in Ambassador Sarek, all the while grumbling about Vulcan physiology. There is a surgical treatment for the defect, but several problems make the surgery risky.

First, McCoy states that he has never operated on a Vulcan. We must assume that most of his training has been in human physiology, with some courses in xenophysiology. And, as he says, that's a lot different from actual surgical experience. You can read, study, watch films, listen to all the lectures, but nothing prepares you for your first sight of a living body under the knife.

Vulcan physiology is different enough from humans for McCoy to be understandably nervous. Organs are rearranged from the human norm, and the blood is the wrong color. While these may seem to be minor differences, their impact could lead to misjudgments and a certain awkwardness.

The open heart surgery proposed takes copious quantities of blood, and Sarek has a rare blood type, T-negative. Spock is the only available donor. The ship does not carry enough Vulcan blood or plasma to start an operation of this type. Spock volunteers to donate the blood, but cannot give enough to supply all that's needed. McCoy and Spock work together with Chapel to research the problem and find a new experimental drug that works on Rigellians to speed up blood production. A drug of this type may be possible in the future, but probably couldn't produce the quantities needed quite so quickly.

McCoy warns Spock that the drug might damage him internally (it would strain the spleen and liver, as well as the blood-producing bone marrow), or it might very well kill him. McCoy's refusal to try it is instinctive, not scientifically deduced, as Spock is quick to point out. He has to use the drug, there is no other way—it's Sarek's certain death against the risk to Spock. McCoy decides to operate.

The operation takes place in the outer room of sickbay. We see Sarek on a diagnostic bed with a metal hood over his chest. This hood must contain lights and the sterile field McCoy asks Chapel to initiate. This field must be very effective, as McCoy wears neither mask nor gloves. Spock is hooked up by plastic tubing carrying his blood for the transfusion. There is a filter to cleanse Spock's blood of its human elements. Sarek does not seem to be getting any kind of anesthesia, certainly not gas or anything we'd recognize. There is no anesthetist, no mask, and Sarek seems to be asleep, but in no way as profoundly anesthetized as an operation of this sort would require.

A nice touch of realism is added by an occasional wisp of smoke coming from under the hood over Sarek. Cautery, or the sealing of open bleeders with heat, is a common practice during surgery, and whether you use electricity or laser, there is always some smoke. Cautery is used because it takes much less time than tying the bleeders off with sutures. (In "City on the Edge of Forever," McCoy finds himself in an historical era where they actually use suture. He raves, "Needles and suture, they used to cut and sew people up like garments . . . oh, the pain." McCoy couldn't abide the thought of such primitive aids, that so much pain couldn't be cured without more pain.)

During the operation, the ship is fired on and the sickbay takes a shaking. McCoy is annoyed and worried about the effects on his patients. He says, "One more like that and I'll lose both these men." Now that's about the most tactless thing McCoy is ever guilty of saying. Even considering the pressures of the moment, it does not sound like the McCoy we have come to know and love. Sarek's wife, Amanda, is standing not six feet away, and Spock, while tranquilized, is not unconscious and turns to look at McCoy when he makes his comment. Hearing is the last sense to fade before unconsciousness, and even patients under anesthetic have been known to report things they were not supposed to be able to hear. We can only assume that McCoy is more frantic than his professional facade will let him show.

The operation is a success, both Sarek and Spock pull through, and McCoy finally gets the last word. But the last word on this whole episode may be, "Why?" Vulcans have the unique ability to enter a healing trance and repair or even regenerate organs. True, it takes time and strength, but why couldn't Sarek repair the defect with Vulcan techniques? It may be that healing trances only work after defects have been repaired and are only useful for dramatically speeding up healing. For example, when Spock is shot in "A Private Little War," he's taken to surgery and uses the healing trance afterward to heal himself quickly. However, if you can direct energies to heal organs, it seems that you could direct repairs to a defective heart and save yourself a long, tedious, dangerous operation.

No discussion of medical techniques or medically oriented episodes would be complete without including "Spock's Brain."

A gorgeous female appears on the bridge, puts everybody to sleep, decides Spock's brain is suitable for her purposes, takes him down to sickbay, and removes it. Does Spock die? No, when McCoy comes to, he slaps Spock on life support to stabilize his condition. Spock survives—unassisted!—without his brain for an unspecified period of time. McCoy attributes this to Vulcan stamina. Then the good doctor calls Kirk down and explains that Spock's brain is missing; it's been surgically removed, a real neat job. McCoy also informs Kirk that Spock can only survive twenty-four hours without his brain. Is it possible for Spock to survive without his brain—without life support and/or constant medical treatment? No, it isn't; you can't have it both ways.

Does Kirk accept the reality of the situation? No, he's going to find Spock's brain, even when McCoy explains he can't replace it. Kirk says that if it was taken, the knowledge must exist to return it. Kirk obviously never watched a two-year-old take apart an old alarm clock.

Then Kirk does the most peculiar thing, in an episode of peculiar things. He turns to Scotty and says, "Get him ready." Do Scotty or McCoy ask, "What do you mean?" No, they must know what he means, but we sure don't. And when we find out, we might wish we'd been left uninformed.

Kirk tracks the woman's ship to a bleak, frozen planet. When he's sure he's found the right place, he has McCoy beam down with Spock . . . *Spock*, wearing a zombielike expression and a device the size of stereo headphones on his head just above his pointed ears. McCoy has a tiny box with lights and buttons on it that he uses to control Spock, making him walk, turn, and stop. We must assume that this is what Kirk meant when he said, "Get him ready." It makes you wonder if this is a common technique, or if they'd had to do something like this before. Granted this is three hundred years in the future, granted the Federation seems to have miniaturization down to a fine art, but this remote-controlled Spock is just too much to believe.

The fundamental agreement between the writer and reader for any kind of science fiction or fantasy (for any kind of fiction, really) is the willing suspension of disbelief. When you give your reader something he cannot believe in, you've violated that agreement, and the reader is then free to throw the book at the wall, or the viewer free to laugh and turn to another channel. That Spock could be ambulatory without life support and controlled by some tiny device is ludicrous. There are hundreds of muscles and thousands of nerves needed to receive messages from the brain for even so simple a thing as balancing to stand. Spock would not be able to see, hear, or even breathe. We find out later in the episode that Spock's medulla oblongata, hooked into the planet's main computer, is pumping water, purifying and circulating air, functions as it does in the human body (so the Vulcan brain must be similar to the human brain). So how is Spock's body managing those functions with no medulla or no life support?

The controls on the box are so simple that any one of the party can operate them by twisting a dial. There just isn't any way that so simple a control could have sent all the signals for something as complicated as walking or restraining one of the women.

Spock's stolen brain is functioning as controller for a vast underground complex. Now that's something that just might be possible in the future. Anne McCaffery wrote several stories about disembodied brains that piloted spaceships and made the notion plausible. But Spock speaking to Kirk over the communicator, *in his own voice*, is a lot of nonsense. Even if could, by some chance, synthesize a voice from inside that black box, it would not sound like his voice. Timbre, pitch, and resonance are all functions of the body, vibrations of vocal cords and chest and sinuses. The body is not speaking, therefore the voice would not be Spock's.

The last portion of the episode is devoted to restoring Spock's brain. McCoy puts a teaching device on his head and learns how to put Spock's brain back, but the knowledge doesn't last. There is no adequate explanation of McCoy's ability to use the teacher in the first place; surely his brain must be different in some essential ways from the priestesses who are meant to use it. There is also no explanation why it would kill him to put it on again when he begins to forget.

The surgery to restore Spock's brain takes place behind a partition that covers only the top of Spock's head. Again, McCoy wears no mask or gloves, and evidently does not have to worry about contamination. No general anesthesia is used, though a local anesthetic might have been. It is possible to use only a local anesthetic in brain operations because the brain itself feels no pain. There is no incision down as far as the neck; McCoy has no access to the base of the brain where the medulla resides. How is he going to put it back?

The most ridiculous part of this implausible episode is Kirk's suggestion that McCoy connect up Spock's vocal cords. Kirk should stick to command and leave medicine to someone who understands it. Spock's vocal cords were never disconnected; they are attached to the inside of the trachea and vibrate to produce sounds. McCoy would have to make an incision in Spock's neck to reattach vocal cords. Spock uses the proper term—speech center—when he begins to talk and direct his own operation. And that's the last straw in this long series of inconsistencies and errors. While Spock might be awake and aware during an operation on his brain (surgery for Parkinson's syndrome is often done while the patient is awake in order to localize the affected area of the brain), the simple instructions he gives McCoy would have occurred to a first-year resident of the time, and involved several different areas of the brain. Spock did not give technical direction, he made generalized comments.

When Spock sits up after the operation, with not so much as a hair out of place, and begins to rattle on about the fascinating things he discovered, you laugh as much out of relief that the whole miserable mess is over as at the idea of Spock, the jolly raconteur.

"Spock's Brain" was a bizarre idea at best, but it could have been worlds better if even minimal care had been taken to find out some basic facts: how a brain works, which portions perform what functions, how the body and the brain wove together, and, at the very least, where the vocal cords are located. A plausible explanation of how the controlling device they built for Spock might work might have been invented. A computer-synthesized voice for Spock when he was in the black box would have been more believable than using his own voice.

Writers have a responsibility to make every effort to have the technology and facts in their stories at least match what is already known. A writer might bend known facts around at times, but it doesn't pay to ignore or misrepresent them. Failing to make exceptions plausible or neglecting research necessary should get the writer just what he deserves—rejection. In a generally excellent show like *Star Trek*, it's hard to justify such sloppiness.

Many episodes conscientiously try to make even the most alien concepts or practices believable. Nona, the *kanutu* witch woman in "A Private Little War," practices a very strange form of medicine, coupling psychic healing with herbal medicine. She cures Kirk of a venomous bite, but seeks to influence him to give her people advanced weapons by using the "sharing of souls" she experienced as part of the healing ritual. Her rituals and culture are alien, yet there is enough background information to help the viewer suspend disbelief.

"The Empath," Gem certainly does not practice traditional medicine, but McCoy's brief explanation of how her healing might work, and his faith in her, give us the opportunity to believe in it.

In "This Side of Paradise," Kirk figures out how to defeat the spores too-benevolent effect by their failure to affect him: strong emotion creates hormonal shifts that render the spores harmless. You cheer Kirk and believe in the cure, although it does seem he could have found a less painful way of freeing Spock from their influence. Spock might have killed him in the fight, and everyone would have been trapped on that Paradise of a planet forever.

However, there are also episodes like "Mirror, Mirror," where the viewer is left wondering how Spock-2 could be so close to death one moment and force a mind meld on McCoy the next. Spock-2 is clobbered over the head hard enough to knock him out. If he was damaged enough to endanger his life, he would wake up—*if* he woke up—with one hell of a headache and probably be dizzy and vomiting. His telepathic abilities would probably be severely scrambled for at least a little while, perhaps days.

In *Star Trek II: The Wrath of Khan*, Khan claims the Ceti eels, creatures resembling slugs, wrap themselves around the cerebral cortex and make a person extremely suggestible. Imagine, if you will, three-inch eels wrapping themselves around the gray matter portion of a brain maybe ten inches long and four or five inches deep. Something that ridiculous jars you out of the carefully constructed fantasy back into the real world.

The representation of medical practice is like anything else in *Star Trek*—some of it outstanding, some of it good, some of it awful. At times, the writers use medicine to point up flaws in characters and civilizations, as well as to illuminate what is desirable in them.

Nona, the witch woman, tries to use her healing to gain power; Gem, the empath, uses hers to save life, and, ultimately, her planet. In "Friday's Child," McCoy uses an old-fashioned right cross to the jaw to convince a pregnant woman to let him examine her, but his healing touch and his attempt to persuade the woman to love and accept her child are as gentle as ever.

While medicine may become more mechanized and computerized in the future, Dr. McCoy shows that flesh and blood will always need TLC—tender, loving care, the presence of someone who can listen and respond to the individual, someone who can understand our fears and dreams. No machine can give us that.

McCoy is particularly valuable as the pragmatic, volatile human whose first reaction to almost any situation is sympathetic, sometimes before he even understands what's going on. His instinct is to pit good old human caring and trust against whatever may threaten. This is the most believable aspect of medical treatment aboard the *Enterprise*.

STAR TREK FANDOM IN AUSTRIA

by Karin Embacher

Awhile back, we ran an article discussing how Star Trek *is seen and appreciated in Germany. This time around, thanks to a native of the country, we have a look at* Star Trek *fandom in neighboring Austria. As usual with* Star Trek, *(to rephrase an old saying) the more things remain the same, the more they change. By the way, although Karin's English is excellent, it is not her first language. We decided to leave most of her article originally as she wrote it, so you fans could enjoy the colorful phrases she uses.*

The Best of Trek is just what I have always been longing for—analytical, explicative . . .

On reading the *Trek Roundtable* I suddenly myself felt the strong urge to write my own feelings and thoughts down. I think mostly because I have nobody around to share my interest in *Star Trek* with. I am afraid *Star Trek* is not so very popular here as it is with your people— but Austrians could never get as excited about any subject or form such big movements as folks in the U.S.A. do. I consider myself quite an ardent *Star Trek* follower, although I am of course practicing my personal fandom quite secretly—as mentioned above, my husband, my friends, my family don't understand my excitement about the show. There is only one girlfriend who just "likes" it. They all laugh about me and everybody would think me to be totally out of my mind if they knew how strong my emotions for *Star Trek* really are. Actually, I myself still shake my head and can't quite understand my affection for it. As others stated in their letters in *The Best of Trek* *#8*, I also felt\totally crazy at the beginning, and finding out there were so many others like me was highly consoling. I love to learn how other Trekkers feel about *Star Trek* and discuss the various questions.

I don't really have much to say, but will just give you sort of a capsule history of my involvement. (I hope my English is not too bad!)

In Austria, the first *Star Trek* episode was broadcast at 9 P.M. on Tuesday, September 4, 1973. (Don't laugh! I know that in the States the series' start was in 1966. We are always back.) I don't recall which episode it was, or whether or not I saw it. I have an article announcing the beginning of a new series with a picture of Spock's ear, headlined OBSERVE THAT EAR! I remember reading that article way back then, but it did not arouse any spectacular interest in me—how should it; I had never been too fond of science fiction, anyway. The first episode I saw was "Tomorrow Is Yesterday." I dropped in somewhere in the middle of the show, seeing men in uniforms running through a building, doors opening automatically in front of persons, the uniformed ones meeting policemen and suddenly vanishing in a sparkle and appearing somewhere else. As I had not seen the beginning, I was quite a mess at first, but by and by I began to understand the plot. I liked it. It was quite funny, too, especially the statements some crew members made.

I gave my okay to the show and decided to see it regularly. But I had counted without my host—or should I rather say mother.

I was only twelve then, and she preferred me in bed at 9:00 P.M. rather than in front of the TV set. She thought it was better to direct one's interest toward Latin, maths . . . than toward science fiction stories. And—most important—on Tuesday there always were cultural programs etc. on the first channel (we only have two), which she was interested in and insisted on seeing. So often I happened to see only part or even nothing at all of the episodes. Wasn't that a shame?

At first we only had a black-and-white TV set, and at school I used every minute to discuss *Star Trek* with my friend Sylvia. Her family had a color TV and she had to give me the uniform colors of each crew member and further information I had missed.

Part of my summer holidays I spent in England. In a bookshop I discovered TV tie-ins for different series, and I decided to give it a try. "Do you have books about the adventures of the "Spaceship *Enterprise*" [that is the title of *Star Trek* here in Austria]?" I asked. The assistant was a little bit puzzled at first, but then she mused I might mean *Star Trek* and told me where to find the books. I got *Star Trek 3, 4, and 5* and felt like having found the greatest treasure in the world.

Back in Austria they finally put the German translation of the Blish stories onto the market, too, and I of course bought them as soon as they were available. Thank goodness they only cost twenty-one Austrian Schilling then, because I only got fifty Schilling monthly pocket money. I watched *Star Trek* on TV as often as I could and even tried to record the sound of some episodes with my cassette recorder—I still have the tapes.

There was a partial rerun of the series then in summer 1977, as *"Schlechtwetterprogramm,"* meaning, whenever the weather was not fine, they broadcast a film on TV in the afternoon so that the kids (being on their summer holiday) who could not go swimming or play outside would not annoy their parents. (We don't normally have programs throughout the whole day.) Can you imagine a sixteen-year-old girl, staying with her cousins in that country, praying for rain or at least many dark clouds? (I think it is ridiculous!)

During another stay in England, in 1979, I saw some episodes. How strange to meet again all the familiar faces but with totally different—yet of course the original—voices! And I managed to get *Log One, Spock Messiah,* and *World Without End.*

And then came summer 1984. I sat there, watching TV, and suddenly I heard an all-too-familiar melody; I saw Spock, Kirk, and the rest on the *Enterprise* bridge. Then the TV speaker announced there would be a rerun of nineteen episodes starting the next Monday. My heart was making unusual jumps, my blood pressure rose to dangerous heights. *Star Trek!* Every day from Monday to Friday! At 6:30 P.M.! I canceled everything that might have endangered these "rendezvous." That was the first time I did not miss a single minute of any episode—

despite the constant mockery of the people around me. On the twentieth day there was a broadcast about science fiction films in general and *Star Trek* in particular. They also showed parts from *Star Trek: The Motion Picture*, and mentioned *The Wrath of Khan*. I noticed I had missed those movies; my family had been out of Vienna for four years and I never studied cinema programs, for there was no time and possibility for me to go there anyway.

Throughout the years that passed at university and during my marriage, my love for *Star Trek* has not diminished. But it had been resting somewhat dormant. I had certainly thought of it from time to time, but as *Star Trek* was not available in any form, I had to push aside my affection for it.

But now it was back again! I started to reread the few books I owned. In them I found lists of titles I did not possess. I developed a real mania to catch up on them. I phoned the British Bookshop and other Viennese bookstores that sold English literature and asked them to order the books for me. I did not realize then what a crusade I had begun.

The three movie tie-ins and three other novels were available at once, but that was it. I highly enjoyed reading them. In December, at last, I managed to drag my husband to Vienna to the cinema. We first saw *Star Trek III: The Search for Spock*, and two weeks later (fortunately) there was a rerun of *Star Trek: The Motion Picture*. I was a little disappointed—not by the films themselves, but I missed so much I had read in the books. Unfortunately a movie can never supply all the background, character, and little side-episodes written work offers. Still, I would have loved to go and see the movies day after day, as long as they were on. (By the way— Spock simply *had* to come back—no *Star Trek* without him!)

I am still in my own *Star Trek* adventure: *Star Trek: The Search for the Books*. Since November, by and by, I received twenty new books (out of, I think, sixty I ordered—in every volume there were new titles listed). You cannot imagine the difficulty of getting books from the U.S.A. or from England, in the twentieth century!

Here, in Austria, if you are lucky at all, it may take up to four or six months to get the books. (I can only hope Kirk and Company have overcome such shortcomings!)

My telephone bill is terrifying. I am constantly calling bookstores. And you cannot rely on them, either. The British Bookshop, for example, told me that *Devil World* was out of print and no longer available, and three days later I found it in another shop. (I wish I were rich and could just go to the U.S.A. myself and buy everything there; and how I'd love to attend the conventions!) But I am tough and do not give in. So I came across *The Best of Trek #8* as well. I am as excited as a child in front of the Christmas tree whenever the postman brings me a new book.

Only last summer I realized that there was organized *Star Trek* fandom in the U.S.A, and that there is much more available in the world of *Star Trek* than I had ever dared to dream of. All the new information I managed to get hold of made me only more devoted to the show. But the more I get and the more I learn, the more I want. I really am a little bit obsessed—especially as it is so difficult for me to take part, being so far away.

And it is only half the fun if you cannot share your thoughts with other people. That is why I am writing all this down. I know this relationship can never be a mutual one, but yet I have the consolation that at least the person who opens this envelope might read the letter and, perhaps, might even appreciate it a little.

Only today I received *The best of Trek #1–7*, which I had ordered in early summer after having read #8 and enjoyed it so very much. I ran through the contents, and when I came upon Charlotte Davis's article "*Star Trek* Lives in Germany" in *BOT #7* , I, out of self-evident reasons, couldn't resist reading it at once.

For me it was like reading "*Star Trek* Mysteries Solved." As Charlotte wrote, the Germans, and we here in Austria as well, were not spoon-fed with too much *Star Trek* anyway. (I envy the Americans who have their reruns permanently.) I got ever so excited and angry when I read what they had done to the episodes. Making all these senseless alterations is a sheer impertinence. This article made much more clearer for me and answered a lot of questions which had been puzzling me tremendously.

I remember seeing "Journey to Babel," and afterward reading the Blish novelization. I was terribly upset and confused because on TV Sarek definitely had called his wife Emily, and Blish named her Amanda. (I was keeping a list of "important *Star Trek* trivias" at that time, and such discrepancies were of course highly disturbing.)

The "Amok Time" (German: "Space Fever") plot-tampering has kept me in confusion throughout my whole twenty-two-year *Star Trek* fandom. Especially as I managed to get the *Amok Time* Fotonovel only three months ago, and it showed the same ending as the book and not as the TV episodes, where it was supposed to have been taken from. I was more disturbed than ever. I would never have imagined that cuts were made or the whole plot of a story changed to dramatically in a film. (Besides, I had never been content with the "nightmare" version.)

But actually I have to admit I was not too surprised to hear about faulty translations. I have read the novelizations of the television series and the motion pictures in German. A lot of absurdities and incongruities that occurred were solved when I later managed to get the books in English. I think it is absolutely mean to confront us not only with so very rare, but also false information. "Normal" people perhaps don't notice, but a fan surely does.

I am going to give you some of the examples I found:

• *The Fate of the Phoenix* was reduced from 262 to 161 pages.

• In *Star Trek III: The Search for Spock* (Saavik and Spock in *pon farr*):

English: "She was not certain that anything she could do would ease his pain. They were not formally pledged, psychically linked . . ."

German:". . . his pain. It was not located, not physically caused . . ."

- In "For the World is Hollow and I have Touched the Sky":

  (Spock studying Fabrini instructions to get behind the altar.)
  English: "Apply pressure simultaneously to the planets indicated."
  German: "Establish pressure equalization with planet's atmosphere."

  English: "Kirk turned to McCoy and Natira. 'Let's get out of this heat,' he called."
  German: "Kirk called to McCoy: 'Get the girl out, doc! Temperature seems to continue rising.' "

- In "Return to Tomorrow":

  English: Kirk: "Lieutenant, have Dr. McCoy report to the transporter room in ten minutes with standard landing-party equipment."
  German: "Lieutenant, have Dr. McCoy report to the transporter room in ten minutes with expeditionary party."

  (Spock mind melding with Sargon in the cave.)
  English: "Kirk flashed an alarmed look at McCoy. It had never been so hard."
  German: "Kirk flashed an alarmed look at McCoy. It had not been so hard for him."

- In "Charlie X": For years I had been wondering why everybody got so excited about a slap on Rand's shoulder, until I found out it actually was a slap on the rump.

Often the alterations and cuts concern sentences and parts that might not necessarily be essential for the plot but for characterization and atmosphere. And, after all, that is what makes a novel or a film a good piece of art—not to be shallow but to go beneath the surface. And that is especially what we love so much about *Star Trek*.

Are there no regulations that prohibit or limit such

alterations? What about copyright, "all rights reserved," and all that stuff?

After all, there are a lot of people who don't understand English, and so never can read or hear the original.

I got the address of the Andromeda Bookshop in Birmingham, England. They specialize in science fiction literature and have almost all the *Star Trek* books, magazines, and fanzines in stock. Had I only known about them at the beginning of my crusade! By now I own almost every novel and some zines (and I usually receive my orders within a fortnight). From Andromeda, I heard about the *Star Trek* Action Group, Britain's largest fan club, and I immediately became a member. (I'm ever so proud.) I was surprised, but of course very grateful as well, that *Star Trek* fandom in Great Britain was almost as common as in the U.S.A. They have everything over there: zines, conventions . . .

I've ordered *Star Trek* merchandise all around the States, and already received quite a number of stills, manuals, blueprints, etc. I also bought *Trek Special #2* from a STAG member. There is so much new information (*The Best of Trek* of course providing a lot of it), it is great! I have to admit that I gained much more knowledge and insight within the past six months than throughout all of my twelve *Star Trek* years together (of course due to lack of sufficient sources of information). I used to consider myself a *Star Trek* specialist—what a joke! But now I am beginning to become a real expert; knowing much more than any other average Austrian *Star Trek* watcher. (I'm sure I still can't compete with a real U.S. Trekker.) But I've fought hard for all that knowledge, believe me! Just think how misguided I was by television and translated books. I highly enjoy it, I love it, I'm terribly proud of being one of the great family!

THE ONE WHO IS SPOCK

By Joyce Tullock

Joyce Tullock really needs no introduction to our readers; she's been writing articles for us for almost ten years now, and remains the most popular of all our contributors. This time around, she turns her attention to everyone's favorite Vulcan, Mr. Spock. And, as usual, she manages to find some new insights into his character, those of his fellow officers, and Star Trek.

Only a few characters from the twentieth century's television explosion have achieved an historically grand stature. That is, they have reached beyond the generation that spawned them and have become truly larger than life. They have surpassed their creators' greatest expectations. There are characters like Matt Dillon of *Gunsmoke*—a series whose well-hewn, adventurous, and tight scripts will no doubt be examined (and plagiarized) by many writers/producers/television executives to come. There is Raymond Burr's *Perry Mason,* who looms on the screen to this day, larger than life, hard-hitting, even legendary. And, of course, there is *Star Trek*'s Mr. Spock, as strong and gallant as Matt, as complex and mysterious as Perry. But their ancestry is different. Matt's origins go back to another, earlier entertainment medium—radio. Perry of course sprang full-blown from the pages of Erle Stanley Gardner's mystery novels. But Spock is a homegrown video original. And he may well be the firstborn child of a new field of study in the American film culture—television.

His roots, alien though they be, are found in the culture of the 1960s. He is the product of that specific time, its daring openness and innocent optimism. He couldn't have been born in the fifties; he was too—well—different. He couldn't have reared his pointed ears in the seventies; he was much too stoical and reserved in thought and practice. And the eighties? No, Spock was too much a thinker to be born in the eighties, although his pointed ears would have probably been all the rage.

Now, of course, having long established his niche in our culture, he is free to be Spock—pointed ears, stoic personality, liberal idealism. He can have it all, because in a very real sense he exists above the maddening crowd as a part of our twentieth-century video heritage, perhaps the first TV-spawned character of grand dramatic proportions. Looking back, it is difficult to find *any* other television character of such dimensions who was not first made popular in another medium. Even the Lone Ranger and Superman had earlier, nontelevised beginnings. And their stature, while huge and legendary, is also a little too camp, lacking the intrinsic dramatic capacity of Spock.

That is probably Spock's secret, in fact. Of all the so-called super heroes, he alone has the capacity to attain moments of a truly dramatic nature. It really kind of puts him in a class of his own. And it most certainly (whether the science fiction establishment likes it or not) opened the door for surrealistic and science fiction filmmaking on a large scale.

Star Trek, led by Mr. Spock (not Captain Kirk, whose character type could have been comfortable as anything from Tom Mix to Bat Masterson), did break new ground. It doesn't matter that many will rave to their graves that science fiction had been around long before. Of course it had! And each of *Star Trek*'s episodes was based on the fantastic literature that preceded it. *Star Trek* was and is an example of the science fiction and fantasy genres, not a literary invention. It never pretended to be anything else. But its pain-filled and stormy existence in the 1960s served to celebrate the best science fiction has to offer. It gave science fiction film a foothold that only grew through such films as *2001: A Space Odyssey* and the *Star Wars* series. Of course, one of those films in science fiction and the other(s) fantasy, but that's the point. *Star Trek,* in its broad approach, merged two genres: science fiction and fantasy.

Star Trek, then, led by Mr. Spock, brought science fiction out of the closet once and for all. And frankly, it's very unlikely that the phenomenon would have occurred without him.

Let's face it, Spock stole the show. One shivers to think how long it might have taken science fiction film as we know and love and detest it to take off if Roddenberry had given in to the pressure to clip the ears.

The ears, of course, represent Spock's physical difference. We don't really care all that much about the differences we *can't* see, like the second eyelid or the heart where his liver ought to be. We're even only marginally concerned about this *pon farr* thing. (Well, some fans *are* terribly troubled by it, poor dears. We'll get to such matters of prejudice later.) Outward appearances meant all the world to us then, and they do now. That's why the pointed ears, though silly and inconvenient, are so important.

That brings up a matter that is absolutely essential to understand: everyone who becomes enchanted by the *Star Trek* universe—most especially by Spock—has pointed ears. Some don't realize it at first, but they discover them soon enough. Most of us, even the most socially successful and acceptable, are instinctively aware of a feeling of being "different" from everyone else. The intensity of this feeling of uniqueness or separateness varies from individual to individual, with an infinity of reasons ranging from upbringing to physique to ethnic heritage. Some of us are better actors than others, but deep inside it is the nature of every human being to feel just a little bit apart from everyone else, a little bit "the alien."

Americans are indeed said to be lonely people. Our advanced technology and independent heritage have helped to build around us a wall of isolation. Like Spock, who is hesitant to even *touch* a fellow crew member, we need living room and we distrust anyone who crosses the imaginary borderline of space we define as "ours."

So, whether we attribute it to the ears, to his need for privacy, or to Spock's near obsession with technology, we can empathize with him. We like him, though we may not every trouble to pinpoint just why. Blame it on the ears, or his sometimes smug and annoying air of superiority. Many admire Spock for his ability to keep cool in a crisis. More than a few longtime *Star Trek* fans admit that they enjoy the famous Spock/McCoy banter more than any other aspect of the series.

On certain levels, then, Spock is really quite easy to understand. That is, from the point of view of the human personality. We know we like him because he reminds us of ourselves—at times. At times, he reminds us of who we'd like to be. But audience identification aside, who is Spock really? As a character of fiction existing within his own *Star Trek* universe, he must be much more complex and—yes—*fascinating* than the first-glance superhero image implies.

The major problem with Spock's tremendous success is that, because of it, he has become part of popular culture. Like poor Admiral Kirk, who is hardly the futuristic Horatio Hornblower he was meant to be, he has been somewhat limited by the whims of those he serves. If he wasn't *liked* so darn much, he might have more impact as a dramatic character.

Today—much of the time—the poetic character and surrealistic poignancy of the half human, half alien is lost on an audience too easily thrilled by the likes of Darth Vader (not to diminish the Dark Lord's masterful evil) and a pack of high-tech gremlins. Spock is a creature of a very different kind of science fiction fantasy, one containing greater warmth than the stark but beautiful *2001: A Space Odyssey* and greater realism than the swashbuckling *Star Wars* saga.

Star Trek has always tried to find a point of balance between hard-core science fiction and the less restrained, but warmer fantasy genre, and it has been primarily successful at this because of its characters. They offer us a tremendous diversity. Kirk, for storybook heroics and his strong but caring macho image. McCoy, for plausibility as the fallible, believable human being. Spock, for the struggling man of the future, trying to reconcile the world of science and cold, hard logic to the world of the human heart. Because of the limited intellectual demands of the 1980s movie-going audience, both McCoy and Spock have been inhibited on the big screen, denied their less glamorous, but rightful place.

But if Spock and McCoy are not the heroes of the eighties, they should take comfort in the fact that they are heroes for all time. It isn't unreasonable to predict that in a future, more introspective era, they will be allowed to approach full potential—because the audience will demand it.

Anyone reading this article already knows what Spock's potential is. Otherwise they wouldn't be bothering with such specialized material. And they understand the complexity of his character. Why? Because they've seen the series. Probably many, many times.

To understand Spock, you have to see the series. It's as cold-blooded and simple as that. You must have a sense of his history, his beliefs, his prejudices and foibles. And it is absolutely necessary to allow for a willing suspension of disbelief so that the character—for fifty minutes—can become real enough to share his experience. It is the suspension of disbelief that builds the fiction of Spock into a very complete creative reality.

Reality can be frightening, especially the irrational reality of dreams and of the creative unconscious. Spock, as a Hollywood alien, has frightening roots. Consider the old movies, the monsters, the eerie aliens of the "B" pictures of the forties and fifties. In those films we find Spock's roots.

Can anyone deny that he is a 1960s version of Michael Rennie's character in the classic *The Day the Earth Stood Still*? Compare the grandness of nature, the elegance of stature and speech, the unaffected air of superiority. Like Rennie's character, Spock is superior to the common crowd because he is inherently disinterested in self. He is more mind than matter, both as a scientist and as a member of society. Like Rennie's aloof, majestic stranger from another planet, Spock is truly civilized. He is socially mature—from an alien standpoint.

Spock's alienness is very important, too. All the more so because it is the one aspect of character most misunderstood and maligned. It's one of the great ironies of *Star Trek* fandom that many fans so resent and so distrust his alienness that they try desperately to make him human. An all-human Spock, they seem to think, would be a happy Spock. One wonders from what frame of reference they speak, and can only conclude that it is a chauvinistic one. Or perhaps it is as we mentioned earlier: they so identify with his alienness (and thereby their own isolation) that they hope to achieve emotional happiness vicariously through him. Catharsis through fiction is fine, but there is something to be said for the sanity of knowing the value of another's creation in its own right. Spock doesn't need tampering; he needs to be understood and respected and examined for who he is.

He was born on an alien planet, Vulcan, of a Vulcan father, Sarek, an a human mother, Amanda. They were good parents, if imperfect. We can assume they didn't always agree about how to raise their son. Spock has struggled with his human half for some years, and in the early days of his service with Starfleet, he experimented with emotionalism. For some reason, he decided to strive more to emulate his father's ways. He tried to become one hundred percent Vulcan.

Perhaps his devotion to his human friends early on had caused him too much pain. We know of his intense capacity for loyalty and that it must have hurt indeed to see his physically inferior, shorter-lived human friends, such as Captain Pike, succumb to injuries and death—while he lived on. Eventually, Spock must have realized that strong attachment to the more fragile human race would bring him repeated emotional pain. It was better to employ his Vulcan tradition and training, denying, perhaps, everything his mother had encouraged in him, and become the stoic, logical Spock we have come to know.

He *chose*, then, to be Vulcan.

For the most part, he *is* Vulcan, despite all attempts to "humanize" him. Of course, there are those who cannot, for whatever reason, allow Spock to be "different" from his half brothers, the Terrans. We know of McCoy's constant nagging and challenging rhetoric. And we also know that there is purpose to what McCoy does. He is Spock's physician, his friend. That gives him a certain "territory," perhaps even a certain kind of obligation to make sure that Spock, as a friend and as a second-in-command of the *Enterprise*, is aware and appreciative of his human half. McCoy may also be conscious of a certain prejudice in Spock toward humans. Well, superior though he believes Vulcans to be, disdain of human nature has no place of a ship manned primarily by humans. McCoy knows that, and considers it his solemn duty to make sure that Spock knows it too.

But while McCoy sometimes pesters Spock about his humanness, he also holds his friend's Vulcan nature in high regard. He may even be in awe of it, as we see in such episodes as "Amok Time," "Journey to Babel," "Operation: Annihilate," and "The Deadly Years." In these episodes, we see a bit more of the Vulcan Spock than usual. In the latter three he shows his Vulcan superiority through his extraordinary physical prowess and his exceptional ability to remain strong in times of pain and stress. In "Amok Time," Spock's logic and presence of mind are challenged almost beyond capacity. McCoy is the first to know something is wrong, and doubtless understands that it has to do with "being Vulcan." Spock even points out that McCoy has guessed his problem—and commends him on his astuteness. What we may take to be a truce in this episode is simply an open expression of the kind of friendship McCoy and Spock have always shared.

Throughout it, McCoy is concerned with how Spock views his fellow humans. So is Kirk to a certain extent, but the captain is—shall we say?—more diplomatic. But, on the whole, there seems to be little curiosity about how Spock, as a Vulcan, views the world in general. What does he see? And how is it so different from the Terran perspective?

In his gruffer moments, McCoy might complain that Spock views the world in black-and-white, as though he were some living machine. But we know that McCoy, a man of tremendous complexity himself, sees that Spock is a being of great, but very *different*, dimensions. Throughout the series and into the movies McCoy comes to understand him, and so do we. But where do we begin? How do we learn to see and comprehend the many dimensions of the alien Spock?

The best way to know a man's philosophy is to observe his behavior. Behavior, even more than words, gives a sort of imprint of our identity. Spock, of course, is a man of few words. That is, unless he is arguing with McCoy, or is taken up with fascination on a certain scientific finding or study. In fact, those are the two things for which he is most remembered in *Star Trek*. His combative relationship with the illogical man (McCoy) and his love affair with science—the logic-based approach to studying the universe. They illustrate something basic to his character.

At first glance, then, we might have to say Spock is confused. He says the most "illogical" things to McCoy sometimes. And he seems to say them with great affection. McCoy, more than any other human Spock has known, brings out the Vulcan's "human half" as he badgers and prods and plays. But it is Spock's Vulcan half that commands the fine intellect to respond as cleverly as it does, and always in defense of the thing Spock loves most.

Order.

Order and logic are Spock's bywords. All of his principles are based on them. It is his religion, just as many humans are devoted to the mythologies and precepts of *their* ancestors. There is a correlation here, too, because Vulcans' love for logic is based on planetary experiences of an earlier time in their racial history.

We know only a little about the development of logic on the planet Vulcan, most of that information gleaned from incidents, remarks, or allusions to the past in such episodes as "The Savage Curtain," "Amok Time," and "All Our Yesterdays." In "The Savage Curtain," we meet Surak, a Vulcan of ancient times who is revered as one who brought the one-time warring planet out of its passionate Dark Ages and into the age of reason and logic. It is clear in the episode that Spock holds this Vulcan in awe; he is to Spock a hero of the greatest magnitude, almost a god.

In "Amok Time," we see how the Vulcans approach the absence of logic. In this episode, Spock must succumb to the sex urge of *pon farr*, and is seen, from the human perspective, as a victim of his passions. McCoy even remarks that the madness of *pon farr* might be the price Vulcans pay for suppressing their emotions the rest of the time. It's a good guess, but we really don't know. It seems to be a truly instinctual drive. What generally puzzles most humans about *pon farr* is the alienness of it. They cannot or will not comprehend that *pon farr* is a *normal* condition that is not of our species. Instead, it is considered by many to be a kind of disease for which there must surely be a cure. A rather bigoted approach, but there you are.

No one stops to think that Vulcans have been dealing with *pon farr* since "the beginning." The race has survived and evolved quite nicely. If Spock seems ashamed of his condition, it is because he is a private person on a ship filled with humans. They know little about his biology or his racial history and have come to expect certain behavior from him. He is the logical one, the "cold-blooded" alien who seems to disdain the concepts of love and romance and sexual pleasure.

But Kirk, McCoy, and Chapel have indeed proved themselves friends in "Amok Time." They see a problem, and try to approach it with compassion, understanding, and diplomacy. The tables are turned here, and it is the humans who are using logic (based on the emotions of love and loyalty). Kirk, McCoy, and Chapel not only figure out Spock's problem, they provide the support he needs to confront both his sex drive and the not-so-logical Vulcan ritual that surrounds that drive. "Amok Time" is one of *Star Trek*'s purest, most perfect episodes. It is rich in the culture of Vulcan and it presents the complexity of Vulcan society in a mysterious, very alien, and very poetic way. We don't get to see that kind of thing again until *Star Trek III: The Search for Spock*.

One thing that bothers humans is that *pon farr*, the Vulcan drive to reproduce, occurs only every seven years. Sex every seven years? Come on, now . . . let's get real. But it was never stated *anywhere* in *Star Trek* episodes that the Vulcan male (or female, for that matter) was subject to the apparent limitations of *pon farr*, *Star Trek* writer Dorothy (D. C.) Fontana insists that the *pon farr* condition is only one aspect of their sexuality. Vulcans, she promises a worried human audience, can have sex whenever they like—just like regular humans. Now that's fine, and it *is* reassuring. It certainly is supported by those occasions in *Star Trek* when Spock is attracted to womankind—"The Cloud Minders," "The Enterprise Incident," "This Side of Paradise," and "All our Yesterdays."

Of course, in a couple of those episodes his Vulcan guard is down, but that doesn't matter. We're talking about physiology here, and it's highly unlikely that outside influences like the spore of "This Side of Paradise" could change his basic physical makeup—unless, of course, they trigger the same biological responses that cause the onset of *pon farr*. We don't really know for sure, but we're pretty safe in assuming he is capable of enjoying sex at any time. It is his intellectuality that usually keeps him the lofty, dispassionate Vulcan.

But the great fuss about Spock's sexuality is interesting for what it says about his human admirers. Are we totally honest in our contention that we admire Spock for the creature he is? Or do we want him to be alien—but not too much so? There are certain rules and limitations, it seems, about how different he can be. He can't, for example, be *too* unemotional. None of us like him so, even Leonard Nimoy. So a little twinge of human emotion must peek through from time to time. And he absolutely *must* have a "normal" human sex drive. To many fans, that's even more important than the emotion stuff. To imagine a being without an ongoing sex drive is—well—just unimaginable! It is more obscene than imagining Spock to be godless.

And, oddly enough, a truly passionate Vulcan—of the old school, that is—does indeed appear to be less than god-fearing. Look at Spock in "All Our Yesterdays." He and McCoy are thrown five thousand years back in time, to a point in history when the Vulcans of his home planet are passionate, raging warriors. Observing Spock's altered behavior in this episode, one does wonder how the race survived. He nearly kills McCoy over the beautiful Zarabeth. And poor Bones isn't even interested in her, he just wants to get home!

Again in this episode we see the role reversal of "Amok Time." McCoy is the logical one; Spock the frantic, passionate lover. "All Our Yesterdays" reinforces what we have seen in "Amok Time," and it becomes easier to understand why the Vulcans have chosen logic as their religion. Reason has indeed become their savior. Here we see McCoy as teacher and friend, confronting Spock with the destructive nature of his passions. It's a microcosmic replay of Vulcan at the time of Surak, only instead of Surak, it is McCoy who lights the way. Here he is nothing less than a preacher striving to redeem the prodigal.

McCoy knows that Spock is alien. He doesn't fool himself with the idea that Spock can someday be as emotional as any human. He recognizes that concept as anathema to all Spock holds sacred. And in "All Our Yesterdays" McCoy sees firsthand proof of the value of the Vulcan logical tradition.

Spock is not like us and he never can be. He doesn't want to be. The Vulcan in him is dominant. We see that in his physiology, his intellect, and his life-style. It is so dominant that in *Star Trek II: The Wrath of Khan* he is able to transfer his *katra* to McCoy as he approaches physical death. That is not a human thing, but a Vulcan thing to do.

And what of his humanness? Isn't he also half human? How does he deal with it? Does he deny his human self? Does he repress it, or does he simply keep it boxed in a convenient, but accessible place to be called upon from time to time?

These questions are hard to answer, and to some extent, the answers *are* a matter of interpretation. Perhaps it is best if we first look at Spock logically. We know that he is half human, half Vulcan. We are pretty sure that the Vulcan genes are dominant. That is, if we go by the evidence. And all we *can* do is go by the evidence as far as a serious discussion of his character is concerned. Once we allow ourselves total conjecture, we have moved out of the universe of Paramount's *Star Trek* into our own private fantasies.

Those who spend any great amount of time with *Star Trek,* either as fans or professional writers, sooner or later find themselves embroiled with someone over the "K/S" syndrome in amateur fan writing. K/S, or "slash" writing as it is sometimes affectionately called, is based upon the theory that Kirk and Spock are lovers. It has become a popular theme with amateur writers because the theory alone presents the author with a storyline. The plot can simply evolve around proving that the concept is plausible. So for nearly ten years, K/S writers have been providing fandom with a steady stream of "apology" stories. The conditions and situations of the stories vary, of course, but the theme is always the same. They are always about how or why Spock and Kirk could become lovers.

K/S writing, from the perspective of Spock the Alien, is very interesting for what it says about humans. Or, more appropriately, what it says about our Western society and its Judeo-Christian ethics. The theory rests, of course, on Spock's isolation and Kirk's vulnerability. But this writer has yet to read a K/S story that is about Kirk and Spock. Generally, one or both of the characters is forced to change his basic nature due to some extenuating circumstance (usually some horrible, at least partially sadistic experience). Perhaps Kirk becomes injured and Spock, stoic though he has always been, must dig deep into his "human" emotions and find the means to comfort Kirk. (McCoy is generally dead by this point in the story, or in any case certainly out of the picture—often relegated to the status of a minor character.) However the plot works, it is designed to force Spock to reach deep into his heart and dramatically rip away the icy, logical, Vulcan exterior to show that he is a "real human" underneath.

At best, the K/S concept is intellectually naive; at worst, it is bigoted. For it assumes that Spock can only be happy if he is totally, passionately, *humanly* emotional. It also displays prejudice by implying that the heterosexual but stoic Spock of the series and movies lacks the basic ability to express love. And finally, it makes the grand, Western mistake of equating love with sex. This is ultimately where it fails, for it lacks the kind of painstaking honesty, intellectual depth, and objectivity that are necessary for the honest interpretation of literature. It ignores or rationalizes away the evidence of the characters of both Kirk and Spock in the episodes and movies. It is a prejudiced approach to the alien Spock, striving desperately to give *human* sexuality and *human* personality to an alien being. The K/S concept is of more interest for what it says about the human need to homogenize and anthropomorphize the behavior of life forms we do not understand. And by such means, K/S commits the primary mistake—it sells the complex Kirk/Spock/McCoy relationship short by looking for easy explanations for the phenomenon of friendship.

Even Captain Kirk has something to say about the concept, as we see in the second chapter of Gene Roddenberry's novelization of *Star Trek: The Motion Picture:* ". . . although I have no moral or other objections to physical love in any of its many Earthly, alien, and mixed forms, I have always found my best gratification in that creature, *woman.*" The suggestion here is that Kirk very possibly *has* experienced many forms of lovemaking, but evidently not with his Vulcan friend. If we interpret Kirk's statement within the framework of the K/S theory, we must draw a very uncomplimentary conclusion as far as Spock's sexual talents are concerned. That is, if they *were* lovers, Spock did not provide Kirk "best gratification." Of course, some claim that Kirk was simply trying to "cover" for Spock here, but that would seem an even greater insult. Kirk would certainly never insult Spock, especially over a matter that must be of only passing interest to those of the reputedly enlightened twenty-third century. Maybe it's time to take the admiral at his word.

In any case, lovemaking for Vulcans is a thing about which we know almost nothing. Even the creators of *Star Trek* show confusion here, as the great debate over whether Vulcans enjoy sex at will or only once every seven years (as Roddenberry suggests in the same footnote) continues. Fact is, as far as Spock is concerned, it really doesn't matter. No doubt he knows that we Terrans will keep insisting on viewing even Vulcan sex habits from a human perspective, regardless of the fact that it's none of our business.

In truth, Spock is neither human nor Vulcan. He is a new being—as far as we know, the only one of his kind in the universe. That places on him a tremendous burden, and he becomes a kind of ambassador of two worlds, two distinct species, two philosophies.

As his experience with humans increases, he seems to strive, not to be like them, but to accept the side of himself that is human and to cherish it. He does not need to be told he harbors human emotion; he knows it. And if it takes a long time for him to accept it, it is only because he recognizes its negative aspects. To learn to love is to learn to hate. To learn to laugh is to learn to cry. And, for a long-lived Vulcan, to find friendship within the human heart is to find a frail, beautiful treasure indeed. The human life span is half that of a Vulcan. And humans are a less hardy species overall than are Vulcans. One wonders—how many times has Spock already had to say good-bye?

We understand his struggle with emotions, and rightly equate it with our own emotional limitations. In his struggle not to be too human, he convinces us of our own value. And with McCoy and Kirk as his mentors, friends, and—at times—his castigators, he observes the virtues and defects of the emotional human.

Throughout the series, there are occasions when Spock is tested and tutored in the experience of his emotional heritage. "The Naked Time," "The Galileo Seven," "This Side of Paradise," "Journey to Babel" (where he must come to terms with his love for his parents and his own need for self-discovery and identity), "Bread and Circuses," "The Paradise Syndrome," "The Tholian Web," "The Empath," and "All Our Yesterdays," to name some important ones.

Each of these episodes deals with some aspect of growth in Spock's character. Whether it is the revelation in "Naked Time" about his own feelings for his neglected human mother or the learning experience of balancing emotion and logic to make command decisions in "The Galileo Seven," Spock begins to understand that emotion and logic must be somehow compatible.

In "The Tholian Web" he learns that logic alone is not enough when dealing with humans during the highly emotional time of a commander's death. It's possible that Spock acquires more diplomacy in this episode than in all the experiences that went before. His friendship with McCoy survives the hardest trial—the apparent death of Kirk—and is subtly changed by the end of the episode, so that we know it is impervious to destruction. It sets the stage for things to come—the challenge of Spock's psychological reversion in "All Our Yesterdays" and the shattering pain of McCoy's sacrifice in "The Empath."

The incidents of "The Tholian Web" and "The Empath" illustrate two things about Spock: he is loyal to his friends with a depth of character that is almost superhuman, and cold, logical Vulcan though he is, he knows *how* to be a friend. In "The Tholian Web" he takes terrible risks, knowing that there is a chance to save Kirk. In "The Empath," he knows how to help his friend face death when the end if imminent. And yet he does not do these things better because he is half human, but because he is half Vulcan. He has learned to care as a Vulcan cares, with logic and grace.

In "The Empath," Spock is much more able to comfort McCoy than Kirk is, not because Kirk doesn't care, but because Spock, as a Vulcan, is able to cast aside his own hurt enough to avoid being debilitated by it. His logic helps him do the compassionate thing. And because he can control his emotions, he ultimately saves McCoy's life as he admonishes Kirk to suppress his emotions long enough to break free of the Vians' force field. (The power field in which Spock and Kirk are trapped grows stronger with intensified emotions. They are literally caged by the emotions.)

So Spock used his life experiences to judge the talents of his Vulcan half and the value of his human half—and found his own unique way to live. Neither human nor Vulcan, perhaps, but successful. And *that* is the important thing. Not that he does it *our* way, but that he finds a way that works for him, the most alien of all the aliens.

After all, in the entire universe of *Star Trek,* there is only one Spock. If other human/Vulcan hybrids came after him, we are not told about it.

Because we are human, we know of what his human half consists, but we must move cautiously when assessing the Vulcan half. Most of us have a very good idea about what it is like to be different, to be an outsider for one reason or another. But we are all humans. We can't see the world any other way. Our perspective is almost hopelessly limited, except for the tiny peephole of the imagination.

In *Star Trek,* it is really only through this peephole that we observe Spock. We know a little of the history of his home planet, that Vulcans were once a warlike, vicious race who nearly destroyed themselves with their passions. Not so different from the natives of Earth? It's hard to say; the connection is there. But the difference seems to be that in *Star Trek,* the human creature, despite all its viciousness, has not yet found it necessary to give up its emotions in order to survive. One might guess that, instead, Terrans have learned to employ their emotions in a constructive manner (as did McCoy in "The Empath").

In fact, one of the themes in *Star Trek* is the positiveness of mankind, suggesting that its ability to use emotions well is its crowning glory. It's all very much in the tradition of IDIC, for similarly the Vulcans' great source of pride is their masterful use of logic.

The Vulcans seem to be a fairly creative race, something which should be surprising when one considers the way they frown on spontaneity. But then again, we really don't know all that much. Perhaps our excellence in music, literature, and the arts is equivalent to Vulcan achievement in the sciences. Most likely, order and discipline are necessary to the development of Vulcan art, music, literature, and philosophy. From one perspective, precision is important in all disciplines. And over the millennia, we can imagine that the beautiful, mathematical precision of the Vulcan mind has unlocked the poetic in all things.

Where the arts are concerned, however, it's nice to imagine the Vulcans envy us a little. (Too bad they can never admit to such a base emotion.)

The logical, Vulcan approach to life is just as pervasive in the family structure, at least if we believe the little evidence we have in "Journey to Babel." Spock's mother makes it clear that (somewhat against her wishes) he was raised as a Vulcan in the truest sense. Perhaps she is also suggesting that Spock (in that episode, at least) is overcompensating in his effort to please his father with his devotion to logic and duty. It is certainly apparent in "Journey to Babel" that Spock is conspicuously Vulcan compared to the self-assured ease of Sarek.

Amanda is a tremendously successful character. Powerful, human, and gracefully defiant. She claims her right as Spock's mother by demanding that he face his own bigoted view of humanity. "Human" is not a dirty word, she reminds him. And by implications, neither is it a failing to show affection. Her great dignity and wisdom actually *demand* that he recognize the value of his human heritage.

Only one other character in the series—McCoy—speaks to Spock with such open, painful honesty. Knowing that, we come to realize how important a part McCoy must have played in the ultimate development of Spock's personality. The doctor's way of boldly chastising Spock no doubt was essential in paving the way for Spock's maturity and eventual self-knowledge. McCoy's unembarrassed human emotions prepared his Vulcan friend for what was to come.

In *Star Trek: The Motion Picture* we find a frightened Spock who has turned away from McCoy and Kirk and the world of humankind in a last-ditch effort to totally "belong" with his Vulcan brothers. The pull of the Vulcan way was always strong, and he hoped to be a part of that world by accomplishing the discipline of *kolinahr*. He almost made it, but Vejur—that long lost relative of humanity and science—came home to roost. Spock's Vulcan mind sensed Vejur's presence out there beyond the system Sol. He felt its power, its all-consuming logic and order. But it is safe to say he also felt something else— danger to his human friends, to a world that was *also* the home of his ancestors.

It's not all that certain if it was Vejur he sought (to answer some personal questions about the logic/emotion debate) or if it was something more subtle but equally profound. But he does come home to the *Enterprise* swiftly, like a prodigal son, embarrassed by the emotional "family," welcome and uncomfortable with the fact that he is still loved (and still trying desperately to deny the fact that he loves in return).

The Spock of the first movie is certainly a character who has tried, very hard, to move away from things human. Quite literally, he had attempted to cleanse himself on the planet Vulcan. It took an entity with no flesh and blood at all to illustrate the value of being human, and to show that his hoped-for "purging of emotions" would have led, not to a superior existence, but to a sterile one.

Spock acquired in *STTMP* a code of values that would change his life forever. Like Decker/Ilia, he found a way to use emotion and logic to constructive, even orderly ends. *Star Trek: The Motion Picture* portrayed Spock's spiritual rebirth, and was no less important to him than *Star Trek III: The Search for Spock*. Probably more important.

It's doubtful, come to think of it, that we would ever have acquired the understanding we now have of Spock if it were not for the events and his behavior in *STTMP*. Spock's personality in this picture is more severe than usual (on the surface, that is); we have never seen him so cold, so isolated, so desperately sad. He is clearly in need of something more than his precious logic. For the first time we are able to realize that perhaps, like Vejur, he is a child still; that just perhaps, for all their extraordinary strength, telepathic powers, and longer life spans, Vulcans do not mature as quickly as humans. It makes sense, when seen from an alien perspective.

So it is that in the cold, sterile, but very logical mind of Vejur, Spock finally discovers the truth: in order for any person to grow, he must acquire an understanding and appreciation of "this simple feeling." What is this "feeling?" Define it as you like—love, friendship, compassion, or simply the ability to recognize the beauty of life. Like so many great discoveries, the power of emotion had been too obvious too long. For Spock's complicated mind, it *was* too simple. He almost missed it.

Some years later, at the time of *The Wrath of Khan*, Spock has indeed matured, no doubt as a result of his transforming experience during the Vejur crisis. His friendship with Kirk is open and appreciative; he seems to have developed an unapologetic warmth and affection for Dr. McCoy's all-too-human temperament. They are friends as in the old days, but are more obvious about it. Spock is no longer ashamed of the human blood coursing through his veins. He carries himself with the proud dignity of his father, and beneath the surface—just beneath—is the wisdom to love openly, his human mother's gift.

It is not just the combination that allows him to give his life for the *Enterprise* and her children. It is the *way* he has come to use his Vulcan and human blood as the galaxy's most alien of aliens. Who could better learn the art of friendship than one who has stood so long separate? When Spock, in *Star Trek: The Motion Picture,* came to understand the magic mixture of his heritage and, even better, how to use it, he welcomed himself home.

If Spock began his life on the planet Vulcan, then there is a very real, very rich poetry in the fact that as death approached he would entrust his *katra*, his living spirit, to the most irascible, most earthy, most human of all humans—McCoy. Amanda would have approved.

So it is that in *The Wrath of Khan* and *The Search for Spock* we see a different Spock than in the series. He has grown as a Vulcan and has assimilated his humanness beautifully. Having matured as the alien from two worlds, his spirit is no longer striving with opposites. He has finally solved the great mystery. He is Spock.

PON FARR AND THE SEARCH IDENTITY

By Kyle Holland

You've told us that the ongoing dialogue between our writers—and sometimes readers, as well—is one of your favorite things about these Best of Trek *books. Not that we plan these debates, you understand . . . They just spring up spontaneously when a reader takes exception to something another reader said in the latest* Best of Trek, *and sits down to write out his own thoughts on the subject. Then the original reader responds, then perhaps another, then the first . . . Fun, isn't it? Here, Kyle Holland presents the latest salvo in the ongoing* pon farr *controversy, and we fully expect it to draw some equally convincing and well-researched return fire.*

I read Katherine D. Wolterink's "In Defense of *Pon Farr*" (*The Best of Trek #11*) with admiration. She has raised this discussion to a new level of sophistication. After considering some of the basic points involved in the *pon farr* issue, particularly as it relates to "Amok Time," I find I am still in disagreement with her. But she has staked out new frontiers for analysis of the role of *pon farr*, and I would like to follow into those regions with my own line of reasoning, with all due thanks to her for pioneering them.

Wolterink clearly lays out the dividing questions between those of us who believe that Spock's *pon farr* in "Amok Time" was false and those of us who think it was genuine. She fairly characterizes my view: that the psychobiological initiative for *pon farr* rests in the Vulcan female, and that *pon farr* as manifested in the male is only a response. I have also hypothesized ("Why Spock

Ran Amok," *The Best of Trek #7*) that in "Amok Time," Spock clearly experiences, albeit at T'Pring's telepathic suggestion, a "false" *pon farr*—that is, a psychosomatic imitation of *pon farr* symptoms that, being false, have no reproductive value, but are more revealing of the psychic tensions within Spock himself. Certainly, Wolterink is persuasive in arguing that a disagreement about the nature of *pon farr* is at base a disagreement about the nature of Vulcan society. Similarly, disagreement over the physiological nature of Spock's *pon farr* experience reveals fundamental disagreement about the nature of Spock and his experiences thus far.

On the particulars of cyclic sexual activity among Terran mammals, I agree with Wolterink that it is hazardous to extrapolate laws that might pertain also to extraterrestrial life. But I am interested in her observation that, as Spock suggests, there may be universal natural principles at work everywhere. Photoperiodicity may, on Earth, be a strong environmental influence on sexual activity. But on Vulcan, or any dual-star system, it seems to me that it might well play a lesser role. Pheremones, whose role in sexual development on Earth is confirmed but not yet well understood, may be a model for the sort of biological environment that stimulates sexual preparedness on Vulcan. But the fact is that as far as Vulcan mating may relate to that elsewhere, we have only Spock's observations upon the necessity of returning to one's natal place. The actual workings of *pon farr* Spock hesitates to compare with any other species; indeed he is outraged at Kirk's remarks about the birds and the bees. So we are left with only empirical evidence.

Is the onset of *pon farr* controlled by the biological state of Vulcan females or is it not? No positive statement is ever offered us concerning the means by which *pon farr* occurs every seven (Vulcan?) years. Let us propose, as Wolterink very reasonably suggests, that it is a matter of coinciding physiological timetables. The bonded pair come to preparedness at the same time; the female does not control the male response, the male does not control the female. Once every seven years this happens, and though we do not know the Vulcan birth rate, let us assume the encounter will in over fifty percent of the cases result in at least one offspring. Without, again, making close assumptions about the length of Vulcan females' reproductive careers, let us at least infer that outside of the Sarek household Vulcan families tend to be large, with a norm of between five and seven children. This would explain the ability of Vulcans to sustain themselves over time in such an inhospitable environment: they have a foolproof reproductive strategy.

This hypothesis rests upon absolute, precise synchronization between the male and female. If, by chance, they should deviate by much as a day, let us say, in the onset of their first mutual *pon farr,* it is unlikely, after a lapse of seven years, that they will ever coincide again, or at least not until they are very old. Let us, again, begin with what we know of species close at hand. In animals that travel in herds, male activity, as Wolterink notes, coincides with the greatest likelihood that the greatest number of females are in estrus. That works out well enough in such sociobiological environments. What about in situations where the males' sexual choices are more limited? Rutting, as a phenomenon, may not be found; the males may instead become more sexually adaptable, and the females may be in estrus more frequently.

Vulcan society, we must infer from what we know, is monogamous. So the principles that are believed to govern certain mammalian behavior on Earth and be relevant to Vulcan mating must pertain to monogamous situations. On Earth, those situations all call for perpetual sexual preparedness on the part of the male. We know for a fact that this is not at all the case on Vulcan. Males (and we assume, females) may reproduce only once every seven years, and there must be absolute synchronization between the sexes for species survival. On Earth, there is tremendous variation in the physiological rhythms of individual primates and humans; regularity on an order that could ensure species survival in the Vulcan scenario is very unusual. If, for instance, the human male was not perpetually prepared for reproduction but had somehow to hope that some onset of rut would coincide with his mate's period of estrus, clearly the species would have disappeared. How have the Vulcans survived? I think it is unlikely that Nature has left the Vulcans to the mercy of coinciding seven-year individual patterns, even if in youth they are synchronized in the affiancing bond.

We have also to consider the biological logic of unresolved *pon farr* resulting in death for the Vulcan male but not, apparently, for the female. The conceiving ability of the Vulcan female, as in the human female, takes primacy over the fertilizing ability of the male; if he cannot fulfill his function, he is disposed of by the workings of his own genes and the female is presumably enabled to form a new bond. I hypothesize that Nature has in the case of Vulcan employed the efficacious strategy of allowing female estrus to control the onset of male rut by means of hormonal or telepathic connections. In fact, I would go so far as to say that we have a clue as to how these work. The initial state is telepathic, perhaps not so different from that which linked Spock to the crew of the *Intrepid;* McCoy commented upon the peculiarity of this telepathy that needed no tactile encounter. The hormonal, or pheremonal, communication that is necessary for full-blown *pon farr* demands proximity of the two parties (logically enough); hence Spock's underscoring the importance of returning to the natal place, where the male will encounter the controlling female.

The question of whether or not females consciously or willfully control the onset of *pon farr* in males is another matter. Before going on to that, I would like to point out that Wolterink's discussion and her suggestions that we may learn some lessons from Terran biology raise some intriguing questions regarding Vulcan social history. Insofar as *pon farr* may be compared to rut, we are forced to wonder whether Vulcan was originally a monogamous society; is it not more likely that pre-Surak Vulcan was sexually chaotic, males and females in *pon farr* mating with any available partner(s) in hopes of evening the odds for species survival? Is *koon-et-kalifi* a ritual remnant from a transitional period from matriarchy to patriarchy, when males simultaneously affected by a female's estrus fought for the right to mate with her? We are also forced to ask whether the Vulcans have not genetically engineered the seven-year cycle for themselves; was a *pon farr* originally a much more frequent occurrence, now limited to seven years in the interests of social stability? Clearly, the survival of Vulcans on their harsh world despite their very inefficient reproductive strategies suggests (a) that *pon farr* does not depend upon individually coinciding physiological schedules over the long term and (b) that the Surak reforms included a major revision of sexual practices, family structure, and possibly a later element of genetic engineering.

If the initiative for *pon farr* rests with the female, is it necessary to assume that she has conscious control of the process? I am inclined to think that the answer to this is not clear even to the Vulcans themselves. T'Pring's explanation of her motives in choosing Kirk as her champion in the *koon-et-kalifi* is not entirely satisfactory. To me, she is very obviously implying that she would be capable of a sexual relationship with Stonn even if her bond with Spock were to remain intact (we never have the least hint that Spock might have the same flexibility). And, like the male death sentence of unresolved *pon farr*, the *koon-et-kalifi* would hardly exist if the female did not have the ability to form and break the psychosexual bond (if this were a male capacity, the females would be battling it out instead). On the other hand, if we look at the case of Sarek and Amanda Grayson, we would have to assume that if the female initiative is willful, then Amanda would have to have become an adept at Vulcan female sexual science before she and Sarek could have taken up conjugal life. I would hypothesize the following: *pon farr* begins in the female with the intuition of estrus, and ends in the female with conception, or a reasonable attempt at it; males are stimulated by change in their bonded female and experience the physiological crisis of *pon farr*, which subsides only after mating has occurred. Females are conscious of what is happening, and all of Vulcan culture affirms the primacy of the female role. The females do not, however, have an extensive ability to willfully manipulate the process, so long as their original partner is within proximity. Hence, Wolterink's concerns about Vulcan females precipitating violent sexual assaults upon their own persons is obviated.

This makes the relationship of Sarek and Amanda much more sensible to me. I am willing to accept Wolterink's suggestion that as two intelligent, sensitive, and loving souls, Amanda and Sarek could tolerate and perhaps even thrive within a celibate relationship. Presumably, in that case, Spock's conception was aided by a considerable amount of medical technology, a suggestion that has been made by several novelists. But I do not think such assumptions are necessary. As a Vulcan male, Sarek must have the ability to respond to his mate's sexual cycle after the establishment of an effective psychic link, whether or not conception is actually possible. If we are going to be nosy about it, we would have to conclude that Amanda's relationship with Sarek would not have the human aspect of sexual expression unmotivated by the reproductive imperative, and here I agree with Wolterink that in all probability Vulcans do not have recreational sex. Fortunately for Sarek and Amanda, human females become receptive to fertilization eighty-four times more frequently than their Vulcan counterparts. I should point out here that I do not share Wolterink's assumption that the evident passion of *pon farr* and the violence of *koon-et-kalifi* implies corresponding violence in mating.

If *pon farr*, as a psychological and as a social phenomenon, is controlled by female Vulcan biology, are we forced to consider Vulcan a matriarchy? Marx and Engels, together with a host of sociologists and archaeologists, hypothesized that matriarchy would be the dominant pattern in all primitive societies; warfare, division of labor, and the development of higher-order political organization all contribute to the shift toward patriarchy. It would not be unreasonable to suggest that Vulcan had a matriarchal prehistory. But unless the *koon-et-kalifi* was in essence a female strategy for selecting the strongest mating partners from among the contenders (and T'Pring's role in Spock's *koon-et-kalifi* suggests that this may have been a possibility), we have also to consider that in some period, perhaps pre-Surak, the transition to patriarchy occurred. There have been many hypotheses put forward regarding Vulcan history and its patriarchal or matriarchal nature. What concerns us here are the implications of *pon farr* for Vulcan society. If *pon farr* is a fixed, unchanging biological process (and I have expressed some doubts about this), does it not present a fixed, unchanging impetus toward matriarchal social and political structures? (I would say there is not necessary implication here.) The bond formed between T'Pring and Spock, even if dependent in its biological aspects upon T'Pring's personal physiology, was nevertheless the result of a social process that neither of them controlled; it was an arranged marriage of a sort well known in many terran cultures, imposed upon minors. Who controlled that process? We do not know. We have no clues.

We must however ask ourselves the meaning of T'Pau's presence at the intended wedding ceremony. Was it merely a ritual appearance, to oversee the ceremonies, by a dignitary of sufficient standing to reflect the status of Spock's and T'Pring's families? Or did T'Pau have a personal interest in the proceedings; had she in fact been a party to the original bonding? Certainly her demeanor toward Spock, T'Pring, and Kirk gives evidence of great personal interest and even great personal control. Though there is no necessary relationship between the biological workings of *pon farr* and a matriarchal Vulcan, independent evidence in fact suggests that women on Vulcan have great power. Of all those involved in the original bonding of Spock and T'Pring, we see only T'Pau as a possible controlling factor. And we are not left in the dark as to T'Pau's standing in Vulcan society, and indeed, in galactic politics. She is without doubt the most powerful living Vulcan to whom we are introduced. Sarek, even with his high professional profile, does not compare to her. We also know that Spock's failed initiation into *kolinahr* is overseen by a priestess, just as T'Lar presided over the return of Spock's *katra* to his body. On the basis of our observations, we have no choice but to see that the highest levels of Vulcan social, political, philosophical, and religious endeavors (if such distinctions are meaningful on Vulcan) are controlled by females. In the absence of evidence to the contrary, we are forced to conclude that, at the very least, Vulcan is a society where females have full access to power and prestige. But weighing the possibilities, we may as easily decide that Vulcan is indeed a society that we might characterize as matriarchal.

Pon farr's object is reproduction, and the foregoing discussion has emphasized the supreme importance of effective reproductive strategy in the survival of the Vulcan race. Given the inhospitable Vulcan environment and the apparent sparseness of its modern population, a minor flaw in the reproductive strategy would be fatal for the species. The ability of a Vulcan male to solve his *pon farr* crisis without mating would present such a flaw. Fortunately for Vulcans, we understand clearly in the early moments of "Amok Time" that such resolution is not possible. Vulcan males must return to their natal place and mate, or they will die. But this is not the way that Spock's *pon farr* is resolved. The emotional crisis catalyzed by his belief that he has killed Kirk dissipates his *pon farr*-like symptoms. I do not see how "Amok Time" can leave any doubts regarding the falseness of Spock's *pon farr*. Moreover, the falseness is basic to an understanding of Spock's experiences, both with and without his *Enterprise* companions.

As I have suggested in "Why Spock Ran Amok," Spock's lived aboard the *Enterprise* during the five-year mission under constant pressure from his human shipmates to prove himself either a man or a Vulcan. Since childhood he had lived as a Vulcan, and we can only guess the identity problems that may have been sparked by the attitudes of his Vulcan classmates and relatives to the half human among them. His fierce determination to live as a Vulcan was what he brought with him aboard the starship—to be met not only with the prejudices of the human officers, but also with constant challenges from Kirk and McCoy to confront his human half. We know he chose to cleave to his often stereotypical, one-dimensional concept of "Vulcanness." But the solution was inadequate: on either side there was the pain of being less than human and less than Vulcan, while keeping up an almost unbearable alien facade.

Given Spock's willful devotion to his Vulcan identity and heritage, it is easy to understand the importance to him of having his sexuality ordered in the Vulcan way. For humans, the involvement of sex and emotion led to confusion, uncertainty, and often intense pain. The possible threat to Spock was profound, and again Vulcanness was a solution, a key to a world in which sex was made secretive, ritualistic, and uncomplicated by emotions. It was the fundamental strategy for Spock's gaining control over his own chaotic inner self, provoked constantly as it was in his contacts with humans.

Often we have had glimpses into the inner turmoil of Spock. In "The Naked Time," his genuine human emotions pour forth. A similar thing happens later in "This Side of Paradise": raw emotions threaten to undermine the ideals of service and loyalty that Spock has spent his mature life pursuing. He is clearly an individual who, in attempting to suppress half of himself, has created a potentially volatile situation. And we know, during the five-year mission, that Spock (like so many humans) is adrift, with no adequate way to conquer the turbulent world within himself.

This is the context within which "Amok Time" occurs. For all we know, this is not Spock's first *pon farr* encounter with T'Pring. He may have experienced *pon farr* symptoms at her prompting previously, and may have fulfilled his role without consciousness of the fact that his symptoms were psychosomatically induced (if not, then he has already had occasion to doubt his ability to experience genuine *pon farr*.) But this time is different. This time there will be fundamental conflict between his drive to fulfill his Vulcan identity and the human drive (which he has suppressed and will continue for some time to suppress) to form bonds of love and respect with others. The power of his repressed human half exposes the falseness of his supposedly insuperable Vulcan physiological imperative. Spock's problems are not solved, but he has, possibly against his will, been moved a pace away from the archetypal Vulcan pose he had assumed to that point.

Spock's psychological development remains unchanged until his meeting with Vejur, and it is significant that he characterizes Vejur (and, by implication, himself) as a child. That certainly corresponds with that we have previously seen in Spock's encounters with his own and others' emotions. But now, Spock's appreciation of his own uniqueness has been deepened by his failure to achieve *kolinahr* and the final confirmation of Vulcan identity it represented. He has clearly been a child, uncomfortable with and resentful of the threat presented by his own feelings, and seeking refuge in a god of total logic. For a time he despairs, seeing the emptiness of Vejur and the emptiness of himself. But the resolution Spock was deprived of in "Amok Time" is found by Vejur in *Star Trek: The Motion Picture*. As James H. Devon has so comprehensively suggested ("Beneath the Surface: the Surrelistic Star Trek"; *The Best of Trek #10*), the movie is a prolonged sexual metaphor. But I think the emphasis here is on metaphor. The underlying urge to unite with another, to not be left alone and meaningless, is a recurrent theme in *Star Trek*, and has often taken the form of a sexual tale. "Amok Time" was in many ways the inverse: the exposure of the false physiological drive Spock had imposed upon himself meant the collapse of an illusory unity built not upon truth and love, but upon fear and suspicion of one's own nature. Spock, after his *kolinahr* failure, Vejur's successful uniting with its creator, and his announcement that his "mission on Vulcan is completed," had far to go in search of himself. To date, the films have not taken him much further along the path.

It is interesting that a sexual confusion similar to Spock's may have affected Saavik. When left alone with the adolescent corporeal Spock on the Genesis Planet, she assumes that his physical discomfort is symptomatic of *pon farr*, and evidently proceeds to take ameliorative measures. Since Spock has jealously guarded the secret of his true, human (or quasi-human) sexual development, it is evidently an honest mistake, and we can presume that Saavik's ignorance of Vulcan culture has not alerted her to the fact that the "Spock" in her care is much too young to be undergoing *pon farr* (immature males, clearly, are not equal to the rigors of *koon-et-kalifi*). Her assumption that a half-Vulcan female could provide helpful service to a Vulcan in Spock's assumed condition may also not have been well founded. In light of this, I am inclined to think that there are many possible reason for her embarrassment before Spock in the last moments of *Star Trek III: The Search for Spock*. In any case, let us hope that her assignment to Vulcan will allow her to clarify these matters.

A COMPREHENSIVE LOOK AT THE KLINGONS

By Adam G. Alsop

Klingons have always been a fascinating part of Star Trek *lore. Almost surprisingly so, as Leslie Thompson pointed out in her first Klingon article way back in* Trek *#1, since they appeared in comparatively few of the television episodes. Still, there is just something about the Klingons that interests and enthralls us . . . perhaps it's simply that they can do the dirty, rotten deeds that we can't, and we get vicarious thrills watching them work their evil ways. Writers of the* Star Trek *novels have not ignored the Klingons, either—in fact, a number of them have managed to expand and explain Klingon lore far beyond anything we ever imagined back in the series days. Adam Alsop guides us through a tour of some of this "new" Klingon information—and we'll betcha there's something here you didn't know.*

Klingon. The very word conveys a sense of violence and "nastiness." As David Gerrold first put it in *The World of Star Trek,* "Klingons are professional villains. They are nasty, vicious, brutal, and merciless. They sharpen their fangs by hand because they think pain is fun." In the five episodes that features Klingons, they were variously portrayed: Kor was ruthless, but intelligent; Kras was ruthless, but careless; Koloth was (surprisingly) somewhat effeminate, while his lieutenant, Korax, was abusive, insulting, and violent (all-in-all, a perfect Klingon); the Klingons we saw in "A Private Little War" were chracteristically violent; Kang was violent, but intelligent and reasonable; and Mara, the only female Klingon we ever saw, was intelligent and strong-willed, but not as violent as her male companions.

When *Star Trek: The Motion Picture* was released, we got another look at the Klingons, but they weren't the familiar swarthy humanoids from the series. These Klingons *looked* mean. The bridge of their battlecruiser was just what we would expect of our favorite villains—dark, smoky, and dirty. These Klingons wore armor-styled uniforms and they spoke an alien language. They were the perfect Klingons (once you got used to their appearance).

Then came *Star Trek III: The Search for Spock,* and we saw yet another type of Klingon (as well as another Klingon female). Kruge and his companions were alien looking, but less so than those from the first movie, and Valkris looked more like an alien than a human female with a lot of eye makeup.

Add to all of this several novels featuring the Klingons, and what do we have? *Confusion and questions!* Why are there so many types of Klingons and why do they act in such varying ways? Well, after reading everything I could find on the Klingons (please forgive me if there is anything I have missed), I have decided to take on the monumental task of tying everything together and explaining any discrepancies.

The Klingon Language

The Klingon language has been presented to us in three main sources: (1) Marc Okrand's *The Klingon Dictionary* (from which the language used in the first and third movies is taken); (2) John M. Ford's *The Final Reflection;* and (3) Majliss Larson's *Pawns and Symbols.* Vonda McIntyre's novelization of *Star Trek III: The Search for Spock* also tells us that the Klingon language consists of three strata and "possessed an almost limitless number of forms and variations, [and that] every utterance had many layers, many meanings." In the aforementioned references, there is virtually no consistency in the language usage. The simplest explanation of these differences lies in a statement from Okrand's dictionary: "Some dialects differ significantly from the current official dialect." Thus, the Klingons in these novels not only speak a dialect of "official" Klingonaase, but also, probably, speak it in different strata.

The Three Strata

Each stratum is determined by a specific inflection and, to a greater degree, by the specific word choice and sentence structure: the higher the level, the greater respect conveyed. The first stratum is the most formal (also known as Court-Klingonaase)—this is the level on which Kruge spoke to Valkris, thus conveying respect to her for her honorable sacrifice. The second stratum is the executive or command level—this is what Kruge and the Klingon commander from the first movie used with their subordinates. The third stratum is the common level—this is how civilian Klingons usually converse with each other.

Within each level, there are three additional substrata. The strata and substrata may be mixed in numerous ways to convey varying degrees of respect or disdain.

The Klingon Home System

The Klingon homeworld, Kazh, is probably populated mostly (at least seventy percent) by the "original" Klingon race, known as the master race, or *wa'DIch tlhIngan* (First Klingon)—Kruge was a wa'DIch Klingon. The cha'DIch tlhIngan (Second Klingons) probably make up about fifteen percent of the population—these Klingons have interbred with other humanoid races (it was these Klingons we saw during the TV series). Roughly five percent are the genetically engineered *chu'tlhIngan* (New Klingons)—they are the battle-class Klingons from the first movie. They have been specifically bred for battle, and their physical strength is superior to the wa'DIch Klingons. Their skulls have thick, bony ridges for added protection.

(We have all wondered why the "other" two Klingon races were never seen in the series. Well, as far as the battle-class Klingons go, there was never an obvious need for them. And as for *wa'DIch* Klingons—well, it should be noted that they do not consider themselves expendable, and only venture forth on the most important of missions. A *wa'DIch* or a *chu'DIch* Klingon demands more respect from others, while the *cha'DIch* Klingons must constantly prove their worth to others.)

The rest of the population is made up of a variety of races that are used as slaves and servants. It is an unofficially acknowledged fact that the practice of keeping *tharavul* and *tharkuve* still exists. *Tharavul* are Vulcan (and possibly Romulan) slaves whose psionic centers have been lesioned; *tharkuve* are deafened slaves.

The Klingon home system consists of five planets. Kazh is the second one out, orbiting the binary orange star *glIngDaj mInDu'*—which translates as "Kling's eyes." It is also known, in the federation, simply as Klingon.

Klingon Life

The average Klingon has a daily routine, probably much like that of most members of the Federation. All Klingons are competitive by nature, but the degree varies with the individual. Usually, the higher one's beginning status, the greater one's ambition—or, as Leslie Thompson aptly put it, "The average Klingon is interested only in his immediate sphere—in elevating his own life-style and comforts. He does not aspire to become Senator-in-Chief, only the head of the department" ("Klingon Update").

Klingon Houses, Groupings, and Families

Klingons have a very strict caste system, which, under normal circumstances, it never violated. There is no such thing as a family on Kazh, and a Kazhian's loyalty is only to himself. All Kazhian children are illegitimate and are raised by the state and cared by for state-owned slaves. Education is by level of intelligence, or, as Leslie Thompson said, "When a Klingon youth fails to pass on to the next level of education, he is trained to serve in a less necessary and less responsible position."

Although mating is rare on Kazh (the actual taking of a mate, not the usual rape), it is not unheard of—though it usually only occurs among the *cha'DIch* Klingons, because the battle-class Klingons are sterile, the *wa'DIch* Klingons frown on it, and slave mating is regulated by the state.

This is not the same on all planets of the Empire—on

many planets, there are extensive Klingon families and religious groupings. The Kazhians, however, consider themselves superior to all other Klingons.

The Rumaly:

This is "a political and ethnic minority on the Klingon homeworld. The highest class of Rumaly often veiled themselves in public" (*Enterprise: The First Adventure*). "Rumaly were not superstitious, at least not about diabolical presences." The Rumaly have extensive family lines—Valkris was a member of the Rumaly.

Klinzhai (Klin Zhai):

This is a planet close to Kazh, were the Klingon culture apparently "co-originated" (most likely due to the intervention of the Preservers). It is also known as the Klingon homeworld, depending on whether one originates from there or not. It is on Klinzhai that the Rumaly exist. The "father" of the Klingon people, Kling, however, was born on Kazh. Klinzhai is the only known Klingon planet to have been ruled by an empress. Kor and Kali (his wife) were from this planet.

Tahrn:

This is the planet that Kang was from. It is said that this is where the Klingon emperor resides (though this has never been confirmed).

Klingon Women

Although I think that Leslie Thompson excellently summed up this area in her article "Klingon Update," there are some additional points that should be mentioned:

"A woman cannot enter the service unless she has a male sponsor or protector. He may not necessarily be her husband." (*The Tears of the Singers*)

"A Klingon woman would never cry before a man. To do so either she is crazy, or he has humiliated her beyond endurance, or . . . she considers him less than a man." (*Pawns and Symbols*)

It seems that women do have their place on the Klingon hierarchy, however, as "(Royal) succession is always through the sister's son." (*Pawns and Symbols*)

On some planets, there are specific restrictions on women—on Tsorn, a rim planet of the Empire, women cannot go outside unless covered by a full-length garment called a *shurdik*. (*Pawns and Symbols*)

Klingon Honor

Klingon honor is an interesting and sometimes complex concept. Honor is extremely hard to gain, but very easy to lose. Honor is usually gained through military victories, but it can be lost in ways too numerous to list.

Kruge said Valkris's name would be remembered with honor for her actions in gaining the information on the Genesis Device and for the way she accepted death.

Klingon Objectives

All Klingons live for the *komerex zha*—the Perpetual Game—and the *komerex tel khesterex*—the Expanding Empire. These concepts are a part of the Klingon philosophy that life is similar to a game—one plays to win, no matter what the cost. The Klingons understand that their survival depends on constant expansion and conquest. Otherwise their society will collapse under its own treachery.

Klingon Customs, Religious Beliefs, and Taboos

Klin Zha is the game of the Klingon Empire. It is similar to chess, but it has many varying forms, such as the *klin zha kinta*—the game with live pieces. The word *klin* translates roughly to "endurance" or "willpower," and *zha* translates to "game." So the *klin zha* is the game of willpower.

Many clans of Klingons (like the Romulans) carry life disks—translucent, colored disks that retain their color only while their owner lives (each member of the clan is given one at birth). They're often used as dueling trophies, and hung from the belt of the victor. After the death of its owner, a life disk becomes colorless and transparent. House members often carry other life disks symbolizing each member of the family.

Military members of these same clans or groups also often carry a blood sword. The sword is made of a sturdy, transparent crystal that absorbs blood and deepens in color with each such exposure.

There is an ancient bonding custom among the majority of Klingon groupings: if a Klingon saves someone's life, then that person is bonded to the Klingon until the Klingon sees fit to release him. "The custom is real, though not often invoked," according to *Pawns and Symbols*.

Several Klingon groups have strong religious customs, beliefs, and myths. Among Kruge's people, there is the myth of Ngarakkani, a Klingon hero who wrestled with demons and defeated them. (*Star Trek III: The Search for Spock*). In *Enterprise: The First Adventure*, the Director believed in, and disliked, what he called "witchcraft."

Among some clans, there is "an ancient taboo against sexual assault with the confines of a dwelling" (*Dwellers in the Crucible*).

Other Klingon deities include Cymele, the goddess of the fields and forests, and the protector of women; and Durgath, the giver and taker of life, and also the god of war.

There are some clans in which the male members take more than one wife. Kang belonged to such a clan and could take up to six wives. The first wife, however, still retains the majority of privileges, such as the right of inheritance (*Pawns and Symbols*).

Klingon Emotion

Like most races of the galaxy, Klingons experience emotions. More often than not, however, they are the darker emotions of hate, anger, envy, greed, etc. However, happiness, and even joy, are not unknown among the Klingons, though many of the things that make Klingons happy are not very pleasant to other races. Klingons experience pain, but rarely grief. John Ford excellently explained these last two in his novel *The Final Reflection:* "Klingons do not weep, as many races do . . . a different set of facial nerves is stimulated by stress. The Klingon in deep emotion bares his teeth, as if to say, 'stay away, until this feeling is past.' "

The Director in *Enterprise: The First Adventure*, appeared highly emotional when he said, "My mind is overwhelmed by the sensitivity, the depth of feeling, the exquisite artistry!"

Kali, Kor's wife in *The Tears of the Singers*, was a very emotional Klingon; she openly displayed great affection for Kor (he often returned it in kind), and several times she was on the verge of tears.

In "Day of the Dove," we see the affection that Kang and Mara have for each other, and Kang and his people even have occasion to laugh at the end.

Miscellaneous Points about the Klingons

A Klingon's chest is vestigally scaled. (*Dwellers in the Crucible.*). In *Enterprise: The First Adventure*, the Director was appalled when Dr. McCoy said that a mint julep would put hair on his chest.

Klingons cannot differentiate between the colors black and red because they lack erythrolabe, the visual pigment of the human eye that identifies the color red. Klingons can, however, see into the ultraviolet end of the spectrum. Their "visual light range runs from about sixty-four hundred Angstroms clear down into the ultraviolet range to about thirty-two hundred Angstroms" (*Pawns and Symbols*).

With all due respect to John Ford and Majliss Larson, I do not believe that Klingons would eat pastries as a main diet or drink fruit juices. It seems more likely that Klingons are avid carnivores, as evidenced by the fact that they have fangs (if the meal has stopped kicking, it's probably overcooked), or at the very least, omnivores with a preference for meat. Those on board starships must be satisfied with processed meals—which only serve to make them that much meaner.

Finally, I would like to present a list of Klingon terminology (as well as several Klingon curses) used in the following novels.

From John M. Ford's *The Final Reflection*:

epetai—an honorific title

epetai-zana—an honorific so high it becomes absurd, an insult

gagny, g'daya—curses similar to "gday't"

gday't—curse; roughly equivalent to "damn"

human zha—chess
humani kuvest'—a paid (Human) worker
kaase—hand
kafei—coffee
kahlesste kaase—Kahless's hand, an honorable compliment
kai—exclamation: good; excellent; well done
kai kassai—a salutory phrase
khest—a curse of many meanings
khesterex—the structure that dies
klin—endurance; willpower
klin zha—the game of the Klingon Empire, it has many variations and is similar to human chess
klin zha kinta—the game with live pieces
komerex—the structure that grows; empire
komerex zha—the Perpetual Game
komerex stela—the large imperial trefoil
kuve—slave; servant
kuveleta—a servitor's half child
kuvesa tokhesa—statement: "I serve willingly."
pozhalasta prishl'yiti bagazh—translates roughly to, "Where are the secret military installations?"
ren—the number three (3)
rom zha—what Romulans call *latrunculo*, details unstated
sa—the number two (2)
sa tel'ren—two out of three
tharavul—Vulcan slaves whose psi centers have been lesioned
tharkuve—deafened slaves
tokhe straav'—willing slave; the vilest name Klingon can call Klingon, an insult only death could redeem
zan—a neutral term, similar to mister
zha—game
zha riest'n tekas tal'tai-kleon—the phrase used at the conclusion of klin zha; it translates roughly to, "A pleasant game . . . my compliments to a worthy opponent."

From Margaret W. Bonanno's *Dwellers in the Crucible:*
komerex tel khesterex—the Expanding Empire
kzantor—a type of shuttlecraft
toH?—equivalent of "Huh?" or "What?"
withiki, cherwtl—birds native to planet Klin Zhai

From Majliss Larson's *Pawns and Symbols:*

aitchnit—disease; a fever

amarklor, kalish—colors, lying in the ultraviolet range.

aydutywa—translated to "unwanted one"

cami—a piece in the game of *tsungu*, extremely versatile

Cymele—goddess of fields and forests; protector of women

Durgath—god; giver and taker of life; god of war

kalimbok—a bush native to Peneli

khizr—equivalent to coffee

Klairos—a recently settled world of the Empire

klibicule—a second-year-bearing grain; a plus-twenty-five-percent protein grain

korin—term of respect for elder males of the maternal line, roughly analogous to uncle.

krelk—a beast of burden; looks like a cross between a llama and a kangaroo

llngen—large trees native to Peneli

lourkain—a truth serum

ngkatha—animals native to Peneli, they are furred and have six legs

Peneli—a planet in the Klingon Empire

persaba—a fruit

pomfrit—a fruit

seyilt—a bamboolike plant

slean—furred predator of the Tahrnian grasslands

siee—exclamation

shurdik—a garment worn by women of Tsorn, covering them from head to toe

theld—house; household

thelerrin—general term for a younger female of a household

thelsa—elder female of the maternal line; older female cousin, aunt-by-marriage, or grandmother

tormin—a rank in the Klingon security forces, roughly analogous to sergeant

tseni—agricultural disease; a virus

Tsorn—a rim planet of the Klingon Empire

tsungu—an intricate game

In closing, five proverbs from John Ford's *The Final Reflection:*

"Sometimes to show teeth is enough—but if you bite, bite deep."

"The only truth about death, is that it is death, and the end."

"Only a fool fights in a burning house" (originally from "Day of the Dove")

"Negotiation may cost far less than war, or infinitely more; for war cannot cost more than one's life."

"If there are gods, they do not help, and justice belongs to the strong; but know that all things done before the naked stars are remembered."

PERMISSION TO COME ABOARD: AN *ENTERPRISE* CREW ROSTER AND BIOGRAPHY

By Jonathan Bell

Do you know who are the members of the starship Enterprise *crew? Well, as many as you can name off the tip of your tongue, you probably can't name them all . . . In fact, if you haven't read all of the episodes or seen all of the movies, you haven't even met them all. Jonathan Bell has, and in the following article, he introduces them briefly to you.*

Aboard the starship *Enterprise* reside over four hundred and thirty souls. Consisting of members of ninety-two Federation worlds, the crew is a "family," experienced and skilled in research and exploration, living and working together for half a decade like a precision-made instrument. Whether assigned to science, engineering, or ship's services, each member of this spacefaring community is important and vital.

Come with me now as I reintroduce you to many members of this family. Each is a qualified member of the *Enterprise* crew roster, having appeared in a live-action or animated episode, or in one of the *Star Trek* novels. Crew members are listed alphabetically (first name is given if known); rank and position follow. The episode or novel in which they appeared or are mentioned appears in parentheses.

Abernathy—Crewman. Position unknown.
Ahmad—Ensign. Helmsman and shuttle pilot. (*Pawns and Symbols*)
Ahrens—Crewman. Position unknown. (*My Enemy, My Ally*)

Al-Baslama, Mohammed—Ensign. Security officer. Was promoted to lieutenant and assigned as chief of security on the *Valor*, but before his transfer, he was tortured and beaten to death by an ancient, evil force. (*Mindshadow: Demons*)

Alden—Lieutenant. Backup bridge officer, communications officer. ("Where No Man Has Gone Before"; *Pawns and Symbols*)

Aledort, Lawrence—Crewman. Serves in NavComp department. (*My Enemy, My Ally*)

Amekentra—Ensign. Dietary services. Female amphibian. As she lay mortally wounded on the *Yorktown* years ago, a "thing" in another reality asked if she were finished with life, and sent her back. (*The Wounded Sky; My Enemy, My Ally*)

Andres—Chief. Engineering technician. (*Mutiny on the Enterprise*)

Arex—Lieutenant. Navigator. Three-armed, three-legged Edoan. (Regular on animated series)

Aristeides, Jenniver—Ensign. Originally a security officer, she transferred to botany. A product of genetic engineering for high-gravity planets, she is two hundred and fifty centimeters tall, has several layers of muscle, thick and dense bone, steel-gray skin, and silver eyes. (*The Entropy Effect*)

Arrunja, Maximo Alisaunder—Crewman. Middle-aged security officer. (*The Entropy Effect*)

Athende—Lieutenant. Maintenance officer. Sulamid. (*The Wounded Sky; My Enemy, My Ally*)

Atkins, Doris—Yeoman. Engineering records clerk. She gave Kirk a fuel consumption report to sign; he later forgot he'd done so. ("The Deadly Years")

Austin—Crewman. Position unknown. (*My Enemy, My Ally*)

Avitts, Candra—Lieutenant. Assistant science officer. She is much attracted to her boss, Mr. Spock. (*The Klingon Gambit; Mutiny on the Enterprise*)

Azuela—Ensign. Communications officer. (*Uhura's Song*)

Bailey, Dave—Lieutenant. Navigator. McCoy believes Kirk may have promoted young Bailey too soon. He becomes a cultural exchange to the First Federation, and supposedly resigned from Starfleet. ("The Corbomite Maneuver")

Banerjee—Lieutenant. Position unknown. Cracked his shoulder when Klingons fired upon shuttlecraft he was in. (*Pawns and Symbols*)

Bardoli—Crewman. Security officer. ("Obsession")

Barnhart—Crewman. Environmental engineering officer. Was killed aboard ship by M-113 salt vampire. ("The Man Trap")

Barret—Yeoman. Position unknown. Lieutenant Richardson is supposedly very interested in finding the air duct to Barret's quarters. (*Killing Time*)

Barrows, Tonia—Yeoman. Position unknown. Attacked by Don Juan on Shore Leave planet; had brief romantic liaison with McCoy. ("Shore Leave")

Bates, Roz—Crewman. Position unknown. (*My Enemy, My Ally*)

Benford—Crewman. Stellar Dynamics. (*The Wounded Sky*)

Berkeley—Lieutenant. Transporter officer. Forgot about Tantalus Colony's security screen when trying to beam down cargo. ("Dagger of the Mind")

Bischoff—Crewman. Position unknown. (*My Enemy, My Ally*)

Bobbie (first name)—Technician. Maintenance. ("The Man Trap")

Boma, Samuel—Lieutenant. Astrophysicist. Court-martialed by request of Commander Scott after the Taurus II incident. Discharged, Boma later became a successful civilian scientist, contributing to Starfleet's dreadnought project. He helped transwarp designer Ursula Mornay steal transwarp technology and offer it to the galaxy. ("The Galileo Seven"; *Dreadnought*)

Brand—Lieutenant. Designer-engineer in PhaserTech. Female. (*The Wounded Sky; My Enemy, My Ally*)

Brassard—Crewman. Position unknown. (*My Enemy, My Ally*)

Brent—Lieutenant. Relief navigator. ("The Naked Time")

Brentano—Crewman. Security officer. (*The Tears of the Singers*)

Bretton—Ensign. Position unknown. Female. (*Mutiny on the Enterprise*)

Briala—Yeoman. Position unknown. (*Web of the Romulans*)

Buchanan—Commander. Position unknown. Female. (*Mutiny on the Enterprise*)

Burke, Lia T.—Lieutenant Commander. Nurse. Substitute for Christine Chapel when she was working on her doctorate. Though Earth-human, home to her is Sa-na-'Mdeihein. (*The Wounded Sky; My Enemy, My Ally*)

Canfield—Crewman. Position unknown. (*My Enemy, My Ally*)

Capra—Lieutenant. Security officer. ("The Time Trap")

Carlisle—Lieutenant. Position unknown. ("The Changeling")

Carstairs—Ensign. Geologist. Has visited the Alpha Carinae region several times. ("The Ultimate Computer")

Carter—Lieutenant. Security officer. Along with Kirk, Spock, and McCoy, aged when drained of energy by race of "siren" women. ("The Lorelei Signal")

Carver—Crewman. Position unknown. (*My Enemy, My Ally*)

Cheung, Marietta—Commander. Navigator (*Enterprise: The First Adventure*)

Ching, Wah—Ensign. Security officer. (*Corona*)

Cho, Sanghoon—Crewman. Engineering officer. Studied with Lieutenant Stryker for a year at Vulcan Science Academy. Kept a pet Venus flytrap. Killed himself while controlled by mysterious, evil force. (*Demons*)

Chou—Yeoman. Position unknown. (*The Tears of the Singers*)

Claremont—Crewman. Position unknown. (*My Enemy, My Ally*)

Clayton—Lieutenant. Shuttle Bay Vehicle Services. ("The Ambergris Element")

Colfax, Rex—Lieutenant Commander. Chief maintenance engineer. Bearded. (*Web of the Romulans*)

Compton—Crewman. Security officer. Died of cellular disruption after being "accelerated" by the Scalosians. ("Wink of an Eye")

Conner—Crewman. Engineering officer. (*Web of the Romulans*)

Cordova, Juan—Lieutenant. Security officer. Killed on gateway by Romulans. Friend of Zar, Spock's son. Creator of "Cordova's Course in Corruption"—booze, gambling, and women. (*Yesterday's Son*)

Dabach—Lieutenant. Position unknown. Female. (*The Wounded Sky*)

D'Amato—Lieutenant. Chief Geologist. Killed by Losira, last of the Kalandans. ("That Which Survives")

Darnell—Crewman. Medical technician. Killed by the salt vampire. ("The Man Trap")

Davidson—Crewman. Security chief. Female. ("The Lorelei Signal")

DeCastro—Lieutenant. Security officer. (*Pawns and Symbols*)

DePaul—Lieutenant. Navigator. ("Arena"; "A Taste of Armageddon")

DeSalle, Vincent—Lieutenant. Originally a relief navigator, he was promoted to assistant chief engineer. (Regular extra)

Dehner, Dr. Elizabeth—Psychiatrist. She died in a mental battle with mutated Gary Mitchell. ("Where No Man Has Gone Before")

Devereaux—Ensign. Security officer. (*Corona*)

d'Hennish Enu-Ma'qe, Niwa Awath-Mane Ri—Ensign. Astrocartographer. A Sadrao, referred to as Ri'niwa d'Hennish. (*The Wounded Sky*)

Dickerson—Lieutenant. Chief Security officer. ("The Savage Curtain")

Dominico, Sergei—Lieutenant. Communications officer. (*Crisis on Centaurus*)

Donnelly—Yeoman. Position unknown. (*Ishmael*)

Donovan—Lieutenant. Biologist. Killed by Klingons on Taygeta. Played guitar. (*The Tears of the Singers*)

Douglas, Heath—Lieutenant. Commander. Chief engineer (temporary replacement). Came close to crossing the line of insubordination concerning engineering affairs. (*Black Fire*)

Drew—Crewman. Nurse. Female. (*Killing Time*)

Eisenberg—Crewman. Position unknown. (*My Enemy, My Ally*)

Elliott—Crewman. Engineering officer. ("The Doomsday Machine")

Evans—Ensign. Security officer. ("Elaan of Troyius")

Farrell, John—Lieutenant. Navigator. (Regular extra)

Finney, Benjamin—Lieutenant. Records officer. Faked his own death in an attempt to ruin Kirk's career. ("Court Martial")

Fisher—Crewman. Position unknown. (*My Enemy, My Ally*)

Fisher—Technician. Geology. Metallic ore on his uniform caused transporter malfunction resulting in duplicate Kirks. ("The Enemy Within")

Flores, Diana Octavia Siobhan "Dossie"—Ensign. Relief helm officer. She makes beautiful harps. (*Crisis on Centaurus; Enterprise: The First Adventure*)

Flynn, Mandala—Lieutenant. Commander. Security chief. Previously served on border patrol. Has fifth-degree black belt in judo. (*The Entropy Effect*)

Freeman—Lieutenant. Ship's operations. Uhura gave him a tribble ("The Trouble with Tribbles")

Freeman, Gerrald—Lieutenant. Xenobiologist. Hobby is converting pre-2200 video dramas to holographic format. (*The Wounded Sky; My Enemy, My Ally*)

Gabler—Crewman. Engineering officer. ("One of our Planets Is Missing"; "Once Upon a Planet")

Gabriel—Ensign. Engineering officer. (*Mutiny on the Enterprise*)

Gaetano—Lieutenant. Radiation specialist. Speared by anthropoid creatures on Taurus II. ("The Galileo Seven")

Galloway—Lieutenant. Security officer. Was a hostage on Eminar VII; later killed on Omega IV by Captain Tracey. ("A Taste of Armageddon" "The Omega Glory")

Galway, Arlene—Lieutenant. Chief of biology. Died of accelerated aging caused by radiation on Gamma Hydra IV ("The Deadly Years")

Garibaldi, Mona—Crewman. Retired from Starfleet to help with reconstruction efforts on Centaurus. (*Crisis on Centaurus*)

Garrovick, David—Ensign. Security officer. Survived encounter with vampire cloud from Tycho IV. His father was Captain Garrovick of the *Farragut*, killed by the creature eleven years before. ("Obsession")

Gilden—Lieutenant. Historical section. Was informed about Guardian of Forever in order to help retrieve

Spock from the past. Has strange habit of playing his own form of solitaire with note cards. (*Ishmael*)

Giotto—Lieutenant. Commander. Security Chief. ("Devil in the Dark"; *Pawns and Symbols*)

Gooch, Mikki—Ensign. Position unknown. (*Demons*)

Gordon—Lieutenant. Life-support systems computer operation. (*The Klingon Gambit*)

Goro, Dr.—Physician. McCoy's second-in-charge at one time. (*The Trellisane Confrontation*)

Grant—Lieutenant. Security guard. Killed by a Capellan when drawing his phaser at the sight of Kras the Klingon. ("Friday's Child")

Green—Ensign. Ship's operations. Killed by the salt vampire who took his form in order to board the *Enterprise*. ("The Man Trap")

Green, Ben—Crewman. Engineering bridge officer. (*Web of the Romulans*)

Grogan—Crewman. Position unknown. Female. (*The Vulcan Academy Murders*)

Hadley—Lieutenant. Relief helmsman and bridge officer. ("A Piece of the Action"; *Pawns and Symbols*)

Haines, Jana—Ensign. Navigator and relief bridge officer. ("The Gamesters of Triskelion")

Hansen—Lieutenant. Relief Helmsman. ("Court Martial")

Harper—Ensign. Engineering officer. Vaporized by M-5 when he tried to disconnect its power source. ("The Ultimate Computer")

Harris—Lieutenant. Security officer. Commanded the excavation party sent to Gateway to remove the archaeologists and their records. (*Yesterday's Son*)

Harris—Yeoman. Position unknown. (*Yesterday Son*)

Harrison—Crewman. Position unknown. Badly wounded on Levaeri V. (*My Enemy, My Ally*)

Harrison,—Technichian. Bridge officer. (*"Space Seed"*)

Harrison, Dr.—Pathologist. After contracting the Psi 2000 virus, he painted (in red) "love mankind" on a corridor wall and "sinner repent" in a turbolift. ("The Naked Time")

Hazarstennaj—Lieutenant. Engineering officer. Of the same race as Snnanagfashtalli. Called "Hazard." (*Enterprise: The First Adventure*)

Helman—Lieutenant. Apprentice navigator. Oxonian. (*The Wounded Sky*)

Helman, Yolanda—Yeoman. Captain's yeoman near end of five-year mission. (*Black Fire*)

Hendorf—Ensign. Security officer. Died on Gamma Trianguli VI from pod-plant poisoning. Kirk knew his family. ("The Apple")

Hudson—Technician. Computer Electronics. (*Crisis on Centaurus*)

Hunters—Technician. Computer technician present in sickbay when Magda Kovas entered. ("Mudd's Women")

Hwavire—Ensign. Junior navigator. Sulamid. Called "Hwa'." (*My Enemy, My Ally*)

Immamura—Lieutenant. Security officer. Wounded on Taurus II by hostile anthropoids while searching for downed shuttlecraft *Galileo*. ("The Galileo Seven")

Iziharry, Constance—Crewman. Nurse, radiation specialist. Chosen by McCoy to help the wounded of Centaurus after an antimatter explosion destroyed the New Athens spaceport there. She resigned in order to remain on the planet. (*Crisis on Centaurus*)

Jackson—Crewman. Position unknown. Killed by Sylvia and returned to the *Enterprise* as a zombie to warn the ship away. ("Catspaw")

Jaeger, Karl—Lieutenant. Geologist, meteorologist, and geophysicist. ("The Squire of Gothos")

Jahma, Mohammed — Crewman. Position unknown. Wounded on Aritani during a Romulan pirate raid. Arabic-speaking North African. Friend of Uhura. (*Mindshadow*)

Jakorski—Crewman. Position unknown. Died during a Klingon attack. (*The Vulcan Academy Murders*)

Jamal, Zahra—Yeoman. Position unknown. ("Operations: Annihilate")

James—Lieutenant. Engineering bridge officer. The duplicate Kirk tried to get him to jump the real Kirk. ("The Enemy Within")

Jaramillo—Yeoman. Position unknown. (*Uhura's Song*)

Johnson, Rusty—Lieutenant. Security officer. ("Day of the Dove"; *Pawns and Symbols*)

Jordan—Ensign. Auxiliary control. Was knocked unconscious by Norman, an android masquerading as a newly assigned officer. ("I, Mudd")

Josephs—Lieutenant. Ship's operations. He found Ambassador Gav's body in a Jefferies tube. ("Journey to Babel")

Kalvecchio, Dr. Laurence—Chief botanist. Regular navy type who demands absolute perfection from his staff. (*Web of the Romulans*)

K'Ang Te—Lieutenant. Head of Biology. Female. ("Eye of the Beholder")

Kaplan—Lieutenant. Position unknown. Killed by one of Vaal's thunderbolts on Gamma Trianguli VI. ("The Apple")

Kazan—Crewman. Security officer. (*Mindshadow*)

Kelly—Crewman. Security officer. Killed by the Horta. ("The Devil in the Dark")

Kelowitz—Lieutenant commander. Biology. He also has experience in security/command. He survived the scrimmage with the Gorns and commanded the search party for *Galileo* on Taurus II. ("The Galileo Seven"; "This Side of Paradise")

Kelso, Lee—Lieutenant. Assistant engineer. Strangled by Gary Mitchell on Delta Vega. ("Where No Man Has Gone Before")

Kerasus, Janice—Lieutenant. Chief of linguistics. Romulan culture expert. (*The Wounded Sky; My Enemy, My Ally*)

Kesselman, Deke—Ensign. Biosupport. (*Mutiny on the Enterprise*)

Khalifa—Crewman. Position unknown. (*My Enemy, My Ally*)

Kinitz—Crewman. Security chief. Killed aboard ship by extremely dangerous prisoners. His overconfidence led to serious mistakes with security procedures. (*The Trellisane Confrontation*)

Kolchek—Lieutenant. Security officer. ("The Infinite Vulcan")

Kopka—Crewman. Engineering officer. (*Web of the Romulans*)

Korren—Crewman. Position unknown. (*My Enemy, My Ally*)

Kouc—Yeoman. Position unknown. (*Web of the Romulans*)

Krejci—Crewman. Position unknown. (*My Enemy, My Ally*)

Krelidz—Lieutenant. Communications officer. (*Mindshadow*)

Kyle, Winston—Lieutenant. Transporter chief and relief bridge officer. He enjoys sculpting and playing Quaestor, a chesslike game based on progressions which, if interrupted, must be replayed from the beginning. (Regular extra)

Kyotomo—Yeoman. Botanist. (*Web of the Romulans*)

Landon, Martha—Yeoman. Position unknown. She and Chekov were "fascinated" with one another and kissed on Gamma Trianguli VI. ("The Apple")

Lang—Lieutenant. Gunnery officer from PhaserTech. Killed on Cestus III. ("Arena")

Langsam—Crewman. Position unknown. (*My Enemy, My Ally*)

Lanz, Rachel—Ensign. Engineering officer. Killed by Romulan raiders on Aritani. Scotty was quite fond of her; she was a "good engineer." (*Mindshadow*)

Latimer—Lieutenant. Navigator. Died on Taurus II. ("The Galileo Seven")

Lawton, Tina—Yeoman third class. Science department. Janice Rand introduced her to Charlie X, but he was not interested. ("Charlie X")

Lee—Crewman. Position unknown. (*My Enemy, My Ally*)

Leonidas, Alexander—Commander. Temporary replacement first officer. While concentrating, he clicks a set of worry beads, making everyone in earshot quite edgy. Despite this, he is well liked by the crew. (*Black Fire*)

Leslie—Lieutenant. Engineering officer, relief helmsman, and substitute bridge officer. (Regular extra)

Levine, Dr. Jonah—Young medical officer. (*Black Fire*)

Lewis—Crewman. Security officer. ("The Devil in the Dark")

Lihwa—Ensign. Position unknown. Andorian female. (*The Wounded Sky; My Enemy, My Ally*)

Lindenbaum—Crewman. Security officer. Killed on Taygeta by Klingons. (*The Tears of the Singers*)

Lindsay—Crewman. Security officer. ("The Devil in the Dark")

Lindstrom—Crewman. Sociologist. He outfitted Sulu and O'Neil in the wrong clothes on Beta III. He later remained there to supervise cultural repair efforts. ("The Return of the Archons")

Litt—Crewman. Position unknown. (*My Enemy, MY Ally*)

Liu, Teresa—Ensign. Position unknown. Killed by "demon controlled" Sanghoon Cho. (*Demons*)

Livenger—Crewman. Position unknown. Died during a Klingon attack. (*The Vulcan Academy Murders*)

London, Robert—Ensign. Position unknown. (*The Wounded Sky; My Enemy, My Ally*)

Lowry—Lieutenant. Security officer. (*Black Fire*)

Lyle—Crewman. Transporter operator. (*Mindshadow*)

Maass, Diana—Crewman. Position unknown. (*My Enemy, My Ally*)

Maass, Donald—Crewman. Orderly in sickbay. (*The Wounded Sky; My Enemy, My Ally*)

MacPherson, Alec—Assistant chief engineer. The crew refers to him and Mr. Scott as "the twins." (*Crisis on Centaurus*)

Maevlynin—Crewman. Medical technician and botanist. Female Estryllian. A telepath with an advanced form of telekinesis. (*Pawns and Symbols*)

Mahase—Lieutenant. Beta shift communicator-in-training. Eseriat. (*The Wounded Sky; My Enemy, My Ally*)

Malkson—Crewman. Position unknown. (*My Enemy, My Ally*)

Mallory—Lieutenant. Security officer. Died on Gamma Trianguli VI after tripping over an explosive rock. His father helped Kirk get into the Academy. ("The Apple")

Marple—Lieutenant. Security officer. Killed by one of Val's people on Gamma Trianguli VI. ("The Apple")

Martin, Thorin—Lieutenant commander. Science officer. Temporary replacement near end of five-year mission. Holds an A6 computer rating. (*Black Fire*)

Martine-Teller, Angela—Ensign. Second-class power specialist. Her wedding to Robert Tomlinson was interrupted by a Klingon attack; he was later killed in action. ("Balance of Terror"; "Shore Leave")

Martinelli—Lieutenant. Position unknown. (*Web of the Romulans*)

Masters—Crewman. Security chief. (*Yesterday's Son*)

Masters—Lieutenant. Position unknown. Female. (*Killing Time*)

Masters, Charlene—Lieutenant. Chemist and dilithium crystal energizer chief. ("The Alternative Factor")

Matlock, Colin—Lieutenant. Security chief. (*The Wounded Sky; My Enemy, My Ally*)

Matshushita, Harry—Crewman. Position unknown. (*My Enemy, My Ally*)

Matson, Larry—Lieutenant. Ship's operations. Substituted for Kevin Riley when Riley reassigned himself to the engineering deck. ("The Conscience of the King")

Matthews—Crewman. Security officer. Middle-aged; pushed down bottomless chasm by Ruk the android on Eko III. ("What Are Little Girls Made of?")

M'Baww—Ensign. Xenobiologist. ("Eye of the Beholder")

M'Benga, Dr.—Assistant chief surgeon in life sciences. A Vulcan physiologist; served for four years at the Vulcan Science Academy. (Regular extra)

McConel, Heather—Chief. Engineering design officer. Scottish. Even fonder of booze than Scotty; runs a secret still, as well as an elaborate gambling machine, once rigged. (*The Klingon Gambit; Mutiny on the Enterprise*)

McGivers, Marla—Lieutenant. Historian and controls systems specialist. Infatuated with Khan, she plotted with him to take over the ship, but recanted. Kirk allowed her to join Khan in exile on Ceti Alpha V. ("Space Seed")

McHenry, Thomas—Crewman. Position unknown. Separated from Starfleet to assist in reconstruction efforts at New Athens spaceport. (*Crisis on Centaurus*)

McNair, Teresa—Ensign. Most junior electronics technician and alien anthropologist. While studying records of the planet Sarpeidon's past, she noticed a painting of a Vulcan face on a cave wall. Her discovery led to the acquisition of Spock's son, Zar. (*Yesterday's Son*)

Mears—Yeoman. Position unknown. Member of the *Galileo* party marooned on Taurus II. ("The Galileo Seven")

Mendez—Lieutenant. Cryptography officer. Female. (*The Tears of the Singers*)

Meyers—Lieutenant. Security officer. ("Eye of the Beholder")

M'Gura—Crewman. Position unknown. Died during a Klingon attack. (*The Vulcan Academy Murders*)

Mikhalis, Giorgo—Crewman. Engineering officer. Killed by Romulan pirate raiders on Aritani. (*Mindshadow*)

Minambres—Crewman. Position unknown. (*My Enemy, My Ally*)

Mitchell, Gary—Lieutenant commander. Chief navigator and second officer. Selected by Kirk to be first officer, but overruled by Starfleet, who chose Spock. He obtained amplified esper powers at the galactic edge, and was killed by Kirk when he became a threat. ("Where No Man Has Gone Before"; *Enterprise: The First Adventure*)

Montgomery—Crewman. Security officer. Instructed to lead Commodore Decker to sickbay, he was knocked unconscious by Decker, who escaped to the shuttle bay. ("The Doomsday Machine")

Moreau, Marlena—Lieutenant. Chemist. Joined the crew in the second year. ("Mirror, Mirror")

Morgan—Lieutenant. Security officer. ("The Infinite Vulcan")

Morris—Crewman. Position unknown. (*My Enemy, My Ally*)

Mosley—Crewman. Ship's stores. (*The Wounded Sky*)

M'Ress—Lieutenant. Communications officer. Caitian; a feline humanoid. (Animated regular)

Mulhall, Dr. Anne—Lieutenant Commander. Astrobiologist. Volunteered the use of her body to the Arretian Thalassa. ("Return to Tomorrow")

Muller—Crewman. Position unknown. (*My Enemy, My Ally*)

Muromba—Lieutenant. Relief helmsman. (*Web of the Romulans*)

Naraht—Ensign. Biomathematics. A Horta, orthomale type B-4A. Helped infiltrate Levaeri V by digesting the hyponeutronium door protecting the computer control room. Due for promotion. (*My Enemy, My Ally*)

Neal—Crewman. Security officer. (*Mutiny on the Enterprise*)

Neon—Crewman. Security officer. She is very quick, has a long, spiked tail, iridescent scales, and an IQ over 200. (*The Entropy Effect*)

Nguyen, Lisa—Ensign. Security officer. (*Demons*)

Niliet—Ensign. Position unknown. An Ielerid. Ielerids are referred to by "hir," not him or her. (*The Wounded Sky*)

Noel, Dr. Helen—Ensign. Psychiatrist. Accompanied Captain Kirk to Tantalus because of her background in rehabilitative therapy. She and Kirk first met at a Christmas party held by science labs. ("Dagger of the Mind")

Nored, Anne—Lieutenant. Security officer. Was engaged to philanthropist Carter Winston when he disappeared. ("The Survivor")

Norton—Crewman. Position unknown. (*My Enemy, My Ally*)

O'Brian—Lieutenant. Position unknown. ("I, Mudd")

O'Connor—Ensign. Navigation officer. Female. (*Mindshadow*)

O'Herlihy—Lieutenant. Ordnance officer. Died during the Gorn attack on Cestus III. ("Arena")

Olaus, Edward—Lieutenant. Chief of security. (*Corona*)

O'Neil—Lieutenant. Sociologist. Was "absorbed" into the Body on Beta III, but later returned to normal. ("The Return of the Archons")

O'Neill—Ensign. Security officer. While searching for the *Galileo* on Taurus II, he was killed by one of the large anthropoids. ("The Galileo Seven")

Onorax—Lieutenant. Security officer. Oxalian. Has flexible, eight-fingered hands and golden hair and skin. (*Web of the Romulans*)

Oranjeboom—Ensign. Position unknown. (*My Enemy, My Ally*)

Orsay, Marie-Therese—Ensign. Engineer. She's expert at building a house of cards. (*Uhura's Song*)

Osborne—Lieutenant. Security officer. He led a search party for the Horta on Janus VI. He later accompanied Kirk to Eminar VII. ("The Devil in the Dark"; "A Taste of Armageddon")

O'Shay—Crewman. Security officer. (*Mindshadow*)

Painter—Crewman. Navigator. ("This Side of Paradise")

Palamas, Carolyn—Lieutenant. Anthropology and archaeology officer. ("Who Mourns for Adonais?")

Palmer—Lieutenant. Relief communications officer. Female. (Regular extra)

Patten—Lieutenant. Chief security officer. (*The Klingon Gambit; Mutiny on the Enterprise*)

Paul—Crewman. Position unknown. (*My Enemy, My ally*)

Pauli—Ensign. Security officer. (*Corona*)

Phillips—Crewman. Astrobiologist. Has explored twenty-nine planets biologically similar to Alpha Carinae II. ("The Ultimate Computer")

Phillips—Yeoman; security officer. Enjoys fencing. (*Yesterday's Son*)

Piper, Dr. Mark—Temporary chief surgeon. ("Where No Man Has Gone Before")

Prox—Ensign. Xenobiologist. ("Eye of the Beholder")

Ragsdale, Fred—Crewman. Security chief. (*The Tears of the Singers*)

Rahada—Lieutenant. Relief helmsman. Female. ("That Which Survives")

Rand, Janice—Yeoman. Captain's aide. When she first boarded the *Enterprise,* she was physically and mentally seventeen, but officially twenty. This discrepancy, caused by traveling in a sublight vessel for several weeks, caused her great despair in coping with her duties, Captain Kirk, and Starfleet Command. She transferred off the *Enterprise,* and returned a year later, prior to the vessel's redesign.

Rawlings—Technician. Computer electronics. (*Crisis on Centaurus*)

Rawlins—Lieutenant commander. Chief geologist. (*"The Ultimate Computer"*)

Rayburn—Crewman. Security officer. Strangled by Ruk the Android of Exo III. ("What Are Little Girls Made of?")

Reems—Second lieutenant. Assistant security chief. (*Mindshadow*)

Reilley—Ensign. Position unknown. Irish; good vocal artist. (*Ishmael*)

Remington, Carl—Ensign. Junior officer, ship's operations. Murdered at Vulcan Science Academy. (*The Vulcan Academy Murders*)

Renner—Lieutenant. Position unknown. She's known for having Sulu steal her clothes at poolside. (*My Enemy, My Ally*)

Richardson, Jeremy J.—Lieutenant. Navigator. A love-sick Romeo: He once fantasized a relationship with Yeoman S'Parva; also (supposedly) spent an entire night searching for the ventilator duct to Yeoman Barret's quarters.

Riley, Kevin Thomas—Lieutenant. Relief navigator, engineering, communications. Under influence of Psi 2000 virus, he took control of the ship, singing "I'll Take You Home Again, Kathleen" over the intercom—terribly. He is one of the survivors of the Tarsus IV executions (his parents were not); he later tried to assassinate the man responsible (Karidian).

Rizzo—Ensign. Security officer. Killed on Argus X by the Vampire Cloud. ("Obsession")

Rodriquez—Crewman. Forensics. (*Demons*)

Rodriquez, Esteban—Lieutenant. Botanist. ("Shore Leave")

Rosen—Crewman. Position unknown. Died during Klingon attack. (*The Vulcan Academy Murders*)

Ross, Anita—Ensign. PhaserTech officer. (*Mutiny on the Enterprise*)

Ross, Teresa—Yeoman. Position unknown. She takes to Viennese waltzes. ("The Squire of Gothos")

Roswind—Crewman. Position unknown. Once a roommate of Janice Rand; cruel-hearted type. (*Enterprise: The First Adventure*)

Rotsler—Crewman. Position unknown. (*My Enemy, My Ally*)

Rowe—Lieutenant. Security officer. Knocked unconscious by Norman in auxiliary control. ("I, Mudd")

Russ—Lieutenant. Engineering officer. ("The Doomsday Machine")

Ryan—Lieutenant. Relief navigator. ("The Naked Time")

Sadady, Mayri—Lieutenant. Chief of astrocartography. (*The Wounded Sky*)

Sajii, Jan—Crewman. Xenobiologist. A well-known artist. (*Yesterday's Son*)

Sakarov—Ensign. Security officer. (*Pawns and Symbols*)

Sam (first name)—Rank unknown. Medical technician. Zapped into nonexistence by Charlie X. ("Charlie X")

Sanchez, Dr.—Pathologist. ("That Which Survives")

Sandage, Judd—Ensign. Ship's services. Called "Scanner"; very knowledgeable in mechanics, has dreams of working in the Sensory. Tennessean with heavy regional accent. (*Battlestations*)

Sanders—Crewman. Security officer. (*Pawns and Symbols*)

Seelens—Lieutenant. Security chief. Female. ("Eye of the Beholder")

Shallert, Johnathan—Crewman. Transporter operator. (*Corona*)

Shea—Lieutenant. Security officer. Reduced to crystal block by Kelvans, then restored. ("By Any Other Name")

Siderakis, Peter—Lieutenant. Helmsman. Native of Centaurus; resigned from Starfleet to help with reconstruction efforts. (*Crisis on Centaurus*)

Singh—Lieutenant. Engineering officer. Assigned to look after Nomad. ("The Changeling")

Sjveda—Lieutenant. Position unknown. Fond of music; gives a seminar in music appreciation.

Smith—Yeoman Captain's aide. Left *Enterprise* when it returned from galaxy's edge. Kirk kept calling her "Jones." ("Where No Man Has Gone Before")

Smith, Beatrice—Crewman. Position unknown. Elderly yogi and close friend of Sulu. (*The Entropy Effect*)

Snnanagfashtalli—Ensign. Security officer. She is a bipedal leopard with a pelt of maroon, scarlet, and cream. The crew sometimes calls her "Snarl"—but not to her face. (*The Entropy Effect; Uhura's Song; Enterprise: The First Adventure*)

S'Parva—Yeoman. In psychology lab. A female Katellan. Katellans have an advanced form of telepathy similar to, but not as advanced as, the Vulcan mind meld. (*Killing Time*)

Spinelli—Lieutenant. Navigator and helmsman. ("Space Seed")

Sru—Crewman. Security officer. (*Web of the Romulans*)

Steinberg, David—Ensign. Security officer. Killed by Romulans on Gateway. Was a friend to Zar, Spock's son. (*Yesterday's Son*)

Stewart—Ensign. Position unknown. (*Web of the Romulans*)

Stiles, Andrew—Lieutenant. Navigator. Was suspicious of Spock, as an ancestor of his fought in the Romulan Wars. ("Balance of Terror")

Stryker—Lieutenant. Engineering officer. Studied with

Snaghoon Cho at Vulcan Science Academy for a year. (*Demons*)

Sturgeon—Crewman. Medical technician. Was killed on M-113 by the Salt Vampire. ("The Man Trap")

Swanson—Crewman. Security officer. ("Obsession")

Tamura, Keiko—Yeoman; Lieutenant. Security officer. Accompanied Kirk to Eminar VII; held Mea 3 prisoner. As lieutenant, was in charge of a pair of Klingon refugees. ("A Taste of Armageddon"; *Pawns and Symbols*)

Tankris—Yeoman. Position unknown. Acted as recorder at Scotty's trial. ("Wolf in the Fold")

Tanzer, Herb—Lieutenant. Chief of recreation. Excellent officer; keeps the crew busy and happy with traditional, holographic, and computer pastimes. (*The Wounded Sky; My Enemy, My Ally*)

Tersarkisov—Crewman. Engineering officer. (*Mindshadow*)

Thomas—Crewman. Security officer. (*The Tears of the Singers*)

Thompson, Leslie—Yeoman. Position unknown. Reduced to crystal block and crushed by Rojan the Kelvan. ("By Any Other Name")

Thule—Technician. Position unknown. ("Space Seed")

Tomlinson, Robert—Ensign. Phaser specialist. Engaged to Angela Martine. Died from phaser coolant leak during battle with Romulans. ("Balance of Terror")

Tomson, Ingrit—Lieutenant. Chief security officer. (*Mindshadow; Demons*)

Tormolen, Joseph—Lieutenant.
Science department. Unknowingly brought Psi 2000 virus aboard *Enterprise;* stabbed and killed himself with a steak knife. ("The Naked Time")

Tracy, Karen—Lieutenant. Psych-tech. Killed by Red Jack. ("Wolf in the Fold")

T'Zeela—Lieutenant. Relief communications officer. Female Vulcan. (*The Tears of the Singers*)

Voung—Lieutenant. Helmsman. (*Uhura's Song*)

Walking Bear, Dawson—Ensign. Relief helm officer. Comanche Indian ("How Sharper than a Serpent's Tooth")

Wallace, Dr. Janet—Endocrinologist. Helped develop a serum for the aging virus. ("The Deadly Years")

Washburn—Crewman. Engineering officer. ("The Dooms-day Machine")

Watkins, John B.—Ensign. Engineer, grade four. Was killed by Losira. ("That Which Survives")

Watson—Crewman. Second engineer. Killed by one of Elaan guards. ("Elaan of Troyius")

Wellman—Lieutenant. Officer of the deck, spacedock. (*Corona*)

Willinck—Lieutenant. Shuttle pilot. (*Pawns and Symbols*)

Wilson—Crewman. Transporter technician. Knocked unconscious by Kirk's evil double. ("The Enemy Within")

Wilson, Bethany—Lieutenant. Life support; engineering. (*The Tears of the Singers*)

Wong, Chu—Crewman. Security officer. Led a small security force on Gateway. (*Yesterday's Son*)

Wyatt—Ensign. Transporter officer. Killed by Losira. ("That Which Survives")

Yimassa—Lieutenant. Navigator. Andorian; like many of his race, expert in his field.

LOVE AND DEATH IN THE
STAR TREK UNIVERSE

By Janeen DeBoard

Love in Star Trek *has been covered quite nicely in these pages, as has been death. But until this article appeared in our mailbox, no one had taken a look at the classical ties of love and death as they appeared in* Star Trek; *how they affect the characters, how they affect each other, even how they now and then come inevitably hand in hand. Indeed, one could even go so far as to say that many episodes were about nothing else; certainly love and death is/are major themes in the last two* Star Trek *movies. Why this seeming obsession? Read on . . .*

In the twenty-third century, life has undergone a great many changes—and so, it seems, has death. The end of life has become as personal a thing as was the life itself; we know this from our observation of the patterns of grief and acceptance displayed by the survivors, for those patterns often differ markedly from those we see today. In the world of *Star Trek,* death is romanticized a great deal, both out of compassion for those who continue, and as encouragement toward risk taking for all who travel in space. Such romanticizing is easily understood once we examine the profound and unbreakable relationship between love and death that exists in the *Star Trek* universe.

"No, I've never faced death. I've cheated death, and patted myself on the back for my ingenuity."

A recurrent idea in *Star Trek* is that love is only truly given when one has accepted the fact that the beloved will someday die, and loves in spite of it.

This idea was probably most evident in the relationship between Dr. McCoy and the priestess Natira in "For the

World Is Hollow and I Have Touched the Sky." She knew that he had contracted a terminal illness and could not be expected to survive as long as she, but loved and married him anyhow.

A more powerful example, however, is found in *Star Trek II: The Wrath of Khan*. When Kirk says that he has never faced death, he is saying that he has never faced love, either. Although he is undeniably a warm and compassionate character, his has been a lifetime of casual relationships with friends and lovers, of distance from a rarely mentioned family, and of no experience with a deep and permanent commitment to another human being. The barriers were always up; the ship and her crew had to come first. This served him well during the chaotic life of a starship captain, but left a piece missing from him nonetheless.

Even after witnessing Spock's death, Kirk has not really been hit by the awful finality of it. He still "can't help wondering about the friend I leave behind." But David, now; David was different. With his son, Kirk had a permanent, irrevocable relationship, always a part of him whether he wished it or not, perhaps the first adult relationship Kirk had ever known over which he had no control. David's death was twice as devastating because the shock of facing both love and death came all at once. This time there was no elegaic reminiscing, as there was for Spock; only a quiet and painful, "Goodbye, David."

Kirk had come to love David wholly, even though he had known him for only a short time. David was the one person with whom Kirk's usual barriers and defenses were useless, and Kirk knew this. His son saw him for what he was, good and bad together, and accepted him that way. No one else, not even Spock, had ever dealt with Kirk on such a level, and it will be interesting to watch Kirk's behavior and the changes it must undergo as a result of this event. Just as Spock was altered by his encounter with Vejur, so Kirk will be altered by the love and death of his son.

"Each of you must evaluate the loss in the privacy of your own thoughts."

Death is romanticized a great deal in *Star Trek*, partly because love is so closely intertwined with it—death is often represented as an heroic sacrifice for love—but also because such idealizations subtly push humans into taking the awful risks that come with space exploration. If no one will be left feeling guilty, or hopelessly devastated, or cruelly abandoned by your death—and will respect your actions even though they ended in your demise—then you may be that much more likely to take some of those risks.

As the ancients drove themselves to superhuman feats and glorious sacrifice "so that the bards will sing of us," so the crew of the *Enterprise* strives without limit to reach the highest possible goals—even at the highest possible price. Their survivors can take comfort in the knowledge that death occurred in the line of duty and so could not be helped. When this valorization of death—of "humanity"—is possible, the agonies of doubt do not occur ("I should have stopped him . . . it should have been me."), nor do excessive grief and guilt. In a sense this romanticizing takes the place of a religious comfort. No mention is ever made of an afterlife; perhaps this, too, is seen only as the personal concern of the lost one.

". . . and we will not debate his profound wisdom in these proceedings."

The twenty-third century puts great emphasis on the individual, including the *responsibility* of the individual for all his or her actions, and death is no exception. It is not for the survivors to question or berate the one who has died, because each person must have the freedom to exert maximum effort in any endeavor—even if it ends in failure. Often the people of the twentieth century agonize that we-who-are-left-behind have been deserted, deliberately abandoned, by someone who has died, but this feeling is not seen in the *Star Trek* universe. Angela Martine could accept Robert Tomlinson's death with quiet dignity; he had done what he had to do, and because she loved him, she allowed him this. Kirk was able to go on living and carry out his duties after Spock's, and even David's, death. They, too, had done what they must; in each case the choice had been theirs, and Kirk respected those choices.

Death is the experience and concern only of the dead. To grieve overmuch is to invade this privacy and rob dignity from the lost one. Neither is any guilt ever carried by the living; it is not wrong to have survived, for it is surely the task of all human creatures to continue for as long as possible. And it is understood by all that each individual assumes for himself the inherent risks of living.

When someone's time has come, the letting-go is as important as the keeping. Dr. McCoy did not use any drastic measures to keep Peter Preston alive for just a little longer, even though he doubtless could have done so, and Scotty does not seem to expect him to. "I know ye tried," he says, not, "I know ye did everything possible"—a subtle but important difference. Spock risked his career to take Christopher Pike to Talos IV, where Pike could be at peace even though Spock would never see him again. Kirk did not try to open the doors to the radiation chamber to rescue Spock even though the Vulcan lay there dying, because it would have put them all in jeopardy and McCoy had already told him that it was "too late."

"*. . . live long and prosper.*"

We have seen that love and death are closely bound in the *Star Trek* universe. So what of immortal characters, those who will never die and need never face death?

Immortal characters are often pictured as shallow, vain, and unfeeling—in other words, "inhuman." We might take "inhuman" to mean "invulnerable" or "insensitive," as in "lacking the capacity to care for one's self or others, since there is no need to do so." Being "human," however, implies that the creature acknowledges it weaknesses and tries to strengthen them so that it might survive, even if only for a short time. By this definition, any life form can be called "human"—and Humanity is what *Star Trek* is all about.

None of the mortal characters ever speaks of wishing for eternal life. When Uhura makes her speech about wanting perpetual youth, her words just don't ring true. Somehow we know it would be out of character for her to wish to live forever and not accept her natural aging and death; to do so would be a denial of her very being, a rejection of her own humanity.

Sargon and Thalassa made the decision to accept and exist in their own forms, imperfect as those were; they did not reject their own version of "humanity." Henoch, on the other hand, wanted to be an immortal at any cost, and he was destroyed.

The Companion offered the ultimate proof of her love for Cochrane by becoming mortal for his sake, and accepting his death and her own.

Apollo insisted upon the worship and station of an immortal god. He offered to make the crew immortal, too, if they would serve him. Such a loss of "humanity," his complete rejection of it, led to his downfall.

Flynt, weary of outliving his loved ones, sought companionship in an android of his own making, Rayna. Flynt rejected the company of humans, but tried to use them to awaken Rayna's emotions. This cold manipulation of another's humanity cost him Rayna's existence.

Roger Korby found immortality for himself through the use of an android body. But he used this status for his own power and prestige, and he destroyed himself rather than face up to Christine Chapel and confront his own loss of humanity.

"The way we face death . . ."

In *Star Trek,* death is always the result of what a creature has chosen to do, be it for good or ill. An individual's true nature is always revealed by the manner of his death.

Death is never a way of redeeming a bad character's actions. "Bad" characters are those who love poorly or not at all; they are selfish creatures who could have died nobly or lived well, but chose not to. They are either killed as a result of their own actions, or use death as an escape from what they feel are unbearable circumstances.

Any character who has twisted love for its own ends is always treated very harshly. This explains why the crew of the *Enterprise* had no pity for the Salt Vampire; it tried to manipulate them by appearing as beloved, trusted friends, when in fact it was only luring them on to the kill. The creature may have been the last of its kind, but such a use of love and trust—of "humanity"—was unforgivable, and the crew had no qualms about destroying the creature.

Charlie Evans, for all his unfortunate situation, also won no sympathy from anyone when it was discovered that he was trying to bully them into love and admiration for him. Even the Thasians knew that such emotional blackmail could not be tolerated, and they took Charlie away to permanent exile.

Gary Mitchell was a character brought down by his own weaknesses. Although he was supposedly a good friend of Kirk, and a well-respected officer aboard the *Enterprise*, his behavior toward Elizabeth Dehner was rude and boorish from the start (when she doesn't drool over him on sight, he calls her a "walking freezer unit"). As soon as his psi powers accelerated, he became cruel, tyrannical, and completely insensitive to the remaining humans. He counted on, and used for his own benefit, Kirk's reluctance to destroy or even imprison him. Dr. Dehner, on the other hand, was slower to gain power than was Mitchell, and was easily talked out of "godhood" by Kirk. Mitchell, however, would not even consider becoming human again, and in the end was killed through the combined efforts of Kirk and Dehner.

Kodos the Executioner, although he may not have believed himself an evil man, nonetheless hid from his drastic decision to destroy half a population so that the other half might live. He never faced his actions, never dealt with the consequences, and so died by his own daughter's hand in her clumsy attempt to help him keep his secret.

Dr. Tristan Adams had a marvelous device that could have been used to help others—it was virtually a cure for even the worst cases of insanity. But instead, he used the machine to control and manipulate others, and in the end was destroyed by it as he lay in its chair, his mind emptied.

Larry Marvick loved the beautiful Miranda, and was jealous of her devotion to the alien being Kollos. He attempted to destroy Kollos and so gain Miranda's affection for himself, but was driven to insanity and death by the sight of the alien.

Dr. Sevrin, the leader of the "space hippies," cared nothing for the fact that he was the carrier of a deadly virus that could destroy any unprotected population. It mattered only that he find his own personal paradise— and when he did, it killed him.

The Gorgon was a clear example of a creature twisting love for its own purposes. He destroyed the adult members of a planetary expedition team, and denied the surviving children their grief in order to gain influence over them. He was shouted back into ugly helplessness by the children once they understood what was happening.

Khan Noonian Singh. Supremely intelligent, supremely powerful—and too good for humanity. Humanity had exiled him and virtually destroyed his own people, and he would have his revenge at any cost—including the remnants of his own humanity. He used the loyalty of Joachim (considered by many to be his own son), then threw away his life. Khan's powers and intellect could have saved himself and his tribe, and aided his fellow humans, but he chose not to do so. He was first exiled; then, when he returned years later, was vaporized in the detonation of the Genesis Device.

Klingon Commander Kruge was certainly the epitome of a character destroyed by his own flaws. The first thing we see him do is vaporize the female who loves him. So selfish and shortsighted was he that he continued to fight and make demands of Kirk in the midst of a disintegrating planet, oblivious to the very real danger all around. He came to the distinctly unheroic end of being kicked into a pool of lava.

"*. . . is at least as important as the way we face life.*"

Some characters meet their deaths not through evil actions or glorious sacrifice, but die in the service of a good cause, or are caught up in the plans or actions of others, or are simply in the wrong place at the wrong time. They are "innocents" who try valiantly to survive, but are overwhelmed by the odds—"humans" by any definition.

Losira tried desperately to keep her people alive on a desolate world, waiting for supply ships that never came. Kirk and his crew were sorry to find out that, even with all the trouble her defenses had caused them, only her beauty survived.

The android Rayna was caught in the struggle between her own emerging humanity and Flynt's desire to own and control her. She could not—or would not—reconcile the conflicting emotions, and was lost.

Miramanee was a victim of Kirk's amnesiac state and her people's superstitious ignorance. She tried bravely to protect him from the angry mob, taking the thrown stone herself, but could not survive the injuries she sustained.

George Samuel and Aurelan Kirk were pioneers of the twenty-third century, living in a strange new world and therefore open to its dangers. Like so many other explorers before them, their lives and deaths taught a great deal to those who would follow.

The powerful Romulan Commander was a man trapped between his weariness of war and the higher call of duty to the Empire. He had little appetite for yet another battle, but still fought with all his strength and cunning against the *Enterprise* so that his own ship might return safely home. When he found that he had been disabled through trickery and would never see his homeworld again, he detonated his ship as the Empire demanded he must. It is hoped that he has at last found a peace that he can accept.

Truly, no one has provided a greater sacrifice than Edith Keeler, unwitting though it was. Ahead of her time in a violent, backward world, she clung to her ideals and tried to make it a better place. But that world had not yet grown up enough for her kind of vision, and so she had to be allowed to die in order for someone else, in another time and place, to bring her ideas to fruition. Undoubtedly, had she known, she would have made the sacrifice willingly.

The Deltan female Ilia made more than one sacrifice for the crew of the *Enterprise*. First, she agreed to live behind the veil of celibacy, which must have been difficult; then she was assimilated by Vejur, who "returned" her in the form of an information-seeking probe. But some part of her own personality survived the transfer, since it is clear that she herself was present when she and Decker were made a part of the mind of Vejur.

On board the Regula space station, a small group of peaceful scientists found themselves in the grip of a raging madman. Though it was too late for them, they still prevented Khan from gaining access to the computer banks holding priceless information about Genesis, as well as buying time for David and Carol Marcus to escape.

Over and over again, it is the security teams of the *Enterprise*—the infamous red-shirts—who put themselves between their captain and danger. Despite their advanced training, many are lost. They should be remembered with all honors, since they put their lives on the line more often than anyone else.

Although not a character in the usual sense of the word, the *Enterprise,* too, became an obstacle to humans struggling desperately to survive, and the great starship became one more bridge for Captain Kirk to burn behind him.

"He did not think his sacrifice a vain or empty one."

The noblest characters in *Star Trek* are those who consciously choose to lay down their lives for the good of others. Although some may ultimately survive the crisis, their willingness to sacrifice themselves is still proof of their love for "humanity"—both their own and that of their companions.

Captain Christopher Pike knew that he was running into deadly danger. The training vessel's baffle plate had ruptured, releasing delta radiation, but he stayed to rescue cadets anyway. The rays should have killed him, but he remained alive, trapped in a grotesque and twisted body, unable to speak or move. He wished for death, but instead was taken by Spock to Talos IV, where he could live out his life within the illusion of being himself once again—as if he had indeed died and been reborn.

Dr. Elizabeth Dehner was well aware of Gary Mitchell's dreadful powers, and could have allowed Kirk to take all the risks. But she chose to reject "godhood," and chose to fight Mitchell with all the powers she possessed, helping to destroy him even though the drain cost her her life.

Fully conscious of the certain death that awaited them, but willing to make the sacrifice, the first Vulcan ambassadors walked openly into the territory of their enemies to ask for peace. Their losses were terrible, but the end result was a culture of pure logic and rationality, the only one known in the galaxy.

Odona knew how her people suffered grievously as a result of overpopulation. She allowed herself to contract a deadly disease so that through her pain and death, others would find the courage to do the same. Fortunately, she did not have to die to accomplish her goals, but the offer was made just the same.

Commodore Matt Decker was not a "bad" character, but he was the one who had made a mistake, and it had cost the lives of the crew of his starship, the *Constellation*. Although it was a kind of escape, he chose to end his life by destroying the deadly "Doomsday Machine" that was rampaging through the galaxy and guided his shuttlecraft directly into its maw.

The entire story of Gem, "The Empath," focused on the sacrifices humans will make for each other. The Vians were not as cold and cruel as they appeared; evidently, they considered the capacity for altruism to be extremely important and were unwilling to save a race that displayed little sign of it. Gem used her highly developed powers of empathic healing when she could, but drew back if there was any threat at all to her own life. The Vians admired the courage of the *Enterprise* crew, their unquestioned willingness to lay down their lives for each other, and hoped to arouse the same qualities in Gem and her race.

Will Decker (*Star Trek: The Motion Picture*) found that he no longer had the place he wanted within the company of humans. Through no fault of his own, his command of the *Enterprise* had been jerked out from under him, and he had lost Ilia to an alien machine. When Vejur demanded to meet its creator in person, it came as no surprise that Decker chose to merge with Ilia and Vejur to become part of an entirely new kind of being, continuing his adventures and together forever with his love.

Lieutenant Marla McGivers first sacrificed her career for the love of Khan Noonian Singh, and later lost her life as a result of her decision to go with him in exile on Ceti Alpha V. It seems strange that she would willingly drop everything to run away with a criminal from the past, but such is the nature of love and sacrifice—sometimes.

"He stayed at his post . . . when the others ran." The epitaph for a very young hero, Scotty's nephew, Peter Preston. Kirk did not lie when he told the boy, "warp speed . . ." because Peter's bravery had helped to save the ship and allow her to again run at warp speed.

Captain Terrell was undoubtedly one of Starfleet's finest captains, and even under the wretched control of Khan and his "pets," he refused to harm Admiral Kirk—deliberately turning the phaser on himself instead.

David Marcus probably never believed that his life would end in a desperate attempt to save another. But when Saavik faced certain death at the hands of the Klingons, he leaped to her defense even though he must have known he had no chance against the Klingon warrior. He did indeed save Saavik's life, and his own brief one had a profound impact on a great many people.

Spock. For him, the choice was clear: sacrifice himself, and save the ship and her crew; live a moment longer, and die along with the rest. A coolly logical decision on the surface, and yet an unparalleled act of heroism. Spock is an excellent example of a creature driving himself to the limits of his abilities in all that he does, right up to the end, and of his death results from that constant striving for the best. Although the crew mourned deeply for Spock, they also recognized that they should not so much grieve his passing as celebrate having known him.

"I have been, and ever shall be, your friend."

The willingness to love in spite of the ever-present specter of death is evidence of the courage at the heart of *Star Trek*. Without accepting this risk, man would have never ventured out of his cave, much less journeyed to the stars. In order for life to continue and the mind to grow, love must be willing to risk loss. Love is our most powerful drive, and our greatest vulnerability. It is the *Kobayashi Maru* of life.

MORE THAN YOU EVER WANTED TO KNOW ABOUT *STAR TREK* BOOKS, OR WHAT UHURA'S FIRST NAME REALLY IS

By William Rotsler

William Rotsler is one of the most prolific and successful writers around, and author of a number of Star Trek *books, yet his name is unknown to a great many fans. Why? William himself explains below.*

I was thumbing through *The Best of Trek #10* when I discovered—to my surprise—not one but three references to my book *Star Trek II Biographies.* I thought you might be interested in reading a few words on these books, and on the references to them.

First of all, the very fact anyone *knows* about the book is astonishing to me. I've gone up to dealers at conventions (but not *Star Trek* cons) who are selling tables of nothing *but Trek* material and they've never heard of the book. This is not to beef up my royalties, for I get none—it and the six other *Star Trek* books were all "buy-outs" as they say in the trade. But that book, over the other six, I thought would be of more than ordinary interest to Trekkies. I've done about three dozen books for Wanderer Books, which is a division of Simon & Shuster, just like Pocket Books. This includes the first six of the "new" *Tom Swift* series (with Sharman DiVono, who wrote the *Star Trek* comic strip for a while), also movie novelizations and originals based on franchised characters. Some of them, including two *Star Trek* books, were interactive (kinda), or "plot-your-own-adventure" books, as the publisher calls them.

The distribution on these books is *terrible.* In checking *over one hundred* book stores in Seattle, San Francisco,

New York, Baltimore, San Diego, Chicago, and Los Angeles, I saw a few of the *Tom Swifts*, but only one or two copies of two or three books.

Anyway, me doing the books was a big surprise to Pocket Books, who thought they had a lock. But they do *novels*, which left me plot-your-own (2), real-little-kiddy-books (2), short stories (2), and the biographies (1). This all was my editor's idea, not mine. So there you have one correction, as one of your writers had me doing novels.

The other correction comes on Uhura's name. I read *The Best of Trek* backward, and so did not come to Nicky Jill Nicholson's "The Naming Game" until I had seen several references to "Penda" Uhura. I totally agree with Nicky's uncompromising statement . . . but perhaps for different reasons.

My editor, Wendy Barish, wanted me to do the biographies of the Starfleet characters and I liked that idea, but I simply did not want to rehash old material. I wanted to give the fans something new . . . and I didn't want to bore myself doing it. So I conceived the "dossier" format. This included full name, serial number, birth place, dates, commendations, etc.

Another thing you must understand is that *Star Trek* is licensed *individually;* that is, the series is licensed separately from each film, each of which is licensed individually, etc. Theoretically, since this book was *Star Trek II,* I could only use material in the second movie. Obviously, you couldn't do the bios on that film alone, so everyone simply paid no attention, tactfully, and firmly.

This format, then, required the addition of first names, family, serial numbers, and so on *where they had not previously been noted.* I used (1) my own memory; (2) Bjo Trimble's *Concordance;* (3) Bjo's memory; (4) other obvious sources. I did *not* read any but the one *Star Trek* novel I had already read—there were simply too many; I had neither time nor inclination. I was, after all, licensed, ordered, and restricted to *Star Trek II* (sorta). So if it wasn't in the series, the two movies, the *Concordance,* or behind-the-scenes-"well-established"-fact, I ignored it.

Example: I had made up a whole history for Sulu, but Pocket Books (who had bowed to the inevitable and the "resident Trekkie" read it and approved) said that Vonda

McIntyre had given Sulu a history, so I used that. My whole idea was to use all reasonable sources, to make it fit in. I used some starship names from another book.

Example: Spock had never had a serial number, so I gave him WR39-733-906, which had been assigned to me some years before by the U.S. Army. McCoy got my phone number as of that date. Kirk graduated from my high school and had my sister's birthday. Chekov had my father's. McCoy had my daughter's, and he was married on the day I was married and divorced on the day I was writing it. Scott was born on my other sister's birthday; Uhura was born on my ex-wife's birthday, which is the same as our daughter's.

Example: Ships, characters, officers are named after fans and friends. (You gotta name 'em sumpin'!)

Example: Naming Uhura was the most fun. I looked through one of those twenty-six-language dictionaries (which never seem to have the word you want) and found *Nyota* under "star." I got Nichelle Nichols's phone number from Bjo—I'd never met Miss Nichols—and called her, told her who I was and what I doing. She was very nice, very polite. I was careful to say I had picked a name for her *character*—not *her*—and had checked it with Gene Roddenberry.

"That's nice," she said.

"It's Nyota," I said.

"Oh, that's nice," she says, still polite.

"It means 'star' in Swahili," I said.

"Oh, *wowww!*" she exclaimed.

You see, I took this attitude: *I* was writing the *official* biographies. What *I* said goes. So "Nyota" is "official," not Penda, not anything else. (And Nichelle liked it.) I admit this is a cavalier attitude, but it was my book, so there.

I *larded* the book with friends, friends' books, puns, and insults (visible only to friends.).

I think the most fun of all was doing the bibliography. Once I had conceived of the format of drawing from reports, letters, official files, etc., it was an obvious step to books. If the *Enterprise* crew had saved the Earth *that* many times, it seems perfectly natural to assume there would be books (or what passed for books, rather, what *will* pass for books then), documentaries, etc. So I jotted down a few obvious titles, quit work, and went in to watch TV. Somewhere in the evening I thought of a title—just popped into my head—*Klingon Cuisine*. About one in the morning or so, my usual beddy-bye time, I stopped by my typewriter to make a note of it . . . and another title occurred to me.

Next thing I knew it was 4:55 A.M. and I had written five thousand words of bibliography. I used the name of every single writer who had worked on the series; I had used most of the membership list of the Los Angeles Fantasy Society (almost always changing first names or using a first and using the street they lived on). For example, Kalisher Pelz became the author of *Klingon Cuisine* because Bruce Pelz lives on Kalisher Street. I used the "real" names of historians and others, mentioned in the *Star Trek* mythos. I switched names—Jim Bearcloud and George Barr live together, so they became the co-authors of *Art of the Stars,* James Barr and George Bearcloud. There is not *one* author who is not based on an "authorized" *Star Trek* character or mixed'n'matched names of friends. Randy Lofficier becomes Randall; Lola Johnson, wife of George Clayton Johnson who we often refer to as Lola Clayton, became L. Clayton Johnson, etc.

For years I have been using the name of Gregg Calkins, ex-WW II marine sergeant, devoted SF fan, and friend—and each time I bumped him a grade. In *Biographies* he is a fleet admiral. I can't get you much higher, buddy . . . except promotion to civilian.

And so on.

This was the most fun to do of the *Trek* books, but later they asked me to cut twenty-five hundred words, so I took it all out of the bibliography and didn't try to balance things out; so probably I lost some of the original series writers.

The two children's books were just "a job of work," as Bob Silverberg calls things like this. The Plot-Your-Own was semifun and I did like the idea of the pre-Logic war Vulcan treasure being hidden and the nature of what they considered treasure.

I did two books of short stories. Originally, I tried to do a story each on the characters, but I found that too often a minor rank would logically have to check with Kirk, or at least Spock, for one thing or another. You really have to isolate the characters, or in most cases of "life and death" people would just call the cops.

In the *Biographies* I thought about the motivation for the Starfleet people to volunteer for five-year missions. After all, this was longer than the two- and three-year missions of Terran sea explorers. You had to be powerfully motivated, I reasoned. So I gave Uhura a wowser of a romance—then killed her lover. Feeling bad about this, I wrote a story where she had a romance with a prince on an idyllic planet . . . well, maybe not so idyllic . . .

One of the books of short stores took place in the microspace between *Star Trek II* and *Star Trek III*. I had no script at first, I didn't know what was going to happen in the third film, so I figured as beat up as the *Enterprise* was it would head for dry dock in earth orbit. I had a midflight breakdown . . . one story . . . then in dry dock, Scott tells a young engineer (Scott is a bit smashed, I'm afraid) a story about Spock . . . Uhura has an adventure in a wildlife preserve in her homeland, the United States of Africa . . . and then, since I seemed to be pressing this idea, two stories taking place in the "regular" *Star Trek* universe. I must say, though, that when I did get a script and I read of the *Enterprise*'s demise I had to reread it. I just couldn't believe it. Not from a logic standpoint of the story, but from the commercial aspect of "What are they going to sell now?"

The experience of writing the seven books was a good one. Writing short stories is easy in the sense that when you are "writing in someone else's universe" (as we writer-types call it) you don't have to explain who these people are, what they are doing there, what their hangups or powers are—you must get right into writing the story. Making certain, of course, that you write the characters true and don't hang inhibition on the writers to follow.

Since the *Biographies* seems to have become a source book for *Star Trek* novelists (and the comic book as well), everyone accepts that it all works better if we agree on certain things, they use what I've done. I was careful to put in brothers, sisters, etc. so that one or another would be available. I've noticed only one error: I sent a copy to Roddenberry's office during filming of *Star Trek III* but they didn't use McCoy's father's name as *I* had written it. Sigh.

When *Biographies* came out I had published approximately forty books. (Total now: fifty three.) All the other thirty-nine books did not generate *together* as much mail as that one book. And no one knows it exists, hardly. The mail is much alike: "Dear Mr. Rotsler: The book was great and long-needed, really swell and terrific and wonderful, but . . ."

After the "but" always came *their* idea of what Uhura's first name was or some other tidbit. Only one writer was right, a man who caught me in a goof on Spock's burial. (And damn, I had gotten a transcript of the film from Paramount to check, too. Note: not the script, but after a film is done, a transcript of what was *actually* said. But my goof was in timing, not words.)

In *The Best of Trek #10*, Jeffrey W. Mason has a great chronology and shakes his finger at me for putting *Star Trek* in the twenty-second century. I think this must be a typo in my book or one of many "corrections" made by a rather eager copyeditor. (I'm not trying to pass blame—I know when it takes place—but that was a copy editor, and they sometimes forget their important function and start to "rewrite creatively." In this case they constantly, in all seven books, no matter what I said, changed Lieutenant, Doctor and Mister—and you can imagine how often those titles are said—to Lt., Dr., and Mr. Now in narrative text that is fine, but in *conversation*? No. We do *not* say *Lit, Dur* and *Mur*. There were other changes I simply did not catch, but were all important. So I apologize to Mr. (Mur) Mason and to Faithful Reader.) (No, I don't, I was just being nice. Screw it.)

Mark Alfred (in *the Best of Trek #10*) notes the discrepancy in the explanations of why Khan recognized Chekov. Vonda McIntyre had one explanation: I another. It's very simple: Vonda was wrong. (There is one thing you must understand about novelizations—you *rarely* see the movie before you do it. You often do not work with the final script. Most of the time you do not have photos, even. I did one hundred pages of *Sinbad and the Eye of the Tiger* without even knowing who was playing the parts and without a real ending. I turned it in, they liked it, the producer liked it, "But you [the publisher] gave him the wrong script." So they paid me twice to make the corrections. So it's obviously easy for Vonda to be wrong. We often say that about her, in fact. (I think I'm in trouble the next time I run into her.)

Writing those books was fun, a *homage* to the best science fiction series ever. In fact, the basic format of *Star Trek* is *the* best format—you go to where the action is and can logically leave after the fun is over, and furthermore, be ordered into places and to do things any sane man would respond to with, "Are you *kidding*?" I felt I had made a small, but interesting contribution, and got paid to do it. I'd do it again.

In fact, I pitched Pocket Books on the idea of three books: *The Starfleet Quartermaster Manuals*, which would have, spread over the books, all the costumes of Starfleet from the beginning to the "present," past and present weapons, including future ones under research and development. (You understand, these are *photographs*, done "manual style" because I have access to many *perfect* replicas by Bruce Wegmann, to Ed Kline's magnificent ray guns, and have others who will make costumes, models, etc., as well as what I do myself.) There would be many things shown, that were referred to but never seen, and things "in the spirit of." Starships, special ships, computers, objects, *things*, aliens, etc.—all real (well, "real") and photographable from different angles.

But that was the period when Pocket Books was having an editor a week and my idea was lost in the shuffle, I guess.

So this is my response to *The Best of Trek #10*. It's 1:46 A.M. and tomorrow I have to go roast Harlan Ellison . . . along with Ray Bradbury, Bob Bloch, Bob Silverberg, Philip De Guere, Stan Lee, some guy named Gerrold and a new kid on his way up, Williams . . . Robert Williams, no, Robin Williams. Poor Harlan.

MONSTERS IN *STAR TREK*— A DIFFERENT PERSPECTIVE

By Miriam Ruff

A different perspective, indeed. Miram Ruff takes a somewhat different look at Star Trek *and comes up with a slightly different interpretation of what should be considered "monsters"—in* Star Trek, *and in real life as well. You think you know what's going to be said here, right? Well, think again.*

Much attention has been given to the role of monsters in the *Star Trek* universe. There have been in-depth analyses of everything from the "classical" monsters—which by nature attack and kill, unable to understand that their actions are wrong, and incapable of being reasoned with—such as the cloud creature in "Obession" or the flying parasites in "Operation: Annihilate," to the misunderstood aliens like the Horta in "Devil in the Dark." Most agree that these monsters, regardless of their type, added a measure of excitement to a story, while those monsters that were merely aliens and acting as a result of a definite, understood need, provided a depth through their interactions with the crew and other characters in the show.

Star Trek was, however, in many ways a subtle show. It was designed to comment on the human condition, its strengths and weaknesses, its failures and successes. As a result, the use of monsters necessarily reflected that approach: the creatures presented, while visually impressive and necessary to the plot, served to a large extent as a reflection of the true monsters of the show, those that exist within ourselves.

The idea that *Star Trek* dealt with human flaws is

certainly not a new one, but few people recognize these flaws for the monsters that they can be. As *Star Trek* showed us, even a tiny flaw can assume monstrous proportions. *Star Trek* was a show about ourselves, our natures, our problems. One message that recurred throughout the episodes concerns the need to recognize, and through that recognition, conquer the monsters hidden within us, before they can conquer us. The use of "real" monsters was necessary in order to dramatize those flaws, to provide a situation where we could see them and take the first, necessary steps toward actively dealing with them.

One of the most vivid examples occurs in "Obession." A cloud creature, which Kirk had encountered eleven years before, reappears on a planet that the *Enterprise* crew is investigating. This creature was of the "classical" type, hardly appearing before it attacked and killed several security men.

Obession, a single-minded fixation on one idea, as Spock has defined it, is one of the strongest of the human monsters. As shown in this episode, it eliminates the capacity for rational thinking and decision making, and if not corrected by some outside or internal force, it will eventually overcome the individual. It is not a side of ourselves that we want to see or even to admit to; it is certainly something that Kirk, as a starship captain, does not want to admit that he is capable of. Yet he blames himself for not killing the cloud creature eleven years ago and allowing it to decimate the crew of the U.S.S. *Farragut*, and becomes obsessed with killing it now, to the point where he puts his command in jeopardy and almost allows himself to destroy the career of Ensign Garrovick, a young officer who reminds him of himself of eleven years ago. Kirk's responds to McCoy's assertion that he is, indeed, obsessed with the destruction of the creature with both shock and anger.

The situation is alleviated by both internal and external events. Kirk, himself, questions the validity of his decisions, his "right" to pursue the course of action he has chosen based merely "on a memory"; he is forced to acknowledge what harm he may be doing when both Spock and McCoy openly question him about his recent behavior. However, because he is ultimately proven correct in his assessment of the creature, he never does confront his obession directly, but merely suppresses it for the time being. We see evidence of it again in later episodes, such as *Star Trek: The Motion Picture,* as he attempts to regain the *Enterprise,* careless of anything or anyone he pushes aside in the process.

Star Trek taught by example: Kirk's failure to fully come to terms with his inner monsters gives us our greatest insight into the human character. We do not want to accept that we, too, are capable of such a flaw; if, by some external process, we are forced to see that darker part of ourselves, we often try to cover it up, so that it surfaces again and again without resolution. It becomes an elusive beast hidden within ourselves.

It is important that there be some external event that releases this monster, at least as far as the series is concerned. Because Kirk is a starship captain and, as such, always must remain outwardly strong, it would not be believable for him to suddenly become obsessed about something without any apparent cause. As a result, a visible monster is used to creature a situation where such a flaw can be brought to the surface, showing us what is hidden within us all.

Another good example of these hidden monsters is found in "Miri." In this episode, there are actually two monsters, the disease that infected both the adults and the children as they entered puberty, and the children themselves.

The first of these, the disease, was a result of life-prolongation experiments conducted by the adults of the planet more than three hundred years before. The experiments extended the life span, but only for the children, the adults becoming increasingly violent, eventually going mad, aging incredibly rapidly, and dying. It was a monster of undefined form, something that had to be fought but was incapable of self-awareness. Interestingly, it had its reflection not in the main characters, but in Miri, one of the children.

Miri was just entering puberty, and was contracting the disease. She had seen its effects on the others, especially Kirk (whom she was attracted to), watching them become increasingly irritable and irrational. Yet she would not accept this fate for herself. The symptomatic blotches appeared quickly as the disease was contracted, but not so quickly that she would not have seen them as they appeared on her body. She vehemently denied that everyone who went through puberty contracted the disease. She refused to look at her arm where the blotches were spreading, refused to accept what was happening to her. Kirk had to physically force her to look, to confront the truth, to confront reality.

This monster, the refusal to accept something we know to be true but is painful for us, is almost as strong, and perhaps more prevalent, than obsession. As Spock has said on occasion, humans have a capacity to believe what they choose. By blocking out the reality of a situation, we eliminate any possibility of rationally dealing with it. The situation will deteriorate until it can destroy us. By refusing to accept that she, too, was becoming one of the "creatures" that she feared, Miri would have let the disease progress in its course until she was dead. It was only after she had been forced to come to terms with it that she took steps to control the situation, by bringing Kirk to the "onlies" so that he could retrieve the communicators and contact the ship.

As with "Obession," we have a visible monster that must be fought and overcome, but the ultimate meaning of the struggle refers us to internal monsters. Only after we have come to terms with ourselves can we come to terms with the external threat. Our internal struggle, our fight for survival against our own weaknesses, gives us the strength and ability to carry on the struggle against the external force. Unknowingly, the creature brings about its own destruction; but only when the human has learned to cope with the situation.

The second monster of "Miri," the children, is not immediately recognizable as such. Children are assumed to be innocents, to lack the experience and knowledge of adults. Yet these children were three hundred years old. They had seen the "grups" hurting and killing in the "before time." They had seen many of the people they had known turn into the "creatures" that they feared and had become cruel and unfeeling themselves. One of the most frightening scenes in the entire series shows Kirk being beaten by the children; the camera close in on a little girl, a cold smile of amusement on her face as she watches the scene.

The children were not aware that were acting like the "grups" they remembered; to them it was all part of another "foolie." We, too, do not like to acknowledge that the violence within ourselves. It goes against everything that we strive for in civilized life. Nevertheless, that tendency is there, and, like the children, we can overcome it—by acknowledging its presence and taking active measures to conquer it.

People rarely recognize their inner monsters without an outside "trigger" of some kind. The visual monsters of *Star Trek* provide such triggers. The monster's presence forces a reaction in the individual, bringing hidden traits to the surface as he searches for means of fighting it. Even as unusual a monster as the children of "Miri" serves as a reflection of our inner selves.

A third example of the external/internal monsters is found in "The Trouble with Tribbles." This is probably one of the least recognized examples of this relationship, yet it is one that brings out one of the most dangerous of our hidden beasts. Cyrano Jones, a trader in rare merchandise, appears at the K-7 space station, where the *Enterprise* is responding to a distress call. In a short while he has sold Lieutenant Uhura a tribble, which she proceeds to bring up to the ship to keep as a pet. The tribbles breed prolifically, soon overrunning the ship and eating everything in sight. Spock realizes their danger, but when he comments that the tribbles are consuming everything and producing nothing, Uhura protests, "They do give us something, Mr. Spock, they give us love. Why, Cyrano Jones says that tribbles are the only love that money can buy."

This statement reveals the full monstrosity of the flaw, the inability to recognize that something can be a major threat when it is cute. Most of the *Enterprise* crew felt that the tribbles were "lovable," and even though they were a nuisance, they just would have to be tolerated. But if the situation had gone on much longer, the tribbles would not only have eaten everything edible aboard the ship, but would probably have caused a number of crucial operating systems to break down, perhaps even causing the crew to abandon ship.

We tend to recognize a threat only when it "looks" like a threat: if it looks cute and furry and harmless, we tend to accept it as such. It is not so much a refusal to accept reality because it is painful, as with the disease in "Miri," as it is an unsubstantiated feeling that appearances are trustworthy. But as Spock told McCoy in "The Empath," "The sand bats of Mynark Four appear to be inanimate rock crystals, until they attack." So, too, while the tribbles appeared to be not much more than little balls of fluff that made pleasant trilling noises, they were in effect parasites, preying on anything that would support them.

Unlike the other external/internal doublings, the internal monster in this episode was one that was a direct response to the nature of the external monster. It is a vague, undefined monster, acting to obscure our judgment and deter us from taking action to correct the situation. In its own way, it can be as devastating as obsession. It prevents us from approaching the situation rationally, making us wait until we feel the creature's bite before we decide that, perhaps, our first impression was not, after all, correct. But by the time we feel that bite, it may be too late: if Kirk and Company had waited any longer before taking action against the tribbles, they would have been powerless to prevent the creatures from overrunning the ship.

"The Doomsday Machine" was an automated machine of immense power that destroyed planets and digested the rubble for fuel. It was left over from a war somewhere outside our galaxy, built by a people long ago destroyed by their own weapon.

Again, it was more the "classical" type of monster; impossible to reason with, attacking and killing without comprehension because that was its very nature.
Nevertheless, its interaction with the characters in the episode demonstrated another powerful internal monster: guilt.

Commodore Matt Decker, the captain of the U.S.S. *Constellation*, sent his crew to the fourth planet in the

L-374 system when it became obvious that they could no longer fight the doomsday machine. But the machine again attacked the ship, damaging the transporter. When the device began destroying the planet and his crew called up begging for help, Decker could do nothing. His entire crew was destroyed because of his error in judgment. Instead of helping the *Enterprise* crew to warn Starfleet about the machine, Decker, driven by guilt, took over command of the *Enterprise,* insisting that the crew attack and destroy the machine, even when Spock repeatedly told him that it was impossible for one ship to do so.

Guilt, like obsession, can eliminate the capacity for rational thinking. Unless a means can be found for overcoming the guilt, it will eventually destroy the person.

Few people, however, see guilt as a form of obsession, and therein lies its monstrosity. Unlike many of the other monsters that we keep hidden, guilt is something that we will often acknowledge. We blame ourselves for things that happen, whether or not they are in our control, seeing in this a means of alleviating the situation. In reality, it only makes the situation worse, merely drives us until we become so obsessed with the past that we lose our capacity to deal with the present.

Decker could not deal with his guilt, and eventually killed himself, flying a shuttlecraft into the doomsday machine in a last attempt to stop it. It is in Decker's failure to conquer his guilt that we see the terrible power of this monster. We like to think that we have the strength to destroy it before it can do any harm. But it is the nature of a true monster to do everything in its power to destroy. The best defense we can take against it is to recognize it, because through acceptance of our fallibility, we can also find our inner strengths and use them to defeat guilt.

Bringing the viewer to awareness was one of the main purposes of *Star Trek*'s monsters. Through the interactions of the characters and these creatures, we could see aspects of ourselves that we might not otherwise see. And this is one of the things that distinguishes *Star Trek* from most other science fiction shows: it had the ability to make us think, to show us subtly but convincingly what we are afraid to see. *Star Trek* made us question who and what we are . . . as well as who and what are the monsters.

DATELINE: STARFLEET

By R. L. Bryant

R. L. Bryant (better known as "Bobby" to friends and readers of our earlier volumes) now works as a reporter for a major newspaper. Here he give us the benefit of his experience in newswriting and newscasting to take a not entirely humorous look at how the media of the twenty-third century might report the exploits of the Enterprise *crew.*

In Nicholas Meyer's 1982 opus *Star Trek II: The Wrath of Khan*, there are a hell of a lot of *happenings*—more than in the average movie, a great many more than in the typical *Star Trek* television episode. Let's recap just a few of these events:

—Khan Noonian Singh, popsickle-frozen refugee from the 1990's, escapes from his prison planet.

—Khan hijacks a scout-class Federation starship, the *Reliant*.

—Khan slaughters the science staff of a top-secret Federation research installation.

—Khan sneak-attacks and severly damages the *Enterprise*.

—Khan steals the Genesis Project, a top-secret device that can re-form matter along any lines its programming dictates.

—After a cat-and-mouse game, *Enterprise* cripples *Reliant*, killing a number of its twentieth-century renegade crew.

—Boom! Khan triggers Genesis, creating a brand-new planet.

—Captain Spock is killed saving the *Enterprise*.

Now, a lot of other things also happen in this story, but

you get the idea. Equally important to the storytelling, for example, is the role played by Kirk's long-lost son, etc. But that's basically a private matter.

What we're talking about here, it follows, is *public*. All the events listed here would be matters of public concern. And any one of these events would be the twenty-third century equivalent of a front-page story—big stuff. If poor old twentieth-century Earth already is, courtesy of mass media, what McLuhan called a global village, then with the obviously greater technology available in the *Star Trek* "future," the Federation must be eyeball-deep in news, twenty-four hours a day, all the time on an infinite variety of broadcast (or whatever) channels and others sources. We're not talking about a global village, but a *galactic* village.

If this is the case, and if the mass media proliferate over the next two hundred and fifty or so years in anything like the fashion they have over the last twenty-five, then we have to assume that any of the events that happen in *The Wrath of Khan* would get major play on thousands of news outlets in the *Star Trek* future. Faced with *all* of them happening virtually back to back, the Federation media would simply go bonkers for extended periods.

Remember what the American television networks alone did in 1985, during the Beirut hostage crisis; or, for that matter, even during the much-more-difficult-to-cover Chernobyl nuclear accident in 1986? Given a Federation media anywhere near the sophistication and tenacity of those we have right now, there would be special reports and bulletins constantly as parts of the story leaked out, along with false reports, denials, and rumors.

Which brings us to the question: how the devil would Admiral Kirk and Company explain all this to the press, even if they could explain it all to Starfleet?

A little exercise in imagination is in order: listen in on a taping of the twenty-third century version of *Meet the Press,* sometime after the events of *The Wrath of Khan*, but before those of *Star Trek III: The Search for Spock*. (I know there wasn't enough time or opportunity between those tales for this to take place, so don't remind me, okay?) Starfleet Admiral James T. Kirk is being interviewed by Mike Wallace IX, a direct descendant of the now-legendary *60 Minutes* commentator, and also by an aging clone of the original Geraldo Rivera.

Wallace: Now, Captain . . .

Kirk: It's Admiral.

Wallace: Of course. Now, Admiral, we'd like to ask you a few questions about the events of Stardate 1267.8—the Khan incident.

Kirk: Certainly. That was, in my opinion, a day of importance to the entire galaxy, a tragic set of events for both me and my crew.

Wallace: First off, Admiral, you must realize how shocking the full story of that event was for the Federation. The general public, you understand, not being privy to the secret files of Starfleet, did not even suspect that Khan was alive, let alone that a shipful of his followers had fifteen years ago taken over your starship, *barely* being put down. Let alone that you decided to exile this criminal to a deserted planet. Let alone the existence of Genesis, a device that could impact on everyone in the galaxy and all of our viewers.

Kirk: Well, I . . .

Rivera: Admiral, how did you feel when that unscrupulous renegade Khan was trying to take over your ship?

Kirk: Well, I wasn't exactly happy—

Wallace: Let me ask you this, Admiral, fifteen years ago, once you had stopped Khan's attempt to seize your ship—

Kirk: And to kill me, don't forget.

Wallace: And to kill you and your crew—

Kirk: To kill us *brutally,* by slow asphyxiation.

Wallace: To kill you all brutally—

Rivera: How did you feel during that time, Admiral?

Wallace: Whatever. Once you had control again, you had, what?—some seventy or eighty of these supermen from the past, these walking history books, in your hands, and yet you on your own authority decided to dump them on this backwater planet, just so you could quote Milton for the record? What about justice? What about history? How could you just drop all charges, multiple counts of conspiracy and assault, and simply put aside their criminal responsibility? Let alone their responsibility to answer for any war crimes they may have committed during the 1990's?

Kirk: Well, Mr. Wallace, if you had experience in Starfleet regs, as I do, and experience in making life-or-death, split-second decisions when the lives of four hundred and thirty crewmen are involved, as I have, you would realize that starship captains have the power to make such decisions. You sound like my old ship's surgeon—

Wallace: I have in my hand, Admiral, a confidential Starfleet report of a special board of inquiry that, to put it bluntly, raked you over the coals for your decision about Khan.

Kirk: Well, I couldn't—

Wallace: I quote the report: "a supremely rash and irresponsible action by a commander who has been criticized before for rash and irresponsible actions." Do you deny it?

Kirk: Well, Mr. Wallace, I really don't know how you got that document, but we can talk about violations of Federation security later.

Wallace: No violation of security, sir; I obtained this report from official sources after it was declassified in the wake of this latest Khan incident. And let me get back to that. Even ignoring your questionable history with this individual and his associates, we now find that Khan escapes—helped by one of your own former crewmen—kills a crew of scientists, and makes off with the Federation's most secret device! A weapon the public did not even know about, stolen and used by a man the public thought dead for more than two hundred and fifty years. The mind boggles, sir, it simply boggles! Has Starfleet never heard of the Freedom of Information Act?

Kirk: Can I have a glass of water?

End of diversionary tale. Now imagine the good admiral having to face this same kind of questioning a hundred more times, and have his actions armchair-quarterbacked countless times across the Federation. (No wonder

Starfleet, in *Star Trek III: The Search for Spock,* clamps a security lid on the whole thing.) It would be enough to make Kirk turn in his gold braid.

The point here (one of them, anyway) is that, while *Star Trek* has always done a pretty good job in making its situations as dramatic as possible, it has never dealt with the question of how the public and press gets checked out on all these crises and disasters. The more sophisticated their technology, the more kinds of news media will exist in a society; just look at the hundreds of magazines, newspapers, radio, and television outlets available directly or indirectly in any sizable American city.

In the *Star Trek* universe, the technology is there in spades—enough for galaxy-wide broadcast networks and millions of specialty publications and broadcasts. Obviously, the peoples of the Federation want and need to know, for example, that a nebula-size amoeba is gobbling up their systems, or that a big machine called Vejur is making a beeline for Earth. Do they get this kind of information? No. At least, not in filmed and televised *Star Trek.*

In many ways, this is simply a fault of the show itself: the apparent assumption that nobody outside of Starfleet knows anything. In some cases, this would be true. The transporter splits Kirk into doubles? Okay, you can keep that one under wraps—it was confined to the ship, nobody got killed, and it was sort of personal, anyway. Stamp it classified; certainly Spock and McCoy aren't going to spread it around.

In many other cases, though, the almighty Starfleet would leak information like a sieve. The *Enterprise* gets knocked back in time to the 1960's? Sorry, Admiral (or Captain)—that's going on the front pages instantly, as soon as somebody on the *Enterprise* gets shore leave and blabs to his girlfriend, or as soon as somebody in the Starfleet bureaucracy talks about this very interesting rumor he heard:

"Hey, word is that something real strange happened to a heavy cruiser last week. Dropped off the boards, then popped back up. Commander said the ship got punched back two hundred years in time, and visited Earth!"

"Jeez. I never heard that."

And so on, until some reporter gets enough to write a story with or without official help from Starfleet.

There are some things Starfleet simply could not keep out of the media, no matter how hard it tried, even if sensitive information were much more restricted than it is today. One of those impossible-to-keep-quiet things is death; the other is serious damage. A Vulcan starship gets eaten by that big amoeba? The Federation media could no more ignore the loss of such a starship than the *New York Times* could ignore the loss of the U.S.S. *Nimitz* with all hands. It would be a major tragedy and would get major coverage. People would protest; editorials would be written; hearings would be held all over the place. (And a really horrifying thought: if the *Enterprise*'s exploits are only a fraction, a tiny sample, of what goes on in the Federation, then what must a typical day be like in the *Star Trek* galaxy overall? And how big a newspaper would it take to report it?)

Here on present-day Earth, the Associated Press is pretty adept at covering all manner of disasters and breaking stories; virtually every American daily newspaper and television station gets a substantial part of its information straight of the AP "wire." The AP is uncluttered information, *Dragnet* style, if you've ever noticed: just the facts, ma'am. The analysis all comes later. Just for kicks, let's take a look at what—in all seriousness—the twenty-third century version of the AP might have to say about the events of public importance in the Star Trek episode, "The Doomsday Machine":

AP/UFPNET 5490AAD-a8092, 0945 ZT
AM/PM PLANETKILL
URGENT
3rd Ld-Writethru, 5490AAD-1
S'fleet finds, stops ancient machine
Will be led/Holos APN 23/T, 24/T, 25/T

STARFLEET HEADQUARTERS, Earth (AP)—An ancient, planet-destroying "doomsday machine" has been destroyed in Federation space after it wiped out at least five uninhabited star systems and killed the entire crew of a heavy-cruiser starship, officials said today.

All 428 officers and crew aboard the starship U.S.S.

Constellation were lost in the incident, according to Starfleet officials and Federation sources. The ship itself, already severely damaged, was blown up in a successful attempt to destroy the "planet-killing" machine.

"There were no survivors" among the crew, said Starfleet in a hastily prepared statement. "This must be counted among the heaviest crew losses in recent history, and possibly the heaviest in peacetime."

Except for the *Constellation*'s commanding officer, Commodore Matthew A. Decker, 51, all crew members died with the destructive alien machine, which apparently was unmanned, attacked an uninhabited planet in the L-374 star system of Epsilon Indii. The machine had earlier crippled the *Constellation*, and the crew had beamed down to the planet for what they believed was safety, informed sources said.

"They all might have survived if they had stayed aboard and had waited for rescue from another ship," said one official involved in the Federation investigation of the incident. "It was just a tragic mistake on somebody's part. The planet-killer would not have apparently considered *Constellation* a threat once it was disabled."

The kilometer-long alien device attacked the planet not specifically to kill the crew, this source said, "but to refuel. It more or less digested matter for propulsion, and it was able to slice up planets with a force beam of some sort."

Decker had apparently remained aboard ship for reasons unknown, but he could not help. Later, when another Starfleet vessel, the U.S.S. *Enterprise*, answered the *Constellation*'s distress calls, Decker died in an apparent one-man attempt to attack the machine, sources said. Starfleet officials would not comment on the exact manner of Decker's death, but *Enterprise* Captain James T. Kirk said in a subspace interview that Decker "died in the line of duty."

Kirk, in the brief interview approved by Starfleet Command officials, said the origin of the alien machine had not been determined, but it was believed to have "wandered into the galaxy" recently.

"Then it did what it does best—it started chopping up planets for fuel," Kirk said. He said preliminary sensor reading indicated the machine was totally unmanned and could have been immensely old. He speculated it was a "doomsday machine" that probably destroyed both sides in some unknown alien war, then kept going until it finally entered Federation space.

Kirk said Enterprise officers, stranded aboard the derelict *Constellation* as the planet-destroyer chased the *Enterprise*, rigged the ship's impulse engines to overload. Kirk then piloted the barely functioning ship "right down that thing's throat" and beamed to the *Enterprise*. "It wasn't even close," he said. "I had plenty of time to spare."

The fusion explosion wrecked the internal mechanisms of the alien machine, Kirk said, but the outside shell remained intact. A team of Starfleet specialists was en route to salvage the remains, which Kirk said had been resistant to phaser fire.

No deaths or serious injuries were reported among the *Enterprise* crew, which, like the *Constellation*'s, is primarily composed of humans. But in its brief statement, Starfleet said it was fortunate that the planet-killer was halted, because it could soon have threatened inhabited planets. No sentient life is know to have existed on the Epsilon Indii worlds—including at least 21 planets in the solar systems L-370, L-371, L,372, L-373 and L-374—which the machine destroyed.

Starfleet officials said a comprehensive news conference would be held simultaneously tomorrow morning at Fleet Headquarters/San Francisco on Earth and at the Academy. Times were to be announced.

"As terrible as our losses were, we must realize they could have been worse," said Federation Undersecretary for Internal Affairs Xavier Millo III in an interview with the AP. "This was war. It was totally unanticipated and unprovoked. If the machine had not been stopped, and if it had attacked populated planets, casualties could well be in the billions."

"As far as we know, this device had no intelligent being aboard and was totally without any external control," Millo said. "If it had, I'm sure we would be on a war footing by now. But there is no evidence of a deliberate aggression by an sentient race we can identify."

Millo confirmed that Federation perimeter defenses were no being placed on alert. "We think there was only one of those things," he said. "We are not expecting another."

So much for the AP, which is traditionally pretty subdued. God knows what the coverage would be like on the Federation equivalent of the Big Three television networks: "Death of a Starship: Special Report." "It Came from Beyond: Ordeal of the *Constellation*." "Unwelcome Visitor: Crisis at Epsilon Indii." "Terror Among the Stars: A Starship's Last Mission."

Not to mention the supermarket tabloids: "I HAD PLANET-KILLER'S BABY," WOMAN SAYS; NAMES CHILD "VEJUR."

STALKING THE WILD STAR TREK: COLLECTIBLE; OR, IN SEARCH OF LOST TREASURES

By Mark Alfred

Many of you may have wondered how and where to find those rare and sometimes valuable Star Trek *items. Well, wonder no more, because Mark Alfred returns to these pages with his tips on how to take a treasure hunt . . . a* Star Trek *collectible treasure hunt. We think you'll be surprised by some of his suggestions, and we hope you'll be inspired to become a* Star Trek *collectible collector yourself! (By the way, prices and values quoted below are for informational purposes only; neither we here at* The Best of Trek—*or Mark believe in collecting for profit; we think fans should collect for the sheer love of it.)*

How many times have you walked into a dealer's room at a science fiction or comic convention and seen a toy or comic book you once owned selling for $20 or $50 or more? If you're like me, you wish for a Guardian of Forever to send you back in time to save what your younger, more foolish self lost or threw out. For example, I feel like enacting *tal-shaya* upon myself when I think of the grocery-bagful of sixties comic books I gave away to the kid down the street when I was ten and he was eight.

Still, all is not lost. Chances are, unless deliberately thrown into the trash, some of those lost treasures have passed from church rummage sale to garage sale to thrift store, and are still waiting, like old friends, for you to redeem them from a lonely shelf life.

Now, you probably won't find the *Star Trek* Walkie-Talkies you lost when you were twelve, or Gold Key's

Star Trek Comics #1, or a first pressing of AMT's *Enterprise* model still shrink-wrapped, but you may be pleasantly surprised by the overlooked wonders out there. Remember that *Star Trek* has nearly always been a hot merchandising property, and that most of the these various products were mass-produced in great quantities.

Most rewarding of all is the thrill enjoyed when you find an unfamiliar item or rediscover an old, lost friend. All you need for this treasure hunt are time, diligence, and—alas—money.

Your chances for success in this endeavor are contingent upon your persistence. As the California forty-niners discovered, the more places you pan for gold, the greater the likelihood of striking paydirt.

(Note: The values of the *Star Trek* items given below are from the 1985 edition of House of Collectible's *Star Trek and Star Wars Price Guide*. I purchase my annual editions at Waldenbooks, and it is available at many other outlets, as well.)

Garage Sales

After many disappointments and a few bargains, I've found that the likelihood of finding a *Star Trek* collectible at a garage sale is fairly low. Toys, books, and such are usually well-worn, and even defective. Very seldom will you find something like-new. Of course, if you have lots of time to spend, or if you stop at garage sales anyway, go ahead and prowl; be assured there will always be plenty of garage sales to investigate.

Church sales are also chancy as to selection, yet their inventory is often in better shape than a garage sale's.

Library Sales

Keep on the lookout at your library or in the paper for your city library system's book sale. Many towns hold these annually.

I once picked up a copy of Leonard Nimoy's album *The Way I Feel*, worth about $25, for seventy-five cents at a library sale. Evidently few people had borrowed it, for it was in very good shape.

At library sales you may also find hardcover editions

of *Star Trek* novels originally available only through book clubs.

Assuming you don't mind "Discarded by Anytown Library" stamped across a book's flyleaf, bargains galore may await you at a library sale.

Used Book Stores

If you aren't deterred by dust or disarray, you can find some nifty books in these places. It was in a cluttered bookstall that I found some Bantam *Star Trek* novels I didn't know existed! Only recently I bought for $5 a first edition of the *Star Fleet Technical Manual,* worth $40 or more.

Be prepared to dig; any book in a jumbled box or at the bottom of a shopping cart might be that first edition of *The Making of Star Trek* you've been waiting for.

The average used-book dealer is a pretty sharp individual. To stay in business, he has to be. So if by chance you come across a superlative bargain—a low price on a book you know is worth much more—that's the time to restrain your eagerness. Remain calm. Don't bounce on your heels with a grin on your face and say, "Boy! You want only a dollar apiece for these Fotonovels? That's cheap!" Not only may the proprietor raise the price on the spot, but if you make an outburst like the above, you can lay odds you'll never find a similar bargain there again. As soon as you leave, the proprietor is likely to make a note to double the price (or more) of the kinds of books you just bought.

By the way, I was indeed able to pick up seven *Star Trek* Fotonovels, worth $10 apiece, for only $1 each. And you can bet I kept my excitement contained behind a face as cool as any Vulcan's.

Thrift Stores

These establishments may be sponsored by the Salvation Army, veterans' groups, or handicapped-aid societies; but their common denominator is that they accept donations of merchandise from groups and individuals and then sell the items to the public.

Donations to thrift stores, and thus the store's stock, vary widely, from unsellable leftovers from garage sales to office equipment donated as a tax write-off to like-new books, toys, and clothing.

There's no telling what you'll find at a thrift store. I've purchased a good-condition copy of Nimoy's album, *Mr. Spock's Music from Outer Space*, worth $35, for $1.29, and a copy of Bantam's rare *Official Star Trek Cooking Manual*, priced at $30, for seventy-nine cents.

Since so many new *Star Trek* items have been licensed in the past twenty years, you'll have to keep an eye on nearly every department. If you inspect only the book and record shelves, you'll miss such items as the following discoveries I've made in the past few years: a 1976 Dr. Pepper glass featuring Kirk from the animated series, worth $10, for twenty-five cents; a 1975 Deka milk mug, worth $4, for twenty-five cents; a "bridge" playset for Mego's eighteen-inch *Star Trek* dolls, worth $65, for $2.98; a *Star Trek: The Motion Picture* lunchbox, worth $10, for seventy-nine cents; a Dinky nine-inch diecast metal *Enterprise*, worth $50, for $2.

See what I mean?

Keep in mind, however, that only persistence and providence will provide a chance for you to come across such valuable rarities. You may find that one store's stock turnover is slow enough that you only need to visit it once a month; another with a more rapid influx of new stock might warrant weekly visits.

Of course, thrift stores offer a wide variety of useful things, so you don't have to feel you're making a special trip to search out *Star Trek* arcana. But what fun if, while making the rounds, you come across a *Star Trek* beach towel, worth $25, for $2, as I have!

A final note: Most thrift stores, unlike used-book dealers or garage sales, will not allow any flexibility or dickering over their prices.

Where Else?

The places to look for "dilithium in the rough" are myriad, besides the locales suggested above. Golden opportunities may be all around you.

When a doll store closed its doors, I bought four-inch-high, finely detailed pewter figures of Kirk and

Spock in TV uniforms for only $3 each. When a huge "toy supermarket" went out of business in 1979, I was astounded by what had been sitting in their warehouses. I bought first-printing *Star Trek* blueprints, priced at $50, for ninety-nine cents a set, and five Mego eight-inch figures, worth up to $40 each, for only twenty-nine cents each, still sealed in original packages!

Check the remainder tables at your local bookstore. I have found copies of the *Star Fleet Medical Reference Manual*, worth $7, for $2.49. Being a frequent patron can pay off in other ways, too. Bookstore managers may give you the promotional materials, such as the colorful headers to paperback book dumps, that are provided by Pocket Books to promote the *Star Trek* novels. These promo items are satisfying to own, because they can't be bought in stores anywhere.

What in the world?

As you become more skilled at sniffing out the offbeat and unknown, you'll be pleasantly surprised at the wide range of *Star Trek* stuff waiting for you. When *Star Trek: The Motion Picture* was released, McDonald's featured *Star Trek* Happy Meals, and at the grocery store you could get three *STTMP* posters free for buying toothpaste. A brand of deodorant soap offered a *Star Trek* kite by mail order a couple of years ago, tied in with *Star Trek III: The Search for Spock*.

The pieces in my collection I'm proudest of belong to the category I call "peripheral *Star Trek*." These items only marginally tie in with mainstream Trekdom, and so the gratification is proportionally increased when they are discovered, because they are not something everyone else has.

Here are ten examples of peripheral *Star Trek* from my bookshelves:

1. *Six Science Fiction Plays*, edited by Roger Elwood (Pocket Books, 1976). This is the only publication of Harlan Ellison's original script for "The City on the Edge of Forever." This version features a sadistic, drug-smuggling, murderous crewman; three ten-foot-tall humanoid Guardians of Forever (how hokey can you get?); and an ending in which Kirk decides to trash all of history so he can keep on enjoying the

favors of Edith Keeler. It is Spock who keeps Kirk from saving her; McCoy is but a minor, unimportant character in this script. Personally, I thank the powers-that-be that the version we saw was rewritten into *Star Trek* material.

2. *The Questor Tapes*, by D. C. Fontana (Ballantine, 1974). This is a novelization of a Gene Roddenberry–Gene L. Coon script, which was filmed as a made-for-TV-movie pilot. The subject is a man-made android searching for its creator. Sound familiar? Still, it's very enjoyable, especially if you're familiar with the film.

3. *I Am Not Spock*, by Leonard Nimoy (Ballantine, 1977). This intriguing autobiography includes dialogues between Nimoy and Spock ("If I'm not Spock, then who is?"). A very interesting book.

4. *Neuron Star*, by Larry Niven (Ballantine, 1968). This collection contains the story "The Soft Weapon," which was rewritten as "The Slaver Weapon" for the animated *Star Trek* series. Niven fans will note that the character rewritten as Spock was originally Nessus, the mad puppeteer featured in *Ringworld*.

5. *Star Wars, Star Trek, and the 21st Century Christians*, by Winkie Pratney (Bible Voice, 1978). This little book (91 pages) is a stream-of-consciousness meditation on the Force's resemblance to and differences from God; Spock's alienation as a model for unredeemed mankind; and so on. Some of the imagery is strained, and some of the terms will make sense only to one versed in traditional Christian doctrine and terminology. Beneath the silly, pseudopoetic format, though, there are some interesting and valuable ideas here, if you can wade through the rest.

6. *Shatner . . . Where No Man*, by William Shatner, Sondra Marshak, and Myran Culbreath (Ace, 1979). Yes, the writing team whose philosophical attitudes ruin some interesting basic story concepts has managed to interview William Shatner at length. The transcripts of these talks are interesting, to be sure. But Marshak and Culbreath twist every incident in Shatner's life to fit their own weird Jungian/alpha male/weeping hero concept of Captain Kirk. On the other hand, the photos are interesting.

7. *The Star Trek and Star Wars Price Guide* (The House of Collectibles, Inc., 1983 to present). This is an interesting little book, published annually, good for hours of browsing. (Did you know that there are four sizes of Saurian brandy bottles available?) But many items are omitted, and some of the prices suggested are pretty silly ($12 for a jigsaw puzzle?).

8. *Mirror Friend, Mirror Foe*, by George Takei and Robert Asprin (Playboy Press, 1979). The main character is Takei's fantasy of himself/Sulu as a ninja warrior and master swordsman of the future. Sulu's swashbuckling dreams come true here, and it's fun to read.

9. *Galaxy 666*, by Pel Torro (Leisure Books, 1968). This is science fiction's version of Sominex. It's only claim to fame is a blurred but immediately recognizable photo of an AMT *Enterprise* model that has been doctored by having a piece from an Erector set glued between the engine nacelles. I don't understand why Paramount didn't sue the publisher into the poorhouse.

10. *Startoons*, edited by Joan Winston (Playboy Press, 1979). This book is 192 pages of cartoons of varying humor relating to *Star Trek, Star Wars,* and science fiction in general. Here's an example of one of the best: The setting is the interior of the shuttle *Galileo* during the action of "The Galileo Seven." Spock says to McCoy, "Perhaps we would have more power if Engineer Scott hooked up your mouth to a generator, doctor."

Another book, though certainly in the *Star Trek* mainstream, is definitely collectible because of its rarity and very limited distribution. You might even own it without realizing its worth.

In October 1982, Pocket Books released the *Star Trek II: The Wrath of Khan Photostory*. Its first press run succeeded in scrambling twenty pages in the middle of the book: the section from McCoy's discovery of the bodies on Regula I to where Saavik tries to call the *Enterprise* after Khan's "buried alive" speech to Kirk. What's interesting about this is that Pocket, recognizing its blunder, reprinted a corrected edition, but without labeling it "second printing."

This denial of error was briefly noted in *Starlog #69*, April 1983, where a two-sentence statement said, "According to Pocket Books, only a small amount of the misprinted Photostories were released. Most books are correctly printed." The second sentence is incorrect, for even the reprints featured upside-down photos of the nebula space battle.

So you see, the misprinted photostory from *Wrath of Khan* is a *rara avis* indeed. It's a definite collectible, sure to increase in value because of its scarcity.

More common items can be found nearly every day. Follow some of the guidelines in this article, beam down to your local rummage sale or thrift store, and get started on filling out your own *Star Trek* collection, all for a fraction of the prices you'd pay in a convention dealers' room.

To close, I offer yet another example. Just last week my three-year-old son Matthew accompanied me to the grocery store, where in the toy aisle he grabbed my hand and said, "*Star Trek*, Daddy!" For fifty-nine cents, I bought him what he'd drawn to my attention, a chrome-coated, plastic "space watch," with a sticker showing "digital" numbers on its face. The watch was shrink-wrapped in a display card. Featured in the center of the card's illustration was an (unauthorized) depiction of the U.S.S. *Enterprise*.

Need I say more? "There are always possibilities . . ."

STAR TREK EPISODE TITLES AND THEIR MEANINGS

By Tom Lalli

What's in a name? Well, in Star Trek, *quite a lot. We editors are lifelong television watchers and critics, and we've always felt that one of the most immediate tipoffs to a quality television program is the presence of meaningful, pertinent, or witty episode titles. It's simply an indication of that little extra measure of care and work that result in a classic show. Naturally enough,* Star Trek *featured some of the most memorable and original episode titles in series history. Very often, however, they were much more than that, as Tom Lalli points out in the following article.*

Star Trek is a show with a distinctly literary bent. This "literariness" is evident in Captain Kirk's frequent speeches and also in many of the episode titles, which frequently contained allusions to famous works of world literature.

The most obvious of these are the *Star Trek* episode titles that allude to the plays of Shakespeare; four episodes derive their names from the Bard's works.

The first of these is "Dagger of the Mind," which derives from this passage in *Macbeth*:

> Is this a dagger which I see before me,
> The handle toward my hand? Come, let me clutch thee.
> I have thee not, and yet I see thee still.
> Art thou not, fatal vision, sensible
> To feeling as to sight, or art thou but
> A dagger of the mind, a false creation,
> Proceeding from the heat-oppressèd brain?
> —*Macbeth*, II.i.33–39

There are several ways of viewing this allusion in light of the episode's story. First, of course, is Dr. Adams's treatment room, truly a "dagger of the mind." The mental pain of the subject in the chair can be so great that he can die of loneliness. Also, like the dagger in the play, the "chamber of horrors" at the Tantalus colony is a "fatal vision." And, like Macbeth, Tristan Adams commits terrible crimes and eventually has to pay for them. His "false creation" becomes all too real, and eventually kills him.

Another first-season episode title that derives from Shakespeare is the "The Conscience of the King." In fact, this episode is replete with homage and allusion to his works, including *Julius Caesar* and *Macbeth* as well as *Hamlet*, from which the title comes. Hamlet suspects his uncle of murdering his father (as Captain Kirk suspects Karidian of being Kodos the Executioner), and he plans to confirm his suspicions:

I have heard that guilty creatures sitting at a play
Have by the very cunning of the scene
Been struck so to the soul that presently
They have proclaimed their malefactions.
For murder, though it have no tongue, will speak
With most miraculous organ. I'll have these players
Play something like the murder of my father
Before mine uncle. I'll observe his looks. . . .
            If 'a do blench,
I know my course. The spirit that I have seen
May be a devil. . . . I'll have grounds
More relative than this. The play's the thing
Wherein I'll catch the conscience of the king.
                              —*Hamlet*, II.ii.596–612

Hamlet is tormented by the spirit of his father, just as Kirk is tormented by the memories of those massacred by Kodos. (Jim Kirk is also likened to Julius Caesar—"Caesar of the stars"—and Kodos to Macbeth.) But Kirk, again like Hamlet, has doubts: "I must be *absolutely* sure." To discover Karidian's true identity, Kirk has him play the part of Kodos for the ship's voice analyzer. Kirk observes Karidian, as Hamlet observes his uncle. Both men use the fiction of a play within a "play" to "catch the conscience of the king."

"By Any Other Name" is part of a famous line in *Romeo and Juliet:* "What's in a name? That which we call a rose, by any other name would smell as sweet." Intelligent species, whether we call them human or Kelvan, are all the same, this episode seems to say.

The fourth Shakespearean *Star Trek* title is the third season's "All Our Yesterdays." Its source is the following speech, also spoken by Macbeth:

> Tomorrow, and tomorrow, and tomorrow,
> Creeps in this petty pace from day to day,
> To the last syllable of recorded time;
> And all our yesterdays have lighted fools
> The way to dusty death. Out, out, brief candle!
> Life's but a walking shadow, a poor player
> That struts and frets his hour upon the stage
> And then is heard no more. It is a tale
> Told by an idiot, full of sound and fury,
> Signifying nothing.
>
> —*Macbeth*, V.v.19–28

This passage, one of the most familiar in Shakespeare, relates to *Star Trek's* "All Our Yesterdays" in that an imminent nova has caused the people of the planet Sarpeidon to escape into their past. Kirk, McCoy, and especially Spock, must live through an adventure that actually happened thousands of years before. As Spock says at the end of the episode, "Yes, it did happen. But that was five thousand years ago, and she [Zarabeth] is dead now—dead and buried, long ago."

Another third-season show, "And the Children Shall Lead," gets its name (slightly modified) from the Old Testament, Isaiah 11:6:

> The wolf also shall lie down with the lamb, and the leopard shall lie down with the kid; and the calf and the young lion and the fatling together; and a little child shall lead them.

This passage actually has little to do with the episode, except perhaps the implication that Gorgan is making promises (prophecies) to the children that he can't keep.

"Those whom God wishes to destroy, he first makes mad."

This, from the Greek dramatist Euripides, gives us the *Star Trek* title "Whom Gods Destroy." This third-season story introduces Garth of Izar, the famous starship captain who became insane. Garth, however, recovers; apparently, God had no plans for his destruction.

The following passage is from Virgil's *Eclogues:* "A sad thing is a wolf in the fold, rain on ripe corn, wind in the trees, the anger of Amaryllis"—a shepherdess. "Wolf in the Fold," the story of an incorporeal entity that was Jack the Ripper and other mass murderers of women, harks back to this maxim. The deaths of countless women caused by "Redjack, Beratis, Kesla," etc., were a "sad thing" indeed.

Juvenal, a Roman satirist of the first century A.D., is the source for the title of a second-season show. He wrote:

> The people that once bestowed commands, consulships, legions, and all else, now concerns itself no more, and longs eagerly for just two things—bread and circuses!

"Bread and Circuses" is an interesting (and probably underrated) *Star Trek* episode that has several subjects working at once. The Roman Empire that the *Enterprise* crew finds on Planet 892-IV has indeed become enamored of their version of "bread and circuses," despite Proconsul Claudius Marcus's claims that their civilization is based on "Roman virtues." We must remember, though, that this "Roman Empire" is also a satire on contemporary American society, especially the references to the television industry (which Kirk describes as similar to the gladiatorial contests he witnesses). Modern American society has been likened to Imperial Rome in its decadence. Both societies are hedonistic and obsessed with entertainment. Claudius Marcus, himself hardly a follower of Roman virtue, would never admit it, but what his society really depends on is the labor of slaves. The episode suggests that Christianity will be a positive influence on the society, and will eventually bring an end to slavery. Flavius Marcus tells Kirk that slaves become discontent only when they learned "the words of the son." The problem with this is that Christianity would be more likely to make the slaves content with their lot, rather than inspiring rebellion. There is no doubt that the society in "Bread and Circuses" (and perhaps, by implication, our own) is decadent and unsound. Whether this is due to a lack of Christian virtue, or to a lack of Roman virtue, is something for the viewer to decide.

"Who Mourns for Adonais" comes from "Adonais," the British poet Shelley's elegy on the death of John Keats:

> Who mourns for Adonais? Oh, come forth.
> Foul wretch, and know thyself and him aright.
> . . . he is gathered to the kings of thought
> Who waged contention with their time's decay,
> And of the past are all that cannot pass away.
> —*Adonais*, st. 47–48

This last line is very fitting in terms of the god Apollo, who in "Who Mourns for Adonais" "cannot pass away" with the other gods. Shelley also wrote a "Hymn of Apollo." Apollo is describing himself when he says:

> I am the eye with which the Universe
> Beholds itself and knows itself divine;
> All harmony of instrument or verse . . .
> All light of art or nature;—to my song
> Victory and praise in their own right belong.
> —"Hymn of Apollo," st. 6

That certainly sounds like the Apollo we *Star Trek* fans know! Apollo was the Greek god of the sun, prophecy, music, medicine, and poetry. The "Apollonian" refers to that which is well-ordered, harmonious, noble, and dignified. Thus, there is irony in Captain Kirk's refusal to worship Apollo, as the lives of Kirk and his crew are nothing if not Apollonian. If they were going to worship a Greek god, it would be Apollo. And perhaps Kirk's eventual demise will prompt someone to ask again, "Who Mourns for Adonais?"

Several *Star Trek* episodes take their names from less high-brow sources. "Mirror, Mirror," of course, comes from *Snow White and the Seven Dwarfs:* "Mirror, mirror on the wall, who's the fairest of them all?" In *Star Trek*'s "Mirror, Mirror," there is no doubt whose is the fairer universe.

"What Are Little Girls Made Of?" comes from the following familiar nursery rhyme:

> What are little boys made of?
> Snips and snails and puppy dog's tails;
> That's what little boys are made of.
> What are little girls made of?
> Sugar and spice and everything nice;
> That's what little girls are made of.

In this episode we learn that Christine Chapel is made of sterner stuff than "sugar and spice," and that she will stand by her captain just as any other crew member would. Nurse Chapel is not the pushover that some may think.

"Journey to Babel" refers to the biblical story of the descendants of Noah's attempt to build a tower to Heaven, only to be punished by an angry God:

> Therefore is the name of it [the tower] called Babel; because the Lord did there confound the language of all the Earth: and from thence did the Lord scatter them abroad the face of all the earth.
> —*Genesis* 11:9

Just as the people of Earth are scattered into various nations, the humanoid races of *Star Trek*'s galaxy are scattered on the various planets, with different languages, cultures, and politics. They must all come together in the Federation of Planets to try to resolve their differences and cooperate. The Federation, by code-naming the site of an important interplanetary meeting "Babel," displayed a sense of humor you might not expect of bureaucrats.

The source material for "Friday's Child" is also well known, another folk poem describing the supposed characteristics of children born on each day of the week:

Monday's child is fair of face,
Tuesday's child is full of grace,
Wednesday's child is full of woe,
Thursday's child has far to go,
Friday's child is loving and giving,
Saturday's child has to work for its living,
But a child that's born on the Sabbath day,
Is fair and wise and good and gay.

The title character of "Friday's Child," named Leonard James Akaar, will become the High Teer of the planet Capella. Since he is "loving and giving," he will probably continue the reforms begun by his mother, Eleen, and the *Enterprise* crew.

A poem called "Jordan" by the seventeenth-century metaphysical poet George Herbert contains the following passage:

Who says that fictions only and false hair
become a verse? Is there in truth no beauty?
                                    —"Jordan," st. 1

This quote fits well with the philosophy of IDIC—Infinite Diversity in Infinite Combinations—which is introduced in the *Star Trek* episode "Is There in Truth No Beauty?" The Medusan is a creature considered by humans to be too ugly to bear. Dr. Miranda Jones questions whether Ambassador Kollos is, rather, too beautiful to bear. Miranda herself hides her vulnerability to avoid being pitied. The inner natures of both Kollos and Miranda turn out to be quite beautiful. The creators of *Star Trek* realized that things other than "fictions and false hair" were suitable topics for drama; real or apparent ugliness and the dark side of life were dealt with often in the show, with the goal of finding meaning in diversity, and beauty in truth.

The artistic beauty of *Star Trek* is apparent in many of its episode titles. "Tomorrow Is Yesterday" . . . "The

Devil in the Dark" . . . "For the World Is Hollow and I Have Touched the Sky" . . . "Let That Be Your Last Battlefield" . . . "Requiem for Methuselah" . . .

"This Side of Paradise" (a title used earlier by F. Scott Fitzgerald for his first novel) is also an intriguing title. One who is under the influence of the spores might say that the planet Omicron Ceti III is "the best thing this side of paradise." Later, we realize that we are seeing another aspect of "paradise," and *this* side of paradise is not a pretty one. Once we achieve "paradise," we realize it is a trap: it only seems like Heaven when we view it with uncritical eyes.

The most popular *Star Trek* episode of them all is "The City on the Edge of Forever." Though it is not my personal favorite, "City" *is* my choice for best *Star Trek* title. Harlan Ellison's script, rewritten by Gene Roddenberry, was one of the best-written *Star Trek* segments, and the title of the show is correspondingly poetic. The ancient, ruined city surrounding the Guardian of Forever is the city to which the title refers; but for Jim Kirk, New York City also become "a city on the edge of forever." This powerful phrase is suited to a story that is both tragic and fascinating.

"Where No Man Has Gone Before" was *Star Trek*'s second pilot, and though it differs in some ways from all the later episodes, it is the epitome of the *Star Trek* philosophy in content as well as its title. Many of the themes that run throughout *Star Trek* begin in "Where No Man Has Gone Before": The ceaseless quest for knowledge and adventure, expressed in Kirk's line, the danger "is probably the best argument to continue the probe [beyond the galaxy]; other vessels will be heading out here one day, they'll have to know what they'll be facing"; the friendship between Kirk and Spock, which begins in this episode (friendship for Spock being "where no man has gone before"); the ever-present temptation for men and women to use their power wrongly, as Gary Mitchell does; the nobility of Kirk, his crew, and their mission. The *Enterprise* crew, in venturing outside the galaxy, and Gary Mitchell and Elizabeth Dehner, by achieving superhuman powers, are all going where no man has gone before.

This is the only episode aired without William Shatner's voice-over introduction. Yet the entire show can be seen as a meditation upon those words: "to explore strange new worlds . . . to seek out new life and civilizations . . . to boldly go where no man has gone before."

Despite the meticulous attention given to *Star Trek* by fans, the episode titles have largely been taken for granted. As many other television series do not even have onscreen episode titles, it is fortunate for the legions of Trekkers that our favorite show did give names to each segment. Imagine the chaos that would have resulted if fan-given titles, or numbers, were all we had to go by. *Star Trek*'s titles, however, are more than a studio filing system or a handy device for fans. They are a special and important part of the creation of Gene Roddenberry and his crew. Suggestive and often lyrical, the episode names are worthy of study and commentary.

SPECIAL SECTION #1: STAR TREK IV: THE VOYAGE HOME

Star Trek IV: The Voyage Home may be the most popular and entertaining Star Trek film so far, at least according to audiences and critics. But with fans, as always, there is something of a different story. Opinions, as they say, vary. Although most of fandom greeted the film with enthusiasm, there were many who did not feel that it was up to the standards of the previous three. Others felt it was the best. Why such a difference of opinion? In the following articles, grouped together to add to the impact of each, several writers examine the film as well as their own feelings about it from a number of differing perspectives. The final conclusion? Decide for yourself . . .

A FLIGHT OF FANCY—
A VOYAGE HOME

By Hazel Ann Williams

Star Trek IV: The Voyage Home is humorous, bright, and light, so light as to border on the insubstantial; it seems intent upon negating the solemnity of the previous *Star Trek* movies. Where *Star Trek: The Motion Picture, Star Trek II: The Wrath of Khan*, and *Star Trek III: The Search for Spock* dealt with the meaning and purpose of life, the next step of man's evolution, sacrifice and loss, grief and maturation, and the duties of love and friendship, *The Voyage Home* deals with . . . vaudeville. Now, I like vaudeville, but not when there are philosophical and moral questions left to be answered, or, at least, explored. In the episodes, *Star Trek* often indulged in social commentary (both blatant and subtle); it often touched on the classic science fiction themes of first contact, new discoveries in science and technology clashing with society, and the technologies so advanced as to first be mistaken for magic or religion. Twice, *Star Trek* proved to be a successful vehicle for pure comedy, and most of the epilogues were humorous. Now, *Star Trek* has broken new ground: ignoring or glossing over the issues and facts to go for laughs.

What was ignored? First, the fate of the *Enterprise* crew, the supposed reason for *Star Trek IV*. Very early on, we see (to paraphrase Kirk) the commander and crew of the late, great *Enterprise* voting to return to Earth to face the consequences of their actions. They have a lot going for them. Kirk and Company have just saved the Federation, the Romulan Empire, and various independent systems from enslavement or destruction. Kirk made sure the Klingons did not get Genesis. Even the flawed Genesis theory would have been an awesome weapon in the hands of the aggressive Klingons. Once the shake-up in the Empire was over—and that kind of power is not dealt out by committee—the Klingons would have turned on the Federation and their Romulan "allies." Galactic civilization could not have survived such a cataclysm. The resulting period of chaos would have made the Dark Ages seem a model of enlightened liberalism. Kirk and his officers spared the galaxy that upheaval by the sacrifice of *Enterprise,* David Marcus, and, nearly, their lives. Given the return, the price was cheap.

Apparently, Misters Nimoy and Bennett felt this was too distant a motive to allow the Federation Council to spare Kirk. Sure, you saved us three months ago, but what have you done for us lately? Enter disaster. A big, splashy (sorry), *immediate* crisis for Kirk *et al* to solve and thus redeem themselves. Saving the Earth is just icing on the cake. Icing can't be substituted for cake, and cake can easily stand alone. The combination is pleasing, but not necessary. Maybe the Federation Council is closer to today's politicians than we'd like to think. The few who were able to grasp the implications of what Kirk had done were unable to convince the others. They needed the immediacy of this last act of heroism to force them toward leniency. Whatever the motive, the saving of Earth is minor compared to the saving of galactic civilization from Genesis.

So we have another crisis, and once again the only ones in a position to act are the senior officers of the *Enterprise*. Once again, Starfleet has been unable to solve the problem. In fact, the Starfleet/Federation seems more eager to explore a mystery than to solve a problem. When *Saratoga* encounters the probe at the Romulan Neutral Zone, Starfleet says they will analyze the signals and advise. Captain Alexander gets no chance to investigate. The probe drains her ship of power before she asks her first question. This is, apparently, Starfleet's first inkling of the probe. Now the time period gets fuzzy, but the movie's emphasis is on things happening *fast*. The Klingons lost two ships to the probe, so it had to swing into the Klingon's sphere of influence. Then the Federation lost two starships and three smaller vessels. Then

Cartwright contacted *Yorktown*, just as *Yorktown* was going down for the count. Soon after, the probe knocks out space dock and goes to work on Earth. To borrow a phrase from E. E. "Doc" Smith, this baby has *legs*. Before Starfleet can even come up with answers, or—as Sarek reminds the president—an understanding of the question, Earth, and thus Starfleet Headquarters, is fighting for survival. Given the incredible speed of events and the vast number of problems SFHQ had to cope with (ships and rescue, handling Earth's population, etc.), they still seemed to do little but observe the events. SFHQ should have adequate resources in manpower and computer to have made some sort of preliminary evaluations before the probe arrived and they were forced to shift their emphasis to survival.

Let's get one point clear. Kirk, Spock, McCoy, Scotty, Uhura, Sulu, and Chekov are Starfleet's and the Federation's best and brightest. They are IDIC personified. There is darned little they can't face and resolve. They're not gods, just individuals of skill and talent, knowledge and judgment, who forge themselves into one unbeatable team. I believe that. I know that. Yet the ease with which they solve this one borders on the miraculous.

Kirk's first reaction to the president's planetary distress call is typical: first, define the problem, then solve it. Here is a conflict of two of the basic approaches to life: a mystery to explore versus a problem to solve. *Star Trek* has always been partial to the problem solvers, albeit with a bit of awe-wonder thrown in for balance. The note of resignation to fate in the president's call goes against everything Kirk believes in.

To define the problem, Kirk first asks, "Why?" It's Spock who helps answer by suggesting the probe has nothing to do with man. After all, the probe's message is aimed at the oceans. Kirk, unlike Starfleet, is very good at marshaling his people's resources. He asks Uhura to modify the signal so they can hear what it would sound like underwater. Bingo! Spock recognizes the sound. Spock? Granted, Spock knows everything, or enough of everything to solve/help solve the problem of the week. Granted, the computer held the sound-song of every type of creature. But why should Spock recognize the song of an alien, extinct species? In the novelization, Vonda Mc-Intyre has an explanation, but that ties in more with her novel *Enterprise* than with this movie. It would be more reasonable for Kirk, with his well-known interest in Earth's history, sailing, and the sea, to be the one to recognize the sound.

Be that as it may, Kirk now has a handle on the situation. What are his options? First, to respond. Though the species is extinct on Earth, does it exist elsewhere? No. They have whale-song recordings, can they play them for the probe? No. They don't understand the language. Second, they could fight and attempt to destroy the probe. Clearly impossible. What's left? As Spock says, they will have to get some whales. This idea appeals to Kirk. McCoy's reaction to the unspoken Kirk/Spock decision is typical and beautifully played.

So what *are* we left with? Time travel. This was used in five episodes:

In "All Our Yesterdays," the people of Sarpeidon escape their exploding sun by fleeing into the past. They are conditioned to exist in the time period of their choice, although they retain their memories of the "future." The issue of whether or not interference in the "past" can change the "future" is never brought up. It is safe enough to assume that the natives would be careful to protect the events that led to the invention of the atavachron, and thus ensure their escape. All other time changes would be irrelevant, as their particular future is a neatly closed loop.

In "The Naked Time," the imploding engines provided the power to blast the *Enterprise* three days into the past. While the crew also retained their "future" memories, they are three days younger and the events that led them to this space-time have yet to happen. This was, to say the least, a messy situation. We'll never know the details. They, perhaps wisely, chose to ignore all the implications and problems inherent in the situation. In *Mudd's Angels*, Blish and Lawrence covered a similar event very tidily. However, "officially" *Star Trek* gives us no clues.

In "Assignment: Earth," Spock says that whatever they did could not be considered interference. After detailed study of their historical banks, they discovered that everything happened as it should have. What? The reason for their mission was to *get* details. In the briefing at the first of the episode, Spock lists some of the important events of the day. He does *not* mention that the launch would malfunction, and the bomb go off a little over a hundred miles above the surface. If he knew it, I feel reasonably sure he would have mentioned it.

If the banks held that little gem, I would think he would know it. After all, he was supposed to have gone through the available information to brief Kirk on the events. It is my belief that history was changed, and changed so thoroughly as to add this new information into the ship's banks.

In "Tomorrow Is Yesterday," *Enterprise*'s crew takes great pains to keep any influence on the present (their past) to a minimum, so as to preserve the future (their present). They discuss the possibility of keeping Captain Christopher, but find they must return him so he can sire a famous son. Therefore, when they slide further into the past, they return their inadvertent guests *before* they become guests, thus causing the events to fall apart. A delicious time paradox that emphasizes the delicacy of time travel.

The most powerful example of the problems of time travel is found in "City on the Edge of Forever." McCoy enters the Guardian of Forever, saves Edith Keeler, and in doing so, destroys his own time. The life of one woman allows the Nazis to win World War II. The Federation is never created; the *Enterprise* never existed. As the Guardian tells the landing party, "Your vessel, your beginnings, all that you knew, is gone." That's a rather definitive statement on the dangers of meddling in time. Kirk is forced to pay a steep price to restore history. He *knows* what will happen if Edith is allowed to live. He *knows* how precious the future is, how and why it must be protected, but still he hesitates. Ultimately, duty wins, honor wins, love wins.

What happened to that caution? Where is the concern? We don't see it in *The Voyage Home*. Kirk is after whales and nothing is going to stop him. Not once did he even pause to consider that they might be endangering the future they'd come to save.

The first run-in with time tampering is explained, or at least mentioned. Needing cash to get around, Kirk sells his antique glasses. As he tells Spock, they were a birthday present from McCoy—and they will be again. Okay, first round covered.

Welcome to round two: transparent aluminum. There's no way they can pay for the acrylic sheeting they need, so they trade the molecular model of transparent aluminum for it. In the film, McCoy objects to this. Scotty easily mollified the good doctor by asking how they know Dr. Nichols didn't invent transparent aluminum. In the novel, Scotty recognizes Nichols as the inventor by recalling the history of his craft. He tells McCoy they're just helping history along by giving Nichols a head start. Unless this is the author's way of covering up or explaining away a film error, that information should have been retained in the film. Giving history a nudge is bad enough, but not even working with this premise is stupid.

Round three involves Chekov's phaser and communicator. His ID is not that incriminating, but remember "A Piece of the Action"? Kirk and Spock berate McCoy for leaving behind his communicator; seems that device contains something called a trans-stater . . . the basis of operation of all Federation equipment. Kirk feared that the imitative Iotians would too quickly achieve a technology level equal to the Federation. Now Earth officials are left with a communicator and nonfunctioning phaser. Granted, they both look to be Klingon manufacture, but the technology has to be similar. What will the lab boys make of them? An argument can be made that the agents will dismiss Chekov as a kook and thus toss his equipment, *but* this kook was mysteriously freed by a group of kooks. That, at least, will bear some investigation.

Round four is a minor point. The prognosis of the old lady McCoy treated was not for a long or happy life. Now she suddenly has a new kidney; she will live longer to be prodded by a score of doctors and undoubtedly the object of numerous papers. What effect her prolonged life will have on future events is questionable. I'm quite sure no one will believe her story. No one will connect her description of McCoy to the outraged surgeon's description. No one will look into the advanced medical skills/techniques McCoy displayed. Right.

The final time-travel event is the most important and potentially the most deadly: bringing Gillian to the twenty-third century. Did she have children? Was she scheduled to make any social, cultural, political, or scientific achievements? Did she lead a pocket of resistance in the Eugenics Wars? Was she destined to die in a traffic accident that afternoon, or would she have had a long, peaceful life? Granted, records of the time period are spotty due to the destruction of the Eugenics Wars, but—blast it all—they didn't even look! Gillian was right, they need her experience and expertise. But no one, not even Spock, did any checking into Gillian's "future." No one objected or even seemed surprised at her presence/inclusion. It boiled down to Kirk. He's already lost one woman to history's demands. He liked her, he needed her, he wanted her in his time, his world, and so he took her along. This has to be Kirk's most irrational moment. He's gone back in time in order to save the future. Yet he takes the chance of destroying, or at least altering, his world and time by bringing Gillian back. As there was a world still remaining to save, as there was no *apparent* change, it seems Kirk's luck is running fantastically high.

The representation of time travel isn't the only thing lost in the shuffle. Science is a necessary element of science fiction. When using science in this genre, you don't have to accurately predict future technology, but you can't be wrong about present technology. If the mass of Earth is in your plot, it had better match today's figures, or you had better explain the discrepancy. For the most part, the *Star Trek* episodes extrapolated from the known into the possible, though not always probable. Using the bugger factor to get around $E = mc^2$, they explain the matter/antimatter engines and warp drive. Artificial gravity is even possible—if gravity waves exist and we learn how to use them. The transporter strains a bit, but it's a well-accepted SF device. There were few glaring science problems in the old episodes. (If you don't mention "The Alternative Factor," I won't.)

The science in the movies didn't fare as well. In *The Wrath of Khan*, there are two blatant examples (as well as many small ones). First, the shifting orbits needed to make Ceti Alpha V look like Ceti Alpha VI makes it hard to believe *any* life—or even any atmosphere—could have survived. Second, the sensors, those most potent devices that have proved their sensitivity again and again, failed to pick up Khan and his survivors. Both are serious errors whose only excuse is that they were necessary to the plot. *Star Trek III: The Search for Spock*'s biggest error is protomatter, a pseudoscience substance that was also created as a plot device. *Star Trek IV: The Voyage Home*, unfortunately, keeps that trend going.

I am not a physicist. I don't pretend to be. I do dabble for fun and I have a growing library of nonspecialist journals and reference books. In high school, we drew up flow charts for fission reactions. Now that was years ago, but I don't remember putting photons on that chart. *The American Heritage Dictionary* describes a photon as: "The quantum of electromagnetic energy, generally regarded as a discrete particle having zero mass, no electric charge, and an indefinitely long lifetime." An old physics book puts it this way: "Particles of light are called photons. . . . Photons of any energy are possible; at least, no upper limit to the energy of photons has yet been ascertained. . . . Any beam of photons, no matter what the photon energy, can be referred to by the general term, electromagnetic radiation."

Was Spock referring to gamma radiation? He says he needs photons to recrystallize the dilithium and proposes collecting them from a fission reactor. Why not just say gamma radiation? Why not say neutrons or call out one of they myriad subatomic particles? If you want simple, low-energy photons, you'll find an abundant supply in sunlight. If you need a photon of a specific energy level, you'd use its specific name. So why the generic term? This sounds more like classic gobbledygook.

Nearly instantaneous power drain/disruption and vaporizing the oceans, thus causing total cloud cover are both . . . possible. The total cloud cover affects the sunlight filtering to Earth, the temperature on the planet, the weather, and, in short, the entire closed ecosystem. When the probe stopped its song, it didn't even hint at doing anything to reverse the situation, it simply stopped and left. I can accept space dock coming back "on" if you explain the probe was draining space dock's power or saying the probe was damping out its ability to generate power, since it was never shown that space dock received the kind of systems damage that the starships sustained. Earth, however, is a closed system. To repair the damage done to the ecology, either the clouds must be allowed to rain themselves out, or some type of energy must be applied to speed up/alter the process. If we needed a dramatic weather reversal to signify victory— and we did—then the probe should have been shown doing *something* to explain the recovery.

A final science gripe. Our respiration depends on a chemical reaction: hemoglobin in the blood combines chemically with oxygen and transports it around the body. To do this, one relies on the bonding ability of oxygen, using the old rule that energy shells want to be full. Allow me another brief quote from the physics book: "An atom or molecule which is not electrically neutral is called an ion. The process of *ionization* generally consists of the removal of one or more electrons from a neutral atom or molecule which then becomes a positive ion."

The president's distress message states that the Earth's atmosphere has been ionized. I submit that situation would not only make it hard to transmit, but darn hard to breathe.

All of the above-mentioned scientific problems could've been easily avoided, often by an extra line or two of dialogue, or a simple word change. The difference in quality would have been well worth the effort. If Mr. Bennett would like someone to look over his future scripts in order to avoid these layman's objections . . . I work cheap.

So much for science. How about simple continuity from *Star Trek III: The Search for Spock*? The most glaring example is the Klingon ship. What happened to *Bounty* during its three-month stay on Vulcan? The bridge is radically different; the doors are different. The whole ship is rustier and dirtier than it is in *The Search for Spock*. Is the red dust of Vulcan corrosive? Did the Vulcans sabotage the ship? Did the set designers forget what it looked like and prayed we would too? Tell me, please, what the heck happened?

My final objections also deal with the technical aspects of the film. First, the bizarre images seen during the trip back to the twentieth century. Nothing like that happened in "Tomorrow Is Yesterday," where the same method of time travel was used. This montage of images stopped a fast-paced sequence of events cold. The time it took up could have been put to better use, like telling us *why* Saavik stays on Vulcan. (The novelization clears that up nicely, but in the film, it's a mystery.)

Leading to my second objection to the film: the editing. One should *not* have to read the novelization to understand the film. Surely, brief scenes or, again, a few extra lines of explanation would clear up any loose ends or ambiguity without hurting the pacing. When the need exists, pacing should be sacrificed to understanding. The ideal, of course, is to say what has to be said in an entertaining way. The myth that an audience won't sit still and enjoy a film for more than two hours was exploded by the phenomenal success of *Amadeus* (to mention just one recent lengthy film). *Quality* is the key to successful filmmaking, not quantity.

Star Trek: The Motion Picture was the worst offender; the expanded version was better, but could have been great with less sight-seeing and more explanatory dialogue. *Star Trek II: The Wrath of Khan* and *Star Trek III: The Search for Spock* both had scenes (in the novelizations) that would have added depth to the story, but were dropped due to running time considerations. *Star Trek IV: The Voyage Home* comes in a close second to *STTMP* for bad editing. Not only were excellent scenes omitted, so too was enough explanation.

My final objection to *The Voyage Home* is the music. While the opening and closing themes, with echoes of Alexander Courage's original music and a nice use of bells, are pleasing, they lack the power of the music in the first three movies. The background music, with the exception of that played during the hospital chase scene, is typical TV background music. I swear some of it came from *Marcus Welby, M.D.* It was insipid and too often downright distracting. The hospital chase scene's music was reminiscent of some in an episode or two. If I could just remember . . . Anyway, it worked.

These objections range from trivial to serious, but they all brought me out of the movie for various periods of time. The success of a movie is gauged by how deeply the viewer immerses himself in it. When you breathe and gasp and cry with the characters, when it takes a moment or two after the lights come up to orient yourself to mundane reality, then you've seen a *good* movie. I go in to any *Star Trek* movie more than willing to suspend my disbelief, to put aside my objections until later, so as to immerse myself in my favorite world and enjoy the *Star Trek* story. *The Voyage Home* made that difficult, but not . . . quite . . . impossible.

Now that you've read everything I think M'Lords Nimoy and Bennett did wrong, you might think I hated *Star Trek IV: The Voyage Home*. You'd be wrong. I enjoyed it. I even liked it. I didn't love it. It missed being great by so many *easily* avoided errors that it breaks my heart, but I *did* like the movie. The aforementioned gentlemen did a lot of things right.

First, one must take the movie on its own terms. It says, "You've been through the wringer. You've followed these people faithfully through grief, tears, and pain. Let's give it a rest. Here are your friends. Let's have some fun." And fun is the name of the game.

The characters we care about are all present. Spock is played with delightful innocence—as he should be. A lifetime of knowledge has been restored, but not integrated into a complete personality. A long chain of learning experiences that left him with the warm, controlled personality we saw in *The Wrath of Khan* must be forged again. He intuitively seeks answers to Amanda's probing questions, as well as those from his friends. Just as T'sai told him on Gol, his answer lies elsewhere. This could have turned out to be a nightmare, but—as with the rest of the movie—the tone is light. The implications of Spock's experience are brushed aside in a very brief Spock/McCoy scene. Part of me agrees with this treatment, part of me misses the . . . possibilities. Yet the important thing is Spock's odyssey toward emotional maturity. From his puzzlement when the computers ask him how he feels, to his confusion over Kirk's angry rebuff over Spock's concern about the mission versus life on earth, from his decisions to rescue Chekov and stand with his shipmates, to his conversation with his father, Spock changes slowly and wonderfully to the being who gave his life for his friends. Even his flirtation with colorful metaphors is logical because Kirk told him no one would take him seriously if they weren't employed. He has no conception of the proper usage or emphasis of said metaphors, though the attempt provides many laughs. Only near the end of the film, when Kirk asks for power, does Spock's reply ring true.

One final word about Spock. His comment about rescuing Chekov, that it was the human thing to do, is not a slam against Vulcan. Spock is half human, half Vulcan, and all Spock. As Amanda said so long ago, he has a home nowhere but Starfleet. Spock learned, and has now relearned, that his life path is unique. His friends and the viewers know his Vulcan side is intact and functioning; with this line we realize his humanity is back in play, too. The only strange moment comes during the horseplay in the water after the weather clears up. Spock's playful laughter as his teammates release their tension is not totally in character, but not too far removed to come under the heading of the bizarre.

McCoy is also a marvel. He is, as he has always been, Spock's opposite and foil. From his first proddings about life, death, and life, to his remarks about guessing, and then comforting Spock about it, McCoy does his best to help his friend . . . the one not working with full thrusters. McCoy's gestures and body English, his expressive eyes and throwaway lines all combine to bring a delightful character to his peak performance. McCoy's gruffness has always hidden a too-vulnerable heart. Being in a hospital full of people he could cure—or at least ease their pain—must have been pure torture for him. He expressed that feeling in his usual manner—anger.

McCoy should have been less worried about Spock and more worried about Kirk. Of all the crew, Kirk seems the most changed. Beginning with the decision to return to Earth's past, Kirk seems to have put himself on hold. His judgment is off. He had to be aware of the political situation on Earth in our time. He'd been involved in it himself in "Assignment: Earth," and the newspaper he glanced at had related stories. Yet he still sent Chekov off to look for nuclear vessels. He just didn't think. Playing fast and loose with time and events, Kirk seemed to be motivated more by the need to act than to reason his way through the situation. In a very short period of time, he met his full-grown son and lost him, he watched his best friend die and then be restored, he was forced to destroy his ship, and to seriously jeopardize his one, true career. Maybe it was all, finally, too much. Although he and his crew had decided to return to Earth, Kirk—after three months of fidgeting on Vulcan—was eager to act, to prove himself and his people. Blind as a bat and out of control describes Kirk's actions to a *T*. Perhaps now, with captain's bars instead of the weight of a flag officer's stars, with a ship of his own, with a future of doing what he loves to do, what he does best, maybe now Kirk can return to the decisive commander we knew and loved.

Someday they're going to start out a film where Kirk has tried to teach Spock how to ski, and they both broke a leg. McCoy has to take care of them, of course. Then, maybe, finally, Scotty, Uhura, Sulu, and Chekov will have some decent roles.

Scotty, the miracle worker, didn't come off too bad in *The Voyage Home*. From his bluster with Dr. Nichols to his awe and wonder in "There be whales here," we got to see more of our favorite engineer than we have in quite a while. Uhura, too, had a bit more to say than hailing frequencies, and even Chekov's scream was subdued. Sulu, unfortunately, was mostly lost in the shuffle, and poor Saavik simply cast aside.

The numerous bits of business and funny lines are definitely the hit of the movie. The heart of the conflict is "culture clash." These people know San Francisco of the twenty-third century, not the twentieth. Its very familiarity makes the confusion stronger. The "triple play" scene that runs from Spock fumbling "logically" over a stylized map and Kirk reading the bus ad, to Sulu, Scotty, and McCoy finding the wall ad urging them to consult the yellow pages, to the Uhura/Chekov with Chekov closing the phone book is delicious. Other *brief* examples: Kirk's face when he sees Spock swimming with the whales; the poetry in stealing power from the *Enterprise;* Kirk's slip of the tongue on "LDS"; "I'm from Iowa; I only work in outer space"; "One damn minute, Admiral"; "Sure you don't want to change your mind?"; "What's wrong with the one I have"; and so on.

The two best scenes in the movie have to be Gillian's gentle dumping of Kirk and the scene between Spock and Sarek. Kirk is surprised by Gillian's ability to take care of herself. She has seen to her own future, and this time it is Kirk, not the lady, who must ask "When will I see you again?" About time, Captain, my friend. The emotional content of the Spock/Sarek scene is different, but still powerful. Sarek loves his son. Vulcans *feel,* they just control their emotions. Here Spock and Sarek are comfortable with each other. They have finally come to appreciate each other. And Spock's message to Amanda perfectly ties the end of the film with the beginning.

Other good points of *The Voyage Home* included getting at least a glance of Chapel and Rand, and wishing we could see more. Also good were the racial differences seen in the Federation Council and Starfleet Command; the quality of the special effects and graphics; and, especially, the probe. We never found out why it came, who—if anyone—sent it, and so forth. But that's all right. Sometimes you *can't* find all the answers. Having the probe mimic a singing whale reinforced the point about communication.

The byplay on the shuttle as our friends try to guess which ship is theirs is nicely done. Kirk's line, "A ship is a ship," gives new meaning to the phrase, "Parts is parts." Scotty's quiet sarcasm brings Kirk back to reality. The second time I saw the film, a woman behind me echoed my initial reaction: "*Excelsior*! They got *Excelsior*!" Then a hiss-gasp, and in a much quieter voice, she went on, "Oh, God, it's *Enterprise*!" To have given Kirk *Excelsior* would have been poetic justice, but would also have been painful for Sulu (who, according to the novel, was slated to command *Excelsior*). To be given a new ship, a new *Enterprise* is . . . well . . . okay. This is not the ship of our past and our dreams, not the ship of battle and shared laughter and quiet tears. This ship was never full of tribbles or chased by angry Klingons or Romulans. It is fresh, new, virginal; it is a new being in a familiar shape. It's a consolation prize, a medal of honor, and a good try. It's . . . okay. I just hope they fix up the bridge before *Star Trek V;* put in a few chairs and give it some paint. The bridge, as it stands, looks ugly and unfinished.

I must add a brief comment on the beginning and end of *The Voyage Home.* The dedication of the movie to the crew of the *Challenger* was moving and appropriate. *Star Trek* is a dream of the future. To make that dream a reality means a lot of hard work. We who follow *Star Trek,* we who want the dream, who wish the stars for our grandchildren or great-grandchildren, must help fulfill that dream. We can work together, or sit back and let it die, maybe along with our race and our world.

THE INTIATION OF SPOCK

By T. C. Johns

Star Trek IV: The Voyage Home is an initiation story in the best tradition of Twain's *Huckleberry Finn*, Knowles's *A Separate Peace*, and Steinbeck's *The Red Pony*. The movie, like these other classic rite-of-passage stories, is about a child passing from the innocence of youth into the first knowledge of manhood. In the case of *The Voyage Home*, however, Spock is not a child in terms of age, but in terms of experience. And by the end of the movie, Spock has become a man, in more than just the traditional sense.

At the end of *Star Trek III: The Search for Spock*, Spock has been resurrected. His body had reached maturity, and after *fal-tor-pan*, his *katra*—his essence, his soul—had been removed from McCoy's care and again placed within the living receptacle, Spock. When Spock says, "Jim. Your name is Jim," we know that all the connections are not quite complete, but we are confident that Spock will soon be his normal self.

What is Spock's normal self? Let us briefly examine the evolution of Spock's character from the beginning. Spock is, as we all know, a hybrid, half human, half Vulcan. Throughout the series much audience fascination has centered around Spock's internal war between the Vulcan philosophy of nonemotionalism and the human propensity to total illogic. With each major "Spock episode" —"The Naked Time," "The Galileo Seven," "Amok Time," "The Immunity Syndrome," etc.—we've seen him come to grips with his dual heritage, each episode showing him, usually enlightened by McCoy, finding new depth to his being—combining steadily the best of Vulcan with the best of human. At the end of the series, Spock has learned intuition, compassion, a little humor, and a little love, but he is not yet at peace, not yet whole.

Star Trek: The Motion Picture is the true turning point of his life. He had almost reached the peace within himself when suddenly the five-year mission was over, and his *Enterprise* family went their separate ways. Dejected and depressed—filled with shameful emotion—he turned to *kolinahr* to absolve *all* emotion once and for all. Nothing could hurt him now. The shell he had built around himself makes him appear cruel, cold, unfeeling in *STTMP*— and we fans reacted very, very negatively to him. Later, when he encounters Vejur, he realizes, again, what it had taken years to learn before: logic without emotion is dead. He cries. He recombines his dual heritage.

In *Star Trek II: The Wrath of Khan* we see the extension of his encounter with Vejur. Now Spock is totally at peace with himself. He knows who he is and he knows his place in the universe. He is a complete being who can unequivocally teach a philosophy of "wholeness" and "uniqueness" to his protégée Saavik. He has become wise, utilizing all his many talents to become the best being he can. And, of all human emotions, he has learned love: "Greater love hath no man than this, that a man lay down his life for his friends" (*John* 15:13). When he died, I did not cry; I rejoiced in the beauty and rightness of the offering. It was if Spock had been translated to a higher mortality, as if he had gone to a heaven reserved for those who achieve their highest potential.

In *Star Trek III: The Search for Spock,* of course, Spock is all body; McCoy has all "his marbles." By the end we are assured that Spock will, eventually, be okay.

So, at the beginning of *Star Trek IV: The Voyage Home,* Spock is back to square one. He has lost that which made him a total being content with himself; he has lost his humanity.

Our first sight of Spock in the film is very significant. He is standing alone on holy Mount Seleya, far above the little pocket of humanity on the plain below. He is dressed in white with his hood up. The sun radiates behind, almost from within, him. Thus we see him in a religious light—pure, white sinless, priestly . . . unearthly.

In the test chamber, we find that Spock's resocialization process has advanced well. He has a firm grasp of the technical language of Vulcan, enough to be proficient in all tests the computer throws at him. But when his mother demands, "How do you feel?" we see the child Spock. Amanda knows that her son is not yet completely well, although he himself does not realize it. Amanda, his human parent, reminds him that he is alive because other humans loved him enough to "foolishly" defy man and nature to rescue him. This is his first lesson in humanity, and though he does not understand it or see the value in it, he files it away for future reference.

In many ways, James Kirk has been as much Spock's father as his friend, teaching the Vulcan and guiding him gently through life's crises, such as *pon farr*. This relationship is underscored when Spock comes aboard the *Bounty:* Kirk welcomes him. "Thank you, Admiral," says Spock. "Jim, Spock, Jim. Remember?" But Spock insists upon the title of respect. "It would be improper to refer to you as Jim while you are in command, Admiral." Like a child with very proper manners, Spock will not any more call the Admiral "Jim" than he would call his father "Sarek" to his face.

Again, the clothing becomes significant. "Also, I must apologize for my attire," Spock says. "I . . . I seem to have misplaced my uniform." I had to laugh, remembering how many mornings my six-year-old and I have undergone the mad shoe search: "Where are your shoes, Trent?" "I don't know, Mom." "Well, where did you take them off?" "I don't remember." Some days we never found them in time for school. So, though Spock has an excellent reason for having lost his uniform, the scene is one every mother can identify with.

McCoy has always been Spock's teacher, especially in less practical areas. In *Star Trek IV: The Voyage Home,* we really see the clash between romantic and realist, poet and pragmatist, in terms of language. Like a child, Spock is working on a very literal, denotative level. All words have only dictionary definitions to him. McCoy says, "Busy?" and Spock precisely clarifies, "Commander Uhura is busy. I am monitoring." Later, McCoy says, "You're joking!" and Spock defines a joke as "a story with a humorous climax." McCoy's language is very colorful and figurative. But all this poetry of human speech has been lost to Spock, as we see when McCoy says, "I may have carried your soul, but I sure couldn't fill your shoes," to which Spock replies, "What would you want to fill my shoes with?" Later scenes suggest the same problem: Kirk says, "Spock, if we play our cards right, we may learn when those whales are really leaving," and Spock answers, "How will playing cards help?" Also, when Gillian asks, "Are you sure you won't change your mind?", Spock wonders, "Is something wrong with the one I have?" Tell a child to go fly a kite, and you'd have a kid out flying a kite. Spock's innocence is shown by this naive literalness.

On 1986 Earth, Spock gets another lesson in the uses of language. On the bus, Spock notes that Kirk's use of language "has altered since our arrival." Kirk says, "You mean profanity . . . Nobody pays any attention if you don't swear every other word." Spock trusts Kirk as any child would trust his father, and later begins imitating him. After the swimming incident, Gillian demands, "What the hell do you think you were doing in there?", to which Spock colorfully answers, "I was attempting the hell to communicate." The humor in this scene is the same as we derive from watching a child trying to act grown up, but not quite making it, and we try not to laugh in his face. Later, of course, the "child's" use of colorful language becomes embarrassing, is no longer "cute." Kirk tells Spock to stop, since he doesn't quite have the hang of it. We see really how inappropriate his swearing is when, out of the blue on the bridge, he tells Kirk to wait "one damn minute."

Spock also exhibits the spontaneity of a child. His impulsiveness both surprises and embarrasses Kirk. On the bus, quite aware of Kirk's annoyance at the punk with the loud radio, he nerve-pinches him to stop the music. Unlike the old Spock, this innocent has no social concept of IDIC because, as he told McCoy earlier, he has not had a chance to study much Vulcan philosophy. Like an immature child, then, he is intolerant of others' behavior. His sole purpose for the action was to make Kirk happy, as a child would, unthinkingly, act to help his father. He does not, unfortunately, learn that intolerance and prejudice are bad; conversely, he learns that they are human qualities to be applauded!

At the Cetacean Institute, Spock jumps into the tank to mind-meld with the whales. It never occurs to him that later might be better. Like a child, *now* is always best. The funniest scene in the entire movie is probably when Kirk sees Spock swimming in the tank. He looks as if he wants to crawl into a hole.

The tank scene has other reverberations when viewed as part of an initiation story. First, of course, water symbolically means rebirth, baptism, cleansing, etc. Ironically, this episode, which occurs almost exactly in the middle of the movie, symbolizes Spock's initiation into the human world, a shift from innocence and purity to man's less noble side. Immediately, he beings to curse. (In the book, incidentally, Spock has an "alcoholic" reaction to sucrose.) He also encounters sex, though innocent and natural: Gracie is pregnant. When he dons his robe, it is no longer a pure garment of religious significance, but merely an absorbent terry-cloth bathrobe to cover his nakedness.

Almost immediately, as well, his apprenticeship begins. When Gillian picks them up, Kirk begins to fabricate a story to cover Spock's behavior: he was at Berkeley in the sixties and into drugs. The adult wants the kid to play along, but the kid either doesn't catch on or is determined to be honest. "So," says Gillian, "you were at Berkeley." "I was not," Spock answers. "Memory problems, too," Kirk lies.

The funniest come-on-kid-play-along scene occurs just moments later: "You guys like Italian food?" Gillian asks. "No," says Spock. "Yes," says Kirk. "No," says Spock. "Yes," says Kirk, "and you do, too!" And Spock nods yes—his first lie. He has learned to play along, to take cues from Daddy. He has learned to lie. He is already more human.

Throughout the ordeal, Kirk is very patient with Spock, but when he beams aboard the *Bounty* after pizza with Gillian, time, and his patience, are running thin. Spock tells him that if they must get wild whales, "The probability is that our mission will fail."

It is Spock's cold, literal, almost euphemistic use of "mission" that makes Kirk explode at the innocent, unthinking Vulcan, who is honestly unaware of the larger social issues at stake. Kirk turns, furious, to face Spock. "Our *mission*! Goddamm it, Spock, you're talking about the end of life on Earth! That includes your father's life. You're half human—haven't you got any goddamned feelings about *that*?"

Spock is stunned. Until now, he has not looked outside himself to see the larger world of which he is part. A child is a very egocentric being, and Spock, in trying to find himself, is also very self-centered. Kirk's rebuke wakes him up, shakes him away from himself, makes him momentarily feel guilt, another human emotion.

Shortly thereafter, Kirk's effectiveness in raising Spock's level of social consciousness is tested. The whales are gone. Kirk debates whether to go after them immediately or rescue Chekov. He deliberately turns to Spock, asking him the most important question of the movie: "What do you think, Spock?" He thereby calls into play all that Spock has learned since Amanda's first lesson on humanity.

After much thought, Spock replies, "We must help Commander Chekov."

"Is that the logical thing to do, Spock?"

"No, Admiral, but I believe you would call it the human thing to do."

Notice that Spock has not yet internalized the deed, making it spontaneous. Instead, "human thing" is something others do, but he is beginning to see his friends' values as his values. His initiation into the human world is not complete, but the first major step has been taken.

Spock's final lesson is from McCoy: the value of intuition. If they are to return to the twenty-third century, they must rely on Spock's calculations. But conditions have altered. Spock is literal; he is honest, and he is also logically precise. When McCoy says he's having difficulty with imprecise calculations, he tells Spock, "You're going to have to take your best shot." "My best shot?" "*Guess*, Spock. Your best guess." "Guessing is not in my nature." Grinning, McCoy lets us know exactly how far Spock has come since Mount Seleya: "Well, nobody's perfect." Again and again, from "This Side of Paradise" to "The Apple,"

Kirk and Company have been ravaging the universe, destroying perfection. In Spock, they have succeeded again.

At the end of the film, an innocent Spock stands with his accused comrades, willing to share their fate. They are exonerated.

In one of the final scenes, Spock stands indecisively for several seconds between Kirk and Sarek. He walks to his father to say goodbye. Sarek, the Vulcan, says that he is proud of his son, implying pride in his son's choice to be both Vulcan and human. Spock, now in touch with his human emotions, tells Sarek to give Amanda a message: "Tell her I feel fine." Then he leaves with Kirk to join the others "at home" on the new *Enterprise*, their own special and private world.

At the end of *Star Trek IV: The Voyage Home*, Spock seems to be somewhat less than the positive character he was when the series ended in 1969. He has a long way to go before he will be as ready for death as he was at the end of *The Wrath of Khan*. As he evolves more in *Star Trek V*, I hope he forgets all the negative lessons in humanity he learned on the Earth of 1986—the cursing, the lying, the materialism—and that he remembers only the positive—the reliance on informed instinct, the sacrificial love, the dedication to ideals. And I hope he trains more in Vulcan philosophy, especially the concept of IDIC. Only by incorporating the positive of both sides of his heritage will he ever again find peace of soul. He is growing, but he is not grown.

STAR TREK IV—FIRST IMPRESSIONS

By Les Leist

The latest movie in the ongoing *Star Trek* saga has unleashed in me a flood of impressions and ideas, which I would like to explore in several sections.

$$I + II + III = IV = I$$

No, it's not a new formula for dilithium crystals. The above represents the key to my reaction to *Star Trek IV: The Voyage Home*. While much will, doubtless, be written praising and analyzing the story and the humor in *The Voyage Home,* my discussion of the film is going to center around one basic and (to me) startling concept:

This sucker is a remake of the first movie!

Let me hasten to say that I don't mean this in a derogatory sense. On the contrary, the repetition adds yet another meaning to the "coming home" idea, beyond the obvious ones depicted in the movie.

In *Star Trek IV: The Voyage Home,* there is a return to the balance between emotion and logic, feelings and technology, that had been slightly askew since the movie series began. As has often been the case in *Star Trek* history, the real-world, practical causes of this imbalance couldn't help having an effect on plot and character development. This imbalance was most prominent, of course, in *Star Trek: The Motion Picture,* not only because of the influence of *Star Wars,* but also because of the natural desire to fully exploit the special effects that had been unavailable in the television series. "Unbelievable technology," Spock says of the robot planet that sent Vejur on its journey back; and that could well serve as the epigraph of *STTMP.* To be sure, this film did have a helping of the familiar *Star Trek* humanity, especially after the longer version was restored; but those endless Vejur interiors and prolonged, repetitive, wide-eyed reaction shots were frequent enough to make even the most devout Trekker wince with embarrassment. (For some reason, Sulu came out looking the worst during these. I think it was the same sort of thing that happened when he was shown at his post moving in time to the music in "The Way to Eden"—the unflappable helmsman acting out of character.)

In *Star Trek II: The Wrath of Khan* and *Star Trek III: The Search for Spock,* the balance gradually started reasserting itself. There were still special effects, and they were very well done, but now the characters and humor were reclaiming their ground. And so we arrive at the fourth movie, *The Voyage Home.* And also at the first movie, as well. But I haven't explained that yet, have I?

I think the best way to begin would be to recall our first impression of each movie; not something we see, but something we hear—the opening music. In *Star Trek: The Motion Picture* we have that solid, four-square march by Jerry Goldsmith. (Yes, I know, *STTMP* also had that wonderfully anachronistic overture that evoked the kinds of feelings we hoped would prevail in the movie, but, as we know now, were to take a backseat.) Though later beautifully adapted into a stately anthem as Kirk (and we) return to the *Enterprise,* it is as a march that this theme characterizes the refurbished ship and all the flashy hardware that dominates the film. In *Star Trek II: The Wrath of Khan,* there are already signs of an opening up with the sweeping, maritime ballad by James Horner. In *Star Trek III: The Search for Spock,* again with Horner, we are nearly there: the themes for Spock and the Genesis Planet are carried over from *The Wrath of Khan* and given greater development in keeping with the plot of this installment.

And now comes *The Voyage Home.* What indeed are we to make of this delightful outburst that assails our ears, this Christmas-like jubilation and baroque style that characterize Leonard Rosenman's score? Why, the first thing we notice is that there doesn't seem to be a definitive, continuous melody, at least not one we can get our hands on right away. Instead, we get a rush of feelings and harmonies, ringing chimes and circles of fifths, interspersed with melodic fragments. Of course, there *is* a melody there, and you'll get it after a few hearings; but it's a fascinating introduction to the general tone of the movie in that the harmonies (feelings) are given a higher priority than a specific melody line (technology).

Then the movie begins. Read through the following checklist of plot details and tell me if I'm talking about *Star Trek I* or *Star Trek IV*:

—Right after the opening credits, a probe of unknown origin is seen approaching Earth. It subsequently threatens to destroy the planet unless it receives a specific type of response.

—Friendship messages are sent to the probe, to no avail.

—Klingon vessels are reported lost after approaching it. (In *The Voyage Home*, as in *STTMP*, they probably fired some torpedoes at it, and we all know how huge mysterious probes feel about *that*!)

—A conversation takes place in which one person talks about needing an answer to the probe, to which the other replies that they don't know the question (Decker and Kirk; the president and Sarek).

—The response is discovered to come from earth's past (old-style radio signal; whale song).

—The crisis in the present had its origins in earthly activities of the past (voyager launched from Earth; whales hunted to extinction).

—Spock performs a mind meld to gain information for a solution.

—Kirk gets the *Enterprise* back as a reward for saving Earth. (To be accurate, in *STTMP* he doesn't so much get it as keep it, knowing there's not much anyone can do to stop him.)

As interesting as these parallels are, what is more revealing are the points where the two movies diverge:

—In *Star Trek: The Motion Picture*, the general gravitation of events is toward the probe (the technological side) rather tan the response. The crew travels toward Vejur; Spock mind-melds with Vejur. In *The Voyage Home*, both Spock and the crew go toward the response, the whales (the emotional side).

—In *STTMP*, Spock has been struggling to rid himself of emotion. In *The Voyage Home*, that struggle is no longer there. On the contrary; when Amanda tells him that his feelings will surface, Spock's almost casual reply—"As you wish, since you deem them of value"—is startling in its calm acceptance. While still primarily Vulcan, he now seems as open to emotions as he would be to any purely intellectual experience. It may be that he no longer has the more unpleasant memories of his hybrid upbringing, such as the taunts of other Vulcan children or the disapproval of Sarek. Notice how, in *Star Trek: The Motion Picture,* he has to be shocked back into acknowledging feelings by the traumatic mind meld with Vejur, whereas in *The Voyage Home*, he arrived more or less on his own at the "illogical" decision that Chekov should be rescued from the hospital, having had only relatively gentle proddings about feelings from Amanda, McCoy, and Kirk. As Kirk would later say about Spock's guessing, "That's extraordinary!"

(I would demur, however, from making any illogical human conclusions that his quite natural grimacing and gasping for breath in the water, while the rest of the crew were splashing around and rejoicing in the whales, could at any time be interpreted as smiling. After all, he is no longer the—you'll excuse the expression—green young officer smiling at ringing plants! He's *not* smiling, you got that? He's *not!*)

We see, then, that *Star Trek IV: The Voyage Home* is a reworking of *Star Trek: The Motion Picture*, with feelings predominant over logic, although the latter will always have its rightful place. *The Voyage Home* even self-confidently takes up a full two hours, a step up from the progressively shorter durations of *The Wrath of Khan* and *The Search for Spock*. Why, Kirk even uses that old chestnut, "Scotty, beam me up!"

When *Star Trek II: The Wrath of Khan* was released, there was a quote from DeForest Kelley, something to the effect that *Star Trek II* was what *Star Trek I* should have been. That quote might now be applied more aptly to *The Voyage Home*. It is indeed a "voyage home"—for Kirk and crew to Earth; for Kirk to a new *Enterprise;* for

Spock to his friends and his feelings. And perhaps in one more way.

Twenty years ago, Gene Roddenberry launched a "probe" into the future. The probe's activities didn't really begin until several years later, after its source had been cut off; then it really took off and began acquiring knowledge, intelligence, and hope. At the far end of its journey, a land of tremendous technology, the beings that found it tried to decipher its programming and gave it the ability to develop on its own. When it finally returned to its origin, it had amassed such an enormous amount of technology that it was almost unrecognizable. What it needed in order to evolve was a human quality, much like the one from which it had sprung. With *Star Trek III* and *IV*, Leonard Nimoy has supplied the missing response that was needed to take the probe to the next step in its evolution. In *Star Trek IV: The Voyage Home*, we have witnessed a birth.

No article about a new *Star Trek* movie would be complete without two things. First, a look at quibbles and questions. Granted that the nature of this movie wouldn't seem to call for the same degree of nitpicking analysis previous movies have, there are still a few queries I might put:

—What happened to the Klingon prisoner Kirk and Company had at the end of the last movie?

—Scotty was able to justify giving the formula for transparent aluminum to Dr. Nichols. But what about the Klingon phaser and communicator Chekov left behind on the U.S.S. *Enterprise*? What happens when twentieth-century scientists analyze them?

—Since we see Kirk taken to a new, ready-to-go *Enterprise* so soon after his court-martial, does that mean that Starfleet had been planning to give it to him all along, even before the events of the movie?

—Saavik tells Kirk that she has not yet had the opportunity to tell him about his son. Yet we have already heard Kirk say they are in the third month of their Vulcan exile. Three months and she doesn't get the opportunity until right when they're about to leave?

—In the beginning, when Kirk is taking the votes of his

crew on whether or not to return to Earth, he addresses everyone formally: "Mr. Scott," "Mr. Sulu," and so on. But Uhura he just calls "Uhura." There seems to be some indecision as to how he should address her formally when not calling her by rank as "Commander Uhura." Should he revert to "Miss Uhura" from the television episodes? Should he adopt the "Ms. Uhura" now found in the novels? Still another choice, albeit a jarring one, would be to address her as he had addressed Saavik: "Mr. Uhura." The latter would at least be in keeping with the greater use of naval protocol that has character-ized the movies, like the "permission to come aboard" routine. My own preference? I'm not sure; it's a hard call.

—Although this movie probably has the best balance yet regarding the spotlighting of individual crew mem-bers, I suppose it's unavoidable that there are one or two more things one could have wished for. We can accept Saavik's reduced role since she had such impressive mo-ments in both *The Wrath of Khan* and *The Search for Spock*. But Sulu and Uhura are still denied their first names; and while it's nice to see Chapel and Rand again, they almost get lost in the shadows during the emergency at Starfleet Command.

—Is Chekov's screaming now to be replaced by his saying "wessel" as often as possible?

—Last but not least, where would we be without a good, old-fashioned blooper? In the hospital, when Kirk goes to melt the door lock, he's holding the phaser in his left hand. In the close-up of the phaser firing, we see it in a right hand. In the next shot, the phaser is back in Kirk's left hand. I would say the chances of the hand in the close-up insert shot belonging to someone other than William Shatner are about one out of one to the fourth power!

The second thing an article like this wouldn't be com-plete without is, naturally, a look ahead to the next movie. Whatever story director William Shatner and his writers come up with for *Star Trek V*, it would be nice if they could include some things, mostly minor touches, that haven't yet been seen, either since the television series, or not at all:

—Mention of the Prime Directive.

—Spock playing his Vulcan harp.

—Uhura singing.

—Andorians and Romulans in speaking roles (and an acknowledgment of Saavik's half-Romulan background).

—Saurian brandy!

—Dress uniforms. In the series, full-dress uniforms made for a nice contrast by showing smarter-looking versions of the familiar yellow, green, blue, and red costumes. Now that the last three movies have firmly established those maroon outfits, why not show dress versions of them?

—Acknowledgment of the events in the first movie. (After all, it *is* part of *Star Trek* lore, and I certainly didn't mean to trash it with my earlier comments.)

—A revival of the tradition, not used since Mark Lenard played a Klingon in *Star Trek: The Motion Picture*, of bringing back favorite guest stars or bit players in other roles.

(My favorite bit player in the film series is Jeanne Mori, who was at the helm of the destroyed *Grissom* in *Star Trek III: The Search for Spock*. In just two short sequences, she created a character with a complete background and life behind her. Her single line, "Standard orbit, aye, aye, sir," spoken with a slightly jaded touch, suggested not only her experience, but also a resigned tolerance for this by-the-book, walking-on-eggs captain she had gotten stuck with. Then, of course, there was her unspoken "Say *what*?" facial reaction upon hearing that Spock had been regenerated on Genesis.)

—Lastly, since there is so often talk of bringing in fresh, new characters, why not finally let us see McCoy's daughter, Joanna? My nomination to play her: Nancy McKeon, who plays Jo on *Facts of Life*.

As to the plot of *Star Trek V*? Well, that's a bit harder. For the first time since the end of *Star Trek: The Motion Picture*, we have nothing left hanging, no loose ends to tie up. The trilogy of *Star Treks II, III, and III* has completed a circle and we are now free to make a fresh start. One thing comes to mind, though: *Star Trek V* should be a straightforward, episodic adventure—nothing threatening to destroy the Earth or take over the galaxy—we've had that several times already. Just as in the better episodes of the television series, there should be characters and surroundings that we encounter for this story only; and the plot twists, conflicts, and eventual resolution should revolve around them, while at the same time serving to further develop our central *Star Trek* characters.

SPECIAL SECTION #2:
THE STARSHIP
ENGINEERING

There is perhaps nothing that symbolizes Star Trek *so much as the unmistakable outline of the starship* Enterprise. *So it was an unbelievable shock when we saw her fall to a fiery death in* Star Trek III: The Search for Spock; *not only was the* Enterprise *a part of the* Star Trek *family, and beloved by all, it seemed insane on the part of Paramount to destroy the very icon of the series and films. Happily, the* Enterprise *lives on, barely changed in configuration, and once again crewed by Captain Kirk and his friends. Even more importantly,* Star Trek *lives on;* Star Trek: The Next Generation *premiered this fall to rave reviews and fan acclaim. And, of course, the ship is named* Enterprise.

But our old friend, the original Enterprise *is still part and parcel of* Star Trek *lore. In the following three articles, our contributors take a look at where she came from, where she went, and, unsurprisingly, where she's going.*

THE ONCE AND FUTURE STARSHIP

By David Gardner

If you're anything like me, on the opening night of *Star Trek IV: The Voyage Home,* you nearly went through the roof at the sight of the new *Enterprise.* But, beyond my elation at seeing my friends coming "home," I had to ask myself where this new vessel came from, and what was its background. These questions led to some interesting lines of thought.

It is, of course, impossible (not to mention illogical) that a new starship had been constructed within the time that the *Enterprise* crew journeyed to Vulcan and the time they stood trial before the Federation Council. Even if we allow for two months between their return from 1986 with the humpbacks and the trial, this could still give us only five months' time for construction. As *Starship Design* (Volume XXXIV, March 2280) lists the construction period for a Belknap/Decatur (MkXX) class vessel as about one year (averaged between seven vessels), and as the Belknap/Decaturs are very similiar in design and technology to the Constitution/Enterprise class, we can assume a similar construction time for a new Mk IX Heavy Cruiser. Furthermore, there is no logical reason why they would build a new vessel based on a design almost forty years old, regardless of whom they would be pleasing by so doing.

The obvious conclusion is that this ship already existed and was modified for Kirk *et al* at some indeterminate time. It is a member of the Constitution class that has somehow been protected and made ready at the request of the Council of Starfleet Command. What kept it intact and yet allowed it to be ready for conversion to NCC

1701-A? And how did it come to be close enough to Earth that its conversion could be completed in so short a time?

As always, there are no easy answers, but if you will bear with me during a few sidetracks, I think we can shed some light on these mysteries.

The *Star Fleet Technical Manual* lists twelve original construction Constitution-class Heavy Cruisers, another twelve second-generation designs, four replacements for destroyed originals, and one hundred and fourteen third-generation ships, a total of one hundred and forty-two vessels. We know that the original complement of twelve were built. By why would they build only twelve? Twelve Heavy Cruisers would never make a dent in a volume of space the size of the Federation, and these ships were chartered to be the workhorses of Starfleet.

Probably the original order called for a dozen vessels, upon which Starfleet could perform testing and evaluation to determine if they would be as spaceworthy as their designers and contractors claimed. As we already know that Starfleet was not entirely happy with the design, and we can prove that at least four ships were lost within a three-to-four year period, the second dozen vessels were probably ordered for the same purpose. This "second generation" (technically the BonHomme Richard class, although I shall refer to all Mk IX vessels as Constitution class) would have included any minor technology upgrades that had come along since the first procurement, and would also have incorporated design modifications reflecting the recommendations of Starfleet's several years' experience with the originals.

The third set of four ships comprised simply "honorary" vessels, probably ships that were already scheduled for construction due to the incredible destruction rate that the class suffered (I'll explain this later), ships that simply had their names changed, retaining their registry numbers. The final set, however, represented a total commitment on the part of Starfleet and the Federation to the Mk IX Heavy Cruiser design. With this order of a hundred and fourteen vessels of the Tikopai class, Fleet Command hoped to have its cruiser design for the next three to four decades.

It is unlikely that Starfleet took delivery of the entire order, however. Consider that a modern military contract often calls for more units than will be constructed or delivered, as before the order can be entirely filled technology has overtaken and passed the current design. This possibility is confirmed in the aforementioned volume *Starship Design;* page 1027 lists Starfleet's procurement plan for the next five years (as of the date of publication), showing several cancellations and additional orders. Further evidence in the booklet of plans for the U.S.S. *Excelsior*, where we find that of five vessels ordered, three have been canceled.

So how many Constitution-class vessels were built, and, of those, how many are extant?

If two shipyards were used for construction of the Mk IXs (as there are for the Mk XX Belknaps), and if construction was carried on at a fairly standard rate for forty years (the rough age of the *Enterprise* at the time of her destruction, not allowing for the fact that she was the second vessel of the Mk IX class to be completed; *Constitution* may have been completed and undergone testing much earlier, but this would change our computation very little) at a rough rate of one vessel per year, it would have added up to a total of eighty vessels completed before Starfleet began their switch-over to the smaller and cheaper Gargarin-and-Reliant class vessels. (It is true that Kirk says of the *Enterprise*, "There are only twelve like her in the fleet," but this statement refers only to the Constitution class, not the BonHomme Richard or Tikopai classes.)

Given the survival rate of the original twelve, and the fact that five are known to have been lost (including, as previously mentioned, four in a three-to-four year span), we can assume that at least fifty percent of the total complement of M1 IXs survived until the *Enterprise* was chosen to become the first to undergo refit to the new technology of *Star Trek: The Motion Picture*. This loss rate is actually a fraction of that portrayed in the series, but if we're going to err, let's do it on the side of caution. It is also logical that, as the Mk IX's service record increased, modifications and minor refits would have been implemented that would have brought the loss rate down to a more acceptable level; otherwise, Starfleet and the Federation might have gone broke building Heavy Cruiser replacements.

One might wonder why so many of these vessels met untimely destruction. Aside from the dangers inherent in space exploration on such a level, most of the answer lies in Vonda McIntyre's novel, *Enterprise: The First Adventure,* wherein we learn that at the time Kirk takes command of the *Enterprise* from Captain Pike, Starfleet Command is embarking on a new galactic exploration program in which the Mk XIs will play a major role. Such missions into the unknown are, by definition, more dangerous than any other type of mission (with the possible exception of a spy mission) for the simple reason that one cannot know what to expect.

If we allow that the destruction rate of six out of twelve probably held true for the entire line, then only forty ships would have survived until the first refit. If we grant, however, that Starfleet's design changes may have upped the survival rate slightly for the second generation, and slightly more than that for the third generation, then it becomes logical to believe that about forty-five to fifty of the ships survived to the time of *Star Trek: The Motion Picture.*

As the Reliant class came on line, the Constitution-class ships remaining in service would have been slowly phased out of front-line duty in order to maintain the limits imposed by the Organian Peace Treaty. Although some do remain in exploratory service (per *Starship Design*), an ever-increasing number would have been broken to such "soft" duty assignments as V.I.P. transports, or, like the *Enterprise,* cadet training vessels. Still others would have been found not to have withstood the test of time, and would have been decommissioned and scrapped. The vast majority, however, would not have a place in the "new" Starfleet, where limitations on the number of vessels in service (due to the Organian Peace Treaty) meant that every vessel had to be optimized for its mission. The remaining Mk IXs that were found to be structurally sound would have been put into a "mothball" reserve fleet.

The mothball reserve would operate similarly to the

reserve fleets of the United States. Vessels that were outdated or that violated treaty limits would be put into "storage"—probably orbiting a lifeless planet in an inhabited, major star system. In this fashion, they would take no valuable space to store and would be near a well-protected and well-guarded area. The mothball reserve concept would also allow these ships to be taken off line, making them irrelevant in terms of the Organian Peace Treaty, but still held ready in case war should break out, providing replacement and reinforcement ships until the Federation economy and industrial military could come into full swing.

At this point numbers become harder to back up with facts, but it seems likely that the destruction rate of the uprated vessels would have dropped off to at least half of what it had previously been. Probably about seventy percent of the uprated vessels survived to see either scrapping, "soft duty" assignments, or mothballing, with the latter group growing every year. This would give us as few as twenty-one, or as many as thirty-five surviving ships of the Mk IX class. Starfleet could, of course, have paid for further refits of these ships, but probably deigned not to when they could have new vessels (the Reliants and the upcoming Excelsiors) instead of forty- to fifty-year-old ships.

The new *Enterprise* is one of these "mothballed" vessels. It has served for about two decades, undergone at least one refit, served for another length of time, and put into mothball storage for possible future duty. Until the events of *Star Trek II: The Wrath of Khan,* there were no openings for a cruiser-class vessel in the Treaty-controlled fleet, but after *Reliant* was destroyed (and her destruction verified by the Klingons, and/or a third, impartial party trusted by both sides to monitor the fleet status of both), an opening was created. Rather than build a new Reliant-class vessel while economically embroiled in the construction, testing, and evaluation phases of the *Excelsior,* Starfleet chose to break out one of the old Mk IXs. A little paint at the last minute was all that was required for our friends to "come home."

It will probably remain impossible to know which vessel was resurrected to become 1701-A, but I think we have some clues to which ships she is *not*. Obviously, she is neither the *Constellation, Farragut, Intrepid, Valiant,* or (need I say it?) the original *Enterprise,* as we have witnessed these ships being destroyed, lost in the line of duty, or made otherwise unusable. (For example, *Farragut* was contaminated with a disease, the only known cure for which was to spend an amount of time on the planet it was found orbiting. While a crew could have been sent to that planet until immunized, the ship itself would have become a carrier of the disease, and would have to be quarantined. It was probably destroyed by a regretful Starfleet.) Furthermore, she cannot be *Saratoga, Excelsior,* or *Yorktown:* the first two have been destroyed, lending their names to vessels of more current designs; the latter has either suffered the same fate, or else it is the original *Yorktown,* uprated, that we see in *Star Trek IV: The Voyage Home.* She also cannot be the *Bon Homme Richard,* as this ship has either been destroyed in order to lend its name to a Belknap-class cruiser listed in *Starship Design,* or has itself been converted to that new design. The *Federation Reference Series #3* lists the *Hood* as destroyed, so she too cannot be 1701-A.

Several of you may have noticed the return of the original, series-era sound effects to the bridge of the new *Enterprise.* If we grant that all the surviving ships did not get the same refit (*Starship Design* does list the Constitution and Enterprise classes separately), and further grant that this ship must have pre-*STTMP* sensor/scanner equipment, then she cannot be *Lexington, Excalibur, Exeter, El Dorado,* or *Krieger,* all of which are listed in *Federation Reference Series #3* as having received the same refit as 1701. (This volume also erroneously lists *Farragut,* 1702, as receiving this refit. Either the printer's computer accessed faulty information, or the *Farragut II,* NCC-1729 actually received the update.)

Unfortunately, at this time we have no way of knowing which of the one hundred and fourteen third-generation ships were actually built, and since more of them are likely to have survived than the first- or second-generation ships, it is likely that 1701-A is one of these vessels.

(This may be an erroneous conclusion. Captain D. G. Tov states in his letter in *Starship Design* that "though their basic designs are similar, [one would find] almost completely different vessels." He goes on to say, "Internal arrangement, armament, and scientific capacity of the [Constitution II, Enterprise, and Tikopai] class cruisers are quite different." If these statements are true, then 1701-A could only be one of a handful of Constitution-class or, possibly, BonHomme Richard–class vessels that we cannot prove were destroyed at an earlier period.)

I said a few paragraphs back that a little paint was all that was required to complete the transformation from Vessel X to 1701-A, but that statement too may have been false. Several fans have assumed, perhaps rightly, that the new *Enterprise* is outfitted with transwarp drive. Does Kirk know something he's not letting us in on when he says, "Let's see what she's got"?

It is difficult to find any evidence to prove or disprove this theory. A friend cited the obvious blue glow from the inboard flux chillers seen before 1701-A went into warp drive in the last scene of *The Voyage Home,* but a little research showed that this glow is present, although not obvious, in the previous three films. It is also certain that the new *Enterprise* used a slightly different effect to denote its transition to warp speed, but we cannot conclude that she has transwarp on the basis of the special effects; *Star Trek IV: The Voyage Home* was, after all, quite a fanciful film, and caution was thrown to the wind in several technical areas.

We can state with some assurance that 1701-A was not refitted with transwarp after being hauled out of moth-ball reserve, as the transwarp units, in and of themselves a new design, would have required much more time to downscale than Starfleet had available. If the ship does have transwarp, it was almost certainly a Starfleet test vehicle for that system, one of handful of different ships on which transwarp prototypes were installed to determine the suitability of the new warp process to military applications (this would have provided yet another use for mothballed vessels—as test units). If this is the case, the ship may have been flying around for some time in its previous incarnation, and then re-retired after the evaluation had been completed, only to be called back to active duty in the procedure detailed above. It is also possible that the ship was not retired a second time, as her weaponry would have had to have been removed and/or disabled before the test process began in the first place; she would not have violated the Organian Peace Treaty and would have remained in service for prolonged observation of the transwarp system. A most interesting service record for one vessel, one that almost rivals the original *Enterprise*.

Interestingly enough, transwarp does not appear to be under any type of security precautions. When Sulu announces that he has heard that *Excelsior* has transwarp (in front of several cadets, no less!), he elicits no reaction from any of the bridge crew, and Scotty seems to understand at least the fundamentals of its operations. This can only lead us to one conclusion. Either the Klingons or the Romulans, or both, already have working transwarp units, and probably have been operating warships with this system, possibly even frontline vessels. This would make information security superfluous as the Federation is playing "catch-up," and the Klingons and Romulans would not need to steal information they already have.

It is also important to note that the possible success of transwarp would not doom the rest of the fleet to the scrap heap; America did not junk its warships and start over with the launch of the *Nautilus*, the first nuclear-powered vessel. If transwarp meets its design criteria, it will still take Starfleet decades to get enough transwarp-equipped vessels on line to even begin to think about decommissioning the nontranswarp ships, and by that time the transwarp drive may, through further research and refinement, become small enough for economically feasible installation on Mk IXs, among other classes (and this may have already taken place if 1701-A was a transwarp test ship).

Whatever the outcome, it is certain that Starfleet and the Federation are on the verge of opening up a vast, new area to exploration and, later, to exploitation. If we assume that transwarp drive is faster, in a relative sense, than warp drive by only a power of one hundred, then warp factor six will jump from a mere 216 times the speed of light to 21,600 times the speed of light!

This will put some areas, such as the Magellanic Clouds,

within a thinkable, if extended, distance. And if we allow that higher factors of warp are likely, nearby galaxies may be opened up to long-distance exploration in the next few decades, and perhaps even to colonization by the end of the century.

It appears that the adventure does, indeed, continue.

A HISTORY OF THE STARSHIP *ENTERPRISE*—A NEW EXAMINATION

By Jeffrey Heine

The written and visual literature on *Star Trek* grows at an unprecedented rate. With its twentieth anniversary now passed, followers of the series now have at their disposal a large selection of *Star Trek* items: novels (appearing regularly), reference books, feature films, videocassettes of the original, uncut episodes in high-fidelity sound . . . in short, a multitude of ways to get a fix of *Star Trek*.

The growing body of literature brings a growing probability of inconsistency as authors reinterpret the *Star Trek* universe, shaping it to fit the needs of their stories. For the most part, the contributing authors have done an excellent job of researching the details of *Star Trek* that already exist, details considered part of the "canon" (i.e., the episodes, the films, certain books). The inconsistencies, for the most part, stem from the works of new authors, who cannot keep tabs on their peers' works, which are often written at the same time. Other novels, while not so inconsistent, are adventures that have no definite frame of reference other than taking place *before* or *after* the first motion picture (as can be determined by references to the characters' military rank, which changed between the series and the movies, as well as allusions to the plot of *Star Trek: The Motion Picture*); such novels are accepted as general action-adventure stories. To find a place for all of them would prove, in the end, quite difficult. In these instances, it is best to resolve the matter by saying that these novels are individual interpretations of the *Star Trek* universe.

Every so often, however, a novel comes along that has

the good fortune to be accepted as an addition to the canon. Such novels tend to be about specific periods of *Star Trek*'s history (*The Final Reflection; Enterprise: The First Adventure*), or else they are written by respected authors who introduce new details (Vonda McIntyre, Diane Duane).

One such accepted novel is Vonda McIntyre's *Enterprise: The First Adventure*. This novel is significant in two ways: it chronicles that nebulous period of time when James T. Kirk took over command of the star ship *Enterprise* from Christopher Pike, and it carries Gene Roddenberry's recommendation. If you'll pardon the pun, it's the real McCoy. This is the way it happened. With the publication of this novel, the bridge between Pike's and Kirk's commands is more clear, making a history of the starship *Enterprise* easier to assess.

However, the previously mentioned inconsistencies make such a venture difficult. Not only does McIntyre's novel refute some basic assumptions held by fandom, but it introduces facts that do not jibe with the television series. These facts must be accounted for. This article will seek to develop a history of science fiction's most famous starship and to examine the source literature with an eye toward establishing some overall unity (including Jeffery W. Mason's articles, "A Star Trek Chronology" [*The Best of Trek #6*], and "A Star Trek Chronology, part Two [*The Best of Trek #10*], and David Gardner's "The Road to the *Enterprise*—And Beyond" [*Trek Magazine #11*].

To develop a history of the *Enterprise*, I had to rely heavily upon books that described the years that specific characters served each other on the *Enterprise*. These books specify crew members' ages while serving aboard the *Enterprise* and the age of the *Enterprise* herself. Unfortunately, it is difficult to find agreement on such matters. Even Gene Roddenberry and Stephen Whitfield's *The Making of Star Trek* (published during the series' run and, for all practical purposes, considered the series' Book of Genesis), is occasionally inconsistent with the series. The task of unifying these disparate sources would not, I saw, be easy.

Let us begin, then, with Captain James T. Kirk, the principal figure in the history of the starship *Enterprise*.

The Making of Star Trek and the third edition of *The Star Trek Writer's Guide* both say that Kirk is about thirty-four years old. *The Making of Star Trek* goes on to say that Kirk joined the Academy as a seventeen-year-old midshipman, receiving command of a destroyer-class starship "while still quite young." According to *The First Adventure,* this would have been the *Lydia Sutherland.* Whitfield also reveals that Kirk has been in command of the *Enterprise* for "more than four years."

This is the earliest allusion to the fact that the starship *Enterprise*'s five-year mission did not begin with Kirk's command assignment to the starship. *The First Adventure* supports this fact. One indication is to be found in the characters' behavior. At the end of the novel, Kirk and Spock's relationship, while significantly better than at the beginning of the book, barely resembles the friendship we would see later. There has to be some time for their friendship to develop to the depth we would see at the beginning of the series.

Another indication found in the novel is that Kirk got command of the *Enterprise* when he was *twenty-nine.* In a scene from the prologue, Kirk reveals his age to Christine Chapel when he stops by to check on his injured friend, Gary Mitchell. He also says that he has known Gary for eleven years.

If Kirk is thirty-four when the series takes place, we are looking at a period of five years between Kirk's assignment and the series' beginnings. Subsequently, in the episode "Where No Man Has Gone Before," Kirk says he's known Gary for fifteen years, making the events of that episode take place four years after the McIntyre novel. Therefore, nearly a year separates the *Enterprise*'s trip to the galactic edge and the first aired episode to acknowledge the fact of a five-year mission.

A gap of a year between "Where No Man" and the rest of the series can be supported visually, as well. The physical makeup of the *Enterprise* in that episode is closer to what we see during Pike's command. The uniforms are in a different style, as well.

The period of time between "Where No Man" and "The Man Trap" could be best explained by the *Enterprise* coming in for a structural refit, much like the one that we see the final hours of in *Star Trek: The Motion Picture.*

The need for a refit is obvious. After the *Enterprise* attempts to cross the galactic barrier, the ship is severely damaged. In order to get home, Lieutenant Kelso has to cannibalize parts from the lithium-cracking station on Delta Vega. Before the starship can go on further extensive voyages, much less a five-year mission, she will need more reliable repairs. Also, she would need a refit for structural improvements and technological advances necessary to aid the vessel on a long-range exploratory mission. Precious time during these years could not be wasted on repair that could be prevented by an upgrading.

Gene Roddenberry, in his novelization of *Star Trek: The Motion Picture,* alludes to the fact that the *Enterprise* went about her five-year mission without putting in much repair time. He describes the ship as "battered" when she finally comes home to Earth.

When we consider the written references to Kirk's command, it is virtually certain that he was captain of the *Enterprise* for nearly five years before the start of the mission chronicled in the television series.

More discrepancies appear when we compare source books. Let's begin with *The Making of Star Trek.*

Spock has been aboard the *Star Trek* for a total of thirteen years (at the time of the beginning of the series): nine years with Captain Pike, and four with Captain Kirk. The four years he served with Kirk jibe with what I've already established, but with one year unaccounted for. Perhaps the *Enterprise*'s refit took close to a year to complete, and Spock would not have served with Kirk during that time. (Kirk, however, would have overseen the refit of the *Enterprise,* as he was assigned to command her exploratory mission; hence *The Making of Star Trek*'s reference to Kirk commanding the starship for "more than four years" and close to five.) Or else, Spock left the *Enterprise* at some point when Gary Mitchell signed on, since the Vulcan knew Kirk originally wanted Mitchell for first officer.

The authenticity of some of the information found in *The Making of Star Trek* can be questioned when compared to "The Menagerie," the first TV episode to show the *Enterprise* under the command of Captain Pike. In "The Menagerie," we see the *Enterprise* as she was thirteen years before the start of Kirk's five-year mission. Spock says that he served with Pike for "eleven years, four months, five days," a quote backed up by Bjo Trimble in her *Star Trek Concordance,* a period of time that is two years longer than the period quoted in *The Making of Star Trek*. The *Concordance* goes on to state that Spock has been on the *Enterprise* for "perhaps fifteen years." This would support the claim that Kirk and Spock had already served together for four years before the start of the series.

However, when Trimble says "fifteen years," of when is she speaking? Has Spock been on the *Enterprise* for fifteen years prior to the first episode, or up to and including the final episode? If prior to the first episode, then, yes, Kirk and Spock served together for four years before the series' inception. If including the series episodes, then this time is cut down to approximately two years.

I agree with the first of these options. It is probably true that five years have passed between *The First Adventure* and the beginning of the television series. The series always hinted that the principal characters have known each other for some time. In "Where No Man Has Gone Before," Dr. Elizabeth Dehner says that Spock and Mitchell have served together "for years." In "The Man Trap," Uhura tells Spock that Kirk is the closest friend he has. The relationship of the principal officers could be more firmly developed over a span of five years, as opposed to two, as well.

Therefore, these years between *The First Adventure* and "Where No Man" are quite clouded. They open up a wide period of time for future adventures to be chronicled (McIntyre left such a possibility open with the unresolved fate of her villain, Koronin), and it is during this period of time that further problems in continuity crop up. One major discrepancy involves the ranking of officers Spock, Scott, and Mitchell. In *The First Adventure*, all three have the rank of commander. At some point between the novel and the start of the series, there were demotions of rank.

Spock and Scott are both lieutenant commander at the start of the series. Spock eventually became a commander, but Scotty was not promoted until the first motion picture. In "Where No Man," Mitchell was also a lieutenant commander.

We can regard this information in four ways. The first would be to regard the discrepancies as a technical slip. McIntyre made an error in calling all three men "commander," a slip that can be corrected in future printings of the novel. (Tolkien did this for the Ballantine edition of *The Lord of the Rings,* so such changes are not unheard of.) Secondly, we could view the reference to "commander" as an abbreviation for the rank of "lieutenant commander." Thirdly, all men could have had brevet, or "field" promotions during the course of alert or warlike conditions, promotions that would not be permanent and would be revoked in times of peace.

The fourth option is harder to swallow, but it would ultimately make an interesting story: for some reason, all three men received reductions in rank. This could have been a result of Kirk's desire to shape up his officers during the first days on the starship; it could have been an edict handed down by Starfleet.

In the case of Mitchell, we see in "Where No Man" that he was a lieutenant commander at the age of twenty-three (according to his service record, which Kirk and Spock examine). It is difficult to believe that he would remain at that rank for eleven years. Given his disposition, however, as seen in "Where No Man," it is likely that he could have been passed by when promotion time came around, despite his obvious popularity among the bridge crew. Given his reduction in position from first officer to serving on the ship's command console, this could have had an effect on future rankings.

What happened to McCoy during those fours years? He is not present in "Where No Man Has Gone Before," although Kirk picks McCoy specifically for chief medical officer in *The First Adventure,* the two of them having known each other for years before Kirk's assignment to the *Enterprise* (their meeting, in fact, is related in Brad Ferguson's novel *Crisis on Centaurus*). In the above episode, we have an older man named Dr. Mark Piper. The

James Blish novelization of the episode says simply that McCoy was on a study leave, but I think Blish was trying to fit the episode into the context of the five-year mission. Nevertheless, the study leave theory works. According to Gene Roddenberry's novelization of *Star Trek: The Motion Picture*, McCoy left the *Enterprise* at the end of the five-year mission to study the Fabrini medical data that had saved his life in "For the World Is Hollow and I Have Touched the Sky." It is possible that he could have taken a similar leave earlier in his career. Piper's appearance in "Where No Man" is even alluded to in *The First Adventure:* Kirk has him in mind for any future need.

Thus, we can see that the four years of Kirk's command before "Where No Man Has Gone Before" contain a stockpile of incidents that would provide for many future volumes of speculation and adventure.

When piecing together a history of the *Enterprise* and her crew, there is one other subject to consider: the starship *Enterprise* herself. To begin with, even her exact age is in question.

We know, for example, that the *Enterprise* has been in existence for at least thirteen years before the start of the five-year mission, since in "The Menagerie" we are told that the *Enterprise* visited the planet Talos IV that many years before.

In the same year that "The Menagerie" takes place, the *Enterprise* found the *Botany Bay* and Khan Noonian Singh in "Space Seed." When the crew encountered Khan again in *Star Trek II: The Wrath of Khan,* Khan says he was found by the *Enterprise* "fifteen years ago."

Therefore, the *Enterprise,* by the time of *The Wrath of Khan,* has to be at least twenty-eight years old.

But in *Star Trek III: The Search for Spock,* which takes place immediately following *The Wrath of Khan,* Admiral Morrow says that the *Enterprise* is twenty years old, and that the time has come to retire the starship. He could have been generalizing; if so, he could have better emphasized his point by saying instead that the *Enterprise* was close to thirty years old.

The inconsistencies do not end there. During *Star Trek's* third season, in the episode entitled "Is There in Truth No Beauty?", we meet Lawrence Marvick, one of the designers of the *Enterprise*'s engines. Marvick is around forty years old (according to the *Concordance*), although he could easily be older. By the twenty-third century, life expectancy for the human race should be higher than it is now. This assumption is backed up by the animated episode "The Counter Clock Incident," where it is revealed that Starfleet's mandatory retirement age is seventy-five—and that age is considered too young by many!

In this same animated episode, we meet Robert April, the first captain of the *Enterprise*. April is seventy-five years old. He has been a Federation ambassador-at-large for twenty years and he became captain of the *Enterprise* on the day of her christening forty years before. Since it is generally accepted that the animated series chronicles some of the fourth year of that five-year mission, April took the *Enterprise* out of drydock thirty-two years before Kirk took command in *The First Adventure*. Taking this into account, the *Enterprise* was approximately fifty-one years old at the time of her destruction above the Genesis Planet in *Star Trek III: The Search for Spock*.

(That is, of course, if we acknowledge the events of the animated series and Alan Dean Foster's novelizations, specifically concerning information on April. A lot of fans ridicule the animated series, saying it is best to ignore it or, at best, consider the episodes as adventures *based* on the exploits of the starship *Enterprise* and her crew. I personally feel it is unfortunate that some refuse to acknowledge the work of Roddenberry, D. C. Fontana, and others who worked to bring *Star Trek* back in 1973. It may have been flawed, but it was *Star Trek*.)

In this same discussion of Captain April, given the time between April's and Kirk's commands, there is a strong possibility that there was another captain of the *Enterprise* between April and Pike. (David Gardner speculates on this possibility in his article as well, and also discusses the issue of Admiral Morrow's problems in counting.)

Obviously Admiral Morrow does *not* know how to count, much less pose a good argument. And Lawrence Marvick would have had to have been a child prodigy if he designed the *Enterprise*'s engines . . . if he had even been born at that time. Or else, there is more information to consider before an exact age for the starship *Enterprise* can be determined.

To begin with, the *Enterprise* was not exactly the same starship throughout her history. There are many interior and exterior structural differences between the *Enterprise* of Captain Pike's years and the *Enterprise* of the television series. The *Enterprise* that appears in the motion pictures is also an almost completely different vessel, more radically redesigned than any previous version.

This newly redesigned and refitted *Enterprise* has been in existence for seven years when Admiral Morrow decommissions the starship. This figure is based on evidence given in the films: Kirk served as head of Starfleet Operations for two and a half years before taking command of the *Enterprise* again. Adding in the five-year mission gives us a total of seven-odd years. After deducting these from the fifteen years Khan claims he's been marooned on Ceti Alpha V, we end up with approximately seven years since the refit seen in *Star Trek: The Motion Picture*.

This "new" *Enterprise* is far from being twenty years old. Despite new technological advances—as shown in the *Excelsior*—Starfleet has invested too much time and money in the *Enterprise* to turn her into scrap after only seven years of service.

At the time of *The Search for Spock*, Kirk has been involved with a ship named *Enterprise* for close to twenty years. Perhaps this is what Morrow meant. The admiral not only wants to decommission the starship, but to end Kirk's career in space as well. At least Morrow does not come across as an idiot—although he still has his decision to decommission the *Enterprise* to answer for.

If the *Enterprise* received the latest in warp drive technology before the start of *Star Trek: The Motion Picture*, it would be logical to assume that the same thing might have happened before, especially if April commanded the *Enterprise* thirty-two years before Kirk. That allows a lot of time for advances in technology.

Earlier advances are hinted at in John Ford's novel *The Final Reflection*. The story is set forty years before the tenth anniversary of the Organian Peace Treaty, which was signed during the first year of the series. (Perhaps slightly earlier than that: *The Making of Star Trek* says that McCoy is forty-five years old; in *The Final Reflection*, McCoy is a diapered infant; Spock is seven years old.) During this time, the Federation's starships could do no better than warp four. Obviously, the *Enterprise* had to have a refit at some point in time, since the ship was built shortly after the events of Ford's novel. In "The Cage," one of Pike's crewmen tells the survivors of the *Columbia* that "the time barrier has been broken," a reference to warp drive technology's development and advancement. I believe a refit of the *Enterprise*'s engines took place before Christopher Pike took command of the starship. Lawrence Marvick could have developed the new engines on the *Enterprise,* the last such update before the first motion picture.

Now, a chronology can be presented. Such a chronology is concerned only with the *Enterprise* and her crew (Mason's chronology of the Federation, as far as I can see, would be difficult to dispute; he has done an excellent job, and I see no need for revision of that portion of the chronology). Of course, this article has been able to utilize *Enterprise: The First Adventure,* where Mason and Gardner both could not.

Mason and Gardner assume that the *Enterprise* was always sent out on missions that lasted five years. After reading *The First Adventure,* I get the feeling that the five-year mission would have to be a new format introduced into the Federation's plans for long-range exploration, since the Federation, at the time of Kirk's assignment, was on the verge of unprecedented exploration. The concept of a five-year mission is perhaps similar to the Soviet Union's five-year economic plans; in the case of both, a period of time is allotted for the completion of specific goals. For the Federation, these goals would involve exploration and establishment of settled territory. A five-year mission, therefore, did not mean that a starship is sent out into space, not to be heard from until the end of that time, it means that goals have been set and the *Enterprise* is given five years to meet them. Since McIntyre hints that the Federation is preparing to expand outward from its current boundaries, I would argue that the concept of the five-year mission was introduced with that expansionist goal in mind.

Mason also assumes—and at the time he wrote his articles, I would have agreed—that Kirk took over after Pike, with the television series beginning immediately thereafter. However, the structural changes seen on the *Enterprise* between "Where No Man Has Gone Before" and "The Man Trap" were not taken into consideration, nor the claims made in *The Making of Star Trek* and the *Concordance* that both Kirk and Spock served on the *Enterprise* for more years than Mason accounted for.

Mason's major obstacle was finding a time frame in which to set the adventures of the *Enterprise*. His sources gave him little help; in the final analysis, he chose to set the five-year mission of the television series during the years 2207–2212.

Star Trek was set in the twenty-third century, although an exact year was never spoken of. The series itself had episodes that did not support this setting, as Mason points out. Whenever the twentieth century is discussed, as in the episodes "Tomorrow is Yesterday" and "Space Seed," it is generally said that only two centuries separate our time and that of the *Star Trek* universe. Mason ultimately settled on a period closer to the twenty-third century.

Star Trek II: The Wrath of Khan opens with the words, "In the twenty-third century . . ." and it is in this film we hear, for the first time, a definitive date. McCoy brings Kirk a present of Romulan ale. Kirk checks the vintage: "Twenty-two eighty-three?" Kirk says. "Well," McCoy jokes, "it takes this stuff awhile to ferment."

It is a brief scene that fans have picked up on and argued about, even here in the pages of *Trek*. How old is the ale? Is the year 2283 based on our calendar or Romulan calendar? Could it be less than a year old, and McCoy's joke is similar to how you or I would joke about the vintage of a screwtop bottle of wine? Could it have been bottled with a vintage label based on a Julian calendar, obviously meant for Federation drinkers? (That would be a nice touch, considering that the ale is supposed to be illegal!)

It would be appropriate, given the film's themes, if *The Wrath of Khan* was set in the waning days of the twenty-third century, on the eve of a new century. Perhaps 2283 was the year when the television series "started."

(If this were true, it puts the birthday scene in a new context. Not only is McCoy commenting on the fact that the ale takes awhile to ferment, perhaps he is also alluding to Kirk's career, as well. If the five-year mission began in the year 2283, then McCoy's comments can be interpreted as meaning that the best years of Kirk's life are yet to come. Anyway, that is another story . . .)

In the end, for the purposes of this article, it is not the exact year, but the exact span of years that is important to set down. To acknowledge Mason's works, I will begin my chronology in the year 2174, with Robert April taking command in 2188.

Chronology of the Starship *Enterprise*

2174—Spock of Vulcan is born. Seven years later, he will meet his first Klingon

2181—Leonard McCoy is born. First Klingon delegation to Earth.

2188—The starship *Enterprise* is commissioned. Robert April serves as her first captain; his wife, Sarah, will serve as his chief medical officer.

2190—James Tiberius Kirk is born. Two year shakedown cruise of *Enterprise* ends.

2195—The S.S. *Columbia* crashes on Talos IV.

2200—April retires as captain of the *Enterprise*. He is promoted to commodore in charge of Constellation-class starships.

2201–2207—During this period, the *Enterprise* is under command of an as-yet-unrevealed captain. Problems in the ship's original design are discovered; an eventual refit is prescribed.

2208—Kirk enters Starfleet Academy as a midshipman.

2209—Christopher Pike is given command of the *Enterprise*. Spock is also assigned to the starship at this time. The ship will be involved in more long-range exploration.

2211—April becomes Federation ambassador-at-large.

2213—The *Enterprise* becomes the first starship to visit Talos IV.

2215—Lieutenant Kirk is commended for his actions during the *Farragut* disaster.

2217—Sulu enters Starfleet Academy. Kirk takes command of the *Lydia Sutherland*.

2219—Kirk awarded Palm Leaf for the Axanar Peace Mission.

2220—Events of *Enterprise: The First Adventure*.

2224—The *Enterprise* visits the galactic barrier. Gary Mitchell is killed.

2225—Refit of the *Enterprise* for upcoming long-range exploration.

2226–2231—The five-year mission of the starship *Enterprise* as chronicled in *Star Trek*.

2234—After a two-and-one-half-year stint as head of operations, Admiral James T. Kirk takes command of a refitted *Enterprise*.

2241—The *Enterprise* is destroyed over the Genesis Planet. United Federation of Planets Starfleet vessel NCC-1701-A, *Enterprise*, is commissioned following James T. Kirk's reduction in rank to captain.

YOU WILL NOT BELIEVE A STARSHIP CAN FLY!

By Maurice Molyneaux

Star Trek has, for the most part, been much better about keeping its continuity intact than most other supposed "science fiction" shows. In the days of the series, the *Star Trek Writer's Guide* explained a lot of important details, and producers Gene Roddenberry and Gene L. Coon would often make pointed comments about inconsistencies in scripts. Things were never perfect, but the series managed to be relatively consistent.

Things have changed with the advent of the *Star Trek* movies. The first film tried to remain consistent with the series; the others haven't. It's gotten so you can't believe anything you see! Unfortunately, the problem has become so severe that I can't even explain away all the continuity gaffes. What's really distressing is that most of these mistakes could be cleared up in the script stage with a few strokes of a blue pencil. What the current *Star Trek* producers need to do is get someone knowledgeable to critique the scripts, point out inconsistencies, and then take those notes and make appropriate changes. Yet, although Bjo Trimble apparently got the chance to make comments on *The Wrath of Khan* script, and noted mistakes, the producer and director apparently chose not to pay attention to her.

One of its strong points of *Star Trek: The Motion Picture* was its careful attention to detail. Roddenberry had all sorts of advisers working on the film, and many technical procedures and processes were written down. Jesco von Puttkamer's detailed discussion of the warp drive (printed in *The Making of Star Trek: The Motion Picture*) is of particular importance, because it describes, in a sense, exactly why the *Enterprise* does not experience the effects of time dilation and other relativistic phenomenon.

Put simply, the warp drive creates intense fields of energy (via the two nacelles) that fold space around the vessel, creating a "subspace," a bubble universe within or *outside* our universe, which carries the ship along. As an example, an air bubble trapped in liquid will sometimes become divided, with a smaller bubble separated from the larger by a thin layer of liquid. This is an extremely simplistic metaphor, but it gives the general idea. This does not mean that the *Enterprise* leaves our universe, but rather creates a tiny, adjoining one. Inside the warp, the ship is apparently at rest, but the warp itself moves at tremendous speed in relation to our universe proper.

The theoretical physics involved are mind-boggling, so I won't go into this subject at all. But I would like to discuss the use and misuse of warp drive and other technology in the various *Star Trek* films.

In *Star Trek: The Motion Picture*, the *Enterprise* doesn't engage warp drive until well beyond the Earth's general vicinity. This is, of course, due to her rushed departure, but it makes sense. The idea of folding the structure of space is a tricky business, and since massive objects like planets already make "dents" in the local fabric of space, it's best to move away from them just a bit before engaging warp drive. The warp effect seen in *STTMP* is by far my favorite. The ship seems to race away, relative to us sublight travelers, blurring into infinity. There follows a "snap" as the space/time fabric "closes" around the ship, making it disappear from our view. Obviously, a ship can scan another ship in warp drive because it can detect the subspace bubble, or warp, surrounding it.

When the ship reaches the desired warp speed, we see a sort of reverse effect, with the ship blurring into sight, and a "snap" behind it. Perhaps, we can imagine, this is the point of view from within the subspace. We still see the snap of space/time fabric closing, but from this point of view we are watching as the outside universe is "closed out." All shots of the *Enterprise* from this point on show her not blurred, but the background stars racing by. This would be, of course, because we are watching the ship from inside the warp, and seeing everything outside the ship moving relative to our self-contained little bubble universe.

I hate the wormhole sequence, and cringe whenever I hear Scotty state that the antimatter imbalance created the wormhole in the first place. Better he should have reported that the imbalance caused the warp field to be to strong, and that the *Enterprise's* subspace bubble crossed so far out of normal space that it entered into a wormhole or temporal tunnel. By disengaging the warp drive, they popped back out of the wormhole. If they'd remained in it, God knows where they would have ended up (the Mirror Universe, perhaps?).

When the *Enterprise* is captured by the Intruder, we must assume that Vejur brings the ship within its own warp field and effectively neutralizes the starship's own warp.

In *Star Trek II: The Wrath of Khan* and *Star Trek III: The Search for Spock,* the warp effect consists of our seeing the ship simply blur away. In *The Search for Spock* we get several shots of a blurred *Enterprise.* This doesn't make any sense, for, since the ship is traveling, in relation to our universe, at several *hundred* times the speed of light, we shouldn't be able to see anything at all. If we were inside the warp with the ship, it shouldn't blur.

In fact, the warp drive seen in the latter films fails to be even marginally convincing. I also wonder why, in *The Wrath of Khan,* after receiving the urgent message from Carol, Kirk set out for Regula I at only warp five? After all, warp six was the maximum cruising speed of the old ship, and warp eight is supposed to be the safe top end for the new version. He must not have been *too* worried.

(Oh, did you know that warp drive, the way it is defined, is too slow for the missions we saw to take place? Officially, a warp factor is figured by cubing the warp number and and multiplying it by light speed. Thus, warp eight is 512 times the speed of light, and warp twelve is 1728 times light speed! This sounds quick, but a little celestial calculation shows that it ain't fast enough! Recall Vonda McIntyre's comments on the Galaxy-class starships in the novelizations of *STTMP* and *The Wrath of Khan*? They were stated to operate most efficiently at about warp twelve. She sent a ship to Andromeda, right? Well, at 1728 times the speed of light, it would take approximately 1273.148 *years* for her ship to cross the *2.2 million* light-years between the galaxies. We've hardly explored our own galaxy, so why waste that much energy going to Andromeda? Even if we took the warp number to the fourth power, making warp twelve equal 20,736 times light speed, it would still take *106.096 years* to go to Andromeda. Actually, this sounds more reasonable, as it fits better with the time frames for travel given in the series.)

On to other comparisons. Impulse power, for example, has been treated even more shoddily than warp drive. In *Star Trek: The Motion Picture*, the impulse engines aren't engaged until the ship is a good distance from the orbital dockyards. A good idea! After all, impulse power is just another name for rocket propulsion. The new impulse engines are said to set off tiny explosions of matter and antimatter, with the resulting energy channeled out the impulse "throats" for thrust. The backup, apparently, is some form of magnetically contained fusion reaction, still not something to take lightly.

Interestingly, a mistake was made in the first film, for when the Klingons approach the warp seven-plus Vejur cloud, their impulse engines are seen to be on!

In *Star Trek: The Motion Picture*, impulse power sends the *Enterprise* racing off. It gets the ship from Earth to Jupiter in a couple of hours at half-light speed. (I don't want to even begin discussing the time dilation this would cause!) But in *Star Trek II: The Wrath of Khan*, going at one-quarter impulse power, the *Reliant* crawls past the *Enterprise*, which is going the opposite direction, and the stars in the background are moving! At any impulse velocity the stars shouldn't appear to budge, and even at one-quarter impulse power, the *Reliant* should have blurred past the *Enterprise* (see, I knew we'd find some use for those blur shots!).

The Search for Spock really upset me, however, because, while *inside* the space station, Kirk orders Sulu to use *one-quarter impulse power*! Not only should the engine exhaust flood the bay with all kinds of radiation, but the ship should rocket forward and flatten itself against a wall. It does neither, but, incredibly, backs up! Explain to me how two aft-facing impulse exhausts can propel a ship backward and I'll nominate you for a Nobel Prize!

Has everyone forgotten what maneuvering thrusters are for?

(And I'd be grateful if somebody could explain to me how the *Enterprise* got all that additional damage in the time between *The Wrath of Khan* and *The Search for Spock*. At the end of *Wrath of Khan*, there were only *three* spots on the port side that had been hit. In *The Search for Spock*, the ship showed damage on all sides!)

Remember "Day of the Dove"? The *Enterprise* fires her phasers at an unshielded Klingon ship, which is instantly vaporized. In *The Wrath of Khan*, the starships fire phaser after phaser, and mostly just burn holes in each other's sides.

Photon torpedoes are interesting, too. In *STTMP*, one torpedo is shown pulverizing a sizable asteroid (the wormhole sequence). In *The Wrath of Khan*, both the *Enterprise* and the *Reliant* are hit with them, with minimal—if any—shielding, and survive. Shields are another question. When Kruge's ship decloaks aft of *Grissom*, Captain Esteban orders "Evasive!" Apparently, he, and his obviously dim-witted crew, never learned to turn on the shields. If nothing else, with that kind of technology, the computer should turn them on automatically.

The Klingon ship bothers me, too. I refuse to believe Klingons would keep "bird of prey" markings on a ship in their use, even if they did get it from the Romulans. Sulu took one look at it and declared it Klingon . . . but how did *he* know? It doesn't appear to have any of the design features of a ship with warp drive. I didn't see any sort of nacelles.

Other points:

In *The Wrath of Khan*, Kirk shouldn't have been a bit worried when Spock told Saavik to "take her out" of the dry dock. After all, Sulu was at the helm. However, if Saavik had been at the controls, *I* would have been worried!

According the *The Making of Star Trek*, a photon

torpedo consists of matter and antimatter charges surrounded and separated by a magna-photon force field. How can you *load* something like that? Come on! It has to be fed from the engines. Then again, if a photon torpedo can travel faster than light (how else can it hit a starship in warp drive?), then it must have some sort of warp-field-generating capability, which would indicate some sort of solid weapon. You tell me which is right!

The torpedo deck seen in *The Wrath of Khan* and *The Search for Spock* could not exist. There isn't enough room for bays like that in the area of the ship the torpedo deck is in. Also, the vertical shaft of the intermix chamber (coming up from engineering) should have passed through that room. The corridor leading forward from engineering, too, cannot exist, because it would go right out the front of the secondary hull! And I still can't figure where there's room for a turbolift to go between the saucer and secondary hull. It should have shown up in both engineering and the torpedo deck.

When the Genesis torpedo was ticking away in *Reliant*, couldn't Scotty have used the transporter to beam it up, and then beam it out into space, scattering its atoms (à la Nomad)? Would a phaser shot have crippled it? Or would either have set it off earlier?

How could the Genesis wave race out, suck up all the material in the Mutara Nebula, and then *turn around* and pull it all back together? That seems to violate the laws of motion. Also, if the torpedo was designed to transform a planet, isn't it neat the way it worked just peachy in a nebula? The programming should have been totally different.

Can you imagine Carol Marcus and her staff of brilliant research scientists being so stupid as not to notice David using protomatter in the Genesis matrix? Real scientists double-check things, and computer simulation would have shown David's unethical work, too.

A lot of people, and some books, have stated that the Genesis torpedo created both the planet and its star. I beg to differ. Stars are not uncommon in nebulae; in fact, many nebulas surround stars or are the remnants of exploded stars. If you recall, in one shot in *The Wrath of Khan*, where the *Reliant* is on a collision course with the

Enterprise, you can see a brilliant light behind Khan's ship. No doubt it was the star that the Genesis Planet would later orbit.

Magnetic fields in flux wouldn't have allowed Spock's tube to soft-land; and the initial velocity of it when launched from the *Enterprise* should have smeared Spock's remains into jelly. And isn't it amazing how the tube didn't open during its fiery descent to the Genesis Planet, but a rejuvenated, baby Spock was able to open it? Thoughtful of Starfleet to put handles on the *inside*. Also, a baby Spock wouldn't have known how to open the tube. If it was airtight, as it should have been, the newly regenerated Spock should have been asphyxiated.

If the Genesis wave regenerated Spock's cells, he should have been found in the same physical form we last saw him. To make him into a child, most of his body mass would have to be removed. Where did it go, and how did he get it back when aging? I didn't see him eating any trees . . .

Kruge's crew was too stupid to scan the *Enterprise* to see that there were only five guys on it? They wouldn't have made it through Klingon summer camp, let alone gotten aboard a starship!

The idea of blowing up the *Enterprise* to take out *six* lousy Klingons makes the mind reel. I knew the Romulans had developed a cloaking device, but not until I saw *The Search for Spock* did I know they'd devised a means for changing the size of objects. When the bird of prey is seen in relation to the *Enterprise* and people on Vulcan, we see that it is quite small. However, when it appears next to the doomed merchant ship early in the film, it dwarfs it. If the Klingon vessel doesn't change size, then I must assume that the entire merchant ship was no larger than my kitchen. Cramped quarters, indeed!

Notice how big the *Excelsior* is in relation to the *Enterprise*. Notice how wide *Enterprise* is in relation to the spacedock doors. Notice that the *Excelsior*'s primary hull was too wide to get through those doors. See physics again defied as it gets out anyway. Maybe the *Excelsior* is equipped with one of those new Romulan size-changing devices.

I find it hard to believe that the spacedock couldn't

have nailed the stolen *Enterprise* with a tractor beam. I'm amazed the *Excelsior* didn't try it (maybe Scotty gummed that up, too?). I'm astounded that Starfleet doesn't have a master-override code to all its ship's computers so that it can take control of them.

I'm amazed that nobody at Paramount ever thinks of these things.

Thank you, and good day.

ABOUT THE EDITORS

Although largely unknown to readers not involved in Star Trek fandom before the publication of *The Best of Trek #1*, WALTER IRWIN and G. B. LOVE have been actively editing and publishing magazines for many years. Before they teamed up to create TREK© in 1975, Irwin worked in newspapers, advertising, and free-lance writing, while Love published *The Rocket's Blast—Comic-collector* from 1960 to 1974, as well a hundreds of magazines, books and collectibles. Both together and seperately, they are currently planning several new books and magazines, as well as continuing to publish TREK.

In the vast intergalactic world of the future
the soldiers battle

NOT FOR GLORY

JOEL ROSENBERG

author of the bestselling
Guardian of the Flame series

Only once in the history of the Metzadan merce-
nary corps has a man been branded traitor. That
man is Bar-El, the most cunning military mind in
the universe. Now his nephew, Inspector-General
Hanavi, must turn to him for help. What begins as
one final mission is transformed into a series of
campaigns that takes the Metzadans from world to
world, into intrigues, dangers, and treacherous diplomatic games, where a strategist's highly irregu-
lar maneuvers and a master assassin's swift blade
may prove the salvation of the planet—or its ultimate ruin . . .